Reforming Elizabeth

OTHER BOOKS BY LORIN GRACE

Waking Lucy

Remembering Anna

Reforming Elizabeth

LORIN GRACE

**CURRANT
CREEK PRESS**

*Elizabeth
Happy
Reading
Lorin Grace*

Dress circa 1785-95 photo credit: The Met Museum Public domain image.
Fichu circa 1795-1800 photo credit: The Met Museum Public domain image.
Cover photos: Piotr Krześlak, Guillermo Avello, Dmytro Sheremeta, and Deposit
Photos

Cover Design © 2017 and formatting by LJP Creative
Edits by Eschler Editing

Published by Currant Creek Press
North Logan, Utah

First printing: May 2017

ISBN: 978-0-9984110-1-9

For Blaine—
"Love alters not with his brief hours and weeks,
But bears it out even to the edge of doom."

Sonnet 116.

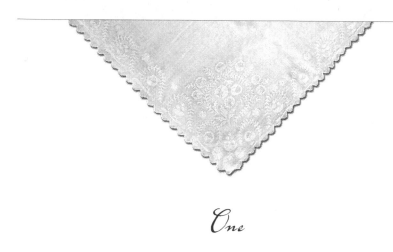

One

MOVEMENT ON THE SNOWY STREET below distracted Elizabeth from her sewing. She rubbed the windowpanes to remove the condensation that had accumulated on the freezing glass and saw the unmistakable broad-shouldered form of Samuel Wilson step out of the parsonage gate. A single set of footprints marked his progress in the falling snow.

He must have managed to annul his ridiculous marriage to that boorish Lucy Simms. Now he could declare himself for her. At tomorrow's Sabbath services, Reverend Woods would make an announcement and try to stanch the scandal. As if Samuel's marriage to his unconscious bride was anything but scandalous. Tomorrow was too long to wait.

She scanned the street. No other people ventured out on this blustery day. This was her chance. Elizabeth rushed down the stairs, careful to not step on the squeaky spots, and grabbed her cloak. She fumbled fastening the silver frog and lifted up the hood. The reflection in the mirror smiled back. Perfect. From the fur-lined wool framing her face, she pulled one golden curl forward and simpered her most practiced of expressions—the one with her mouth slightly parted, the smile she used only for the most eligible of bachelors.

One step from the door, she pivoted back to the gilded mirror and ripped the fichu from around her neck and shifted her stays lower. The cloak opened at the perfect angle to show off her womanly assets, which her favorite crimson gown flattered more than any other, then she stuffed the lacy scarf up her sleeve and ran out the door before she could rethink her boldness or be seen by her father.

—✠— ❈ —✠—

Magistrate Ebenezer Garrett dipped his pen in the inkwell and corrected another error on the report his clerk had delivered earlier. Saturday or not, he'd sequestered himself in his study to review the document. This time his analysis would bring him to the attention of Governor Increase Sumner. The information must be flawless that he might obtain an appointment to a committee or higher judicial post. The monotony of his work in the tiny North Shore town wore on him. Anything would be more exciting than issuing a handful of marriage certificates and charging Abner Sidewall with public intoxication—again—or listening to petty complaints involving roosters, fence lines, and swearing on the Lord's day.

The front door slammed, rattling the study's windows in their wooden frames.

"What in tarnation? No interruptions. After twenty years as a magistrate, people should leave me alone on Saturday," he muttered as he straightened the papers on his desk and sat up a bit taller.

When no knock came at the mahogany door separating his domain from the rest of the house, Ebenezer leaned back in his chair. Who would slam the door, if not the careless maid letting in some impatient citizen who couldn't wait to meet with him until Monday?

No sound echoed in the hall. He adjusted his spectacles and returned to reading the report. The snow fell harder, dimming the room, and he turned up the lamp. Outside, a flash of red amid the snowflakes caught his eye. *What's the commotion in front of the parsonage?*

He laid aside the papers and stepped to the window for a closer look. His Elizabeth owned a cloak the same color. *What on earth?* He rubbed the pane, hoping to clean the wavy glass, but the combination of condensation and snow made a clear view impossible. A woman came from the parsonage and joined the man and woman near the sleigh.

"Samuel Wilson and his new bride, Lucy," he grumbled. "What is Elizabeth up to now?" Ebenezer had made a habit of muttering to himself to make up for the lack of intelligent conversation in his home.

Not caring to answer his own question, Ebenezer turned from the sight when the newlyweds climbed into the sleigh.

Just as he reached the desk, a screech filled the air. Startled, his hand brushed the uncapped inkwell, tipping the bottle over on the desktop and soaking the report.

The shriek outside decrescendoed into a wail, not unlike the cry of a panther he'd heard in his youth. Ebenezer's voice mingled with the woman's cries as he took in the damaged papers.

"Elizabeth!" Ebenezer ran from the room faster than most men of his age or bulk were capable.

He didn't bother to shut the front door as he rushed into the street where his daughter knelt screaming. To his credit, he did look for blood before hauling Elizabeth to her feet, the swift movement instantly stifling her scream and causing her cloak to fall back, revealing more of his daughter's chest than any father would be comfortable viewing. Without a word, he propelled her into the house and thrust her into a chair in his study.

Elizabeth gasped for air. Her blonde hair tumbled out of its confines on one side, a hairpin dangling dangerously near her eye. She swatted it out of the way. For a moment, Ebenezer caught himself wondering if his daughter were deranged as his gaze fell from her face to her bared chest. He turned away.

"Cover yourself at once!" His bellow echoed throughout the house and brought his wife, Rebecca, scurrying from the direction of the kitchen.

She stopped in the doorway. "Is something wrong?"

"Look at the mess!" Ebenezer wiped a blotting cloth over the spilled ink, smearing it farther.

"Oh, my! Don't try to clean it that way. Elizabeth, go tell Cook—"

Elizabeth darted from her chair, her cloak falling to the floor.

"Stop! You are not leaving this room." Ebenezer's voice echoed off the ceiling.

Elizabeth obediently sat back down.

"I said to cover yourself this instant!" Ebenezer demanded, his face flaming with more than anger.

Rebecca turned her attention to her daughter for the first time. "Good heavens! Where is your fichu?"

When Elizabeth pulled the length of cotton from her sleeve, Rebecca snatched it out of her hand and let out a little gasp. She wrapped the scarf around Elizabeth's neck, then blocked her husband's view as Elizabeth tucked the ends into her bodice.

"Why ever did you take it off?" Rebecca asked.

Elizabeth's gaze moved from her mother's perplexed face to her father's enraged one, and she began to sob into her hands. Her mother spouted endearments and patted Elizabeth's shoulder.

Ebenezer pulled Elizabeth's hands down, revealing dry eyes. "I told you before—she only pretends to cry. Now stop your coddling and leave us. This time I will take our daughter in hand. She shall not embarrass us again."

—∗— ※ —∗—

The following morning Elizabeth pled a headache, mostly true, and begged to remain home from church services. Wrapped in her dressing gown, she reclined on her bed, sipping the willow-bark tea her mother had sent up.

The two antiquated ensembles her father had asked the maid to bring down from her grandmother's trunk in the attic hung near the window, which she'd propped open a half inch. Both frocks stank of camphor wood—the stale odor the only thing worse than the out-of-fashion excuses for clothing. Drab-brown and washed out gray, with necklines four inches higher than the least-fashionable gown she owned and made of homespun!

Appearing at church services in either dress would be as bad as walking in with a pet skunk. Elizabeth's cheeks burned as she thought about the fool she made of herself yesterday. Samuel had rebuffed her every move. Then Lucy had appeared from who knows where and smiled at her husband, giving every indication they were indeed a very happily married couple despite rumors to the contrary. The soft gaze Samuel had given his wife ruled out any annulment. Never had

Elizabeth been put down so thoroughly. No wonder her frustration had come to the surface, screaming itself out in the street. Perchance she'd experienced a moment of madness. Usually she maintained her emotions until in private.

The image of Samuel's mortified face as she'd leaned toward him flashed through her mind. Perhaps she'd gone too far in removing the fichu.

She sipped her tea and tried to think of ways to modify the horrid dresses. Her only consolation became the hemlines, and for the first time in her life, she let out the hem of a skirt. Grandmother Patience had stood just under five feet—two inches shorter than Elizabeth. Not that she minded being shorter than most women. Men seemed to enjoy the way her small frame could be tucked under their arms.

Her father had forbidden her to wear any of her own clothing until she demonstrated she could dress modestly. Her elegant gowns were to have the necklines raised to more "appropriate levels," which meant to the Puritan level her grandmother had worn her entire life. Of course, she must do this herself. She wouldn't trust anyone else to the task. Elizabeth's sole talent was with the needle, and father couldn't tell basting from a finished seam.

For the rest of the week, Elizabeth dressed simply, remained indoors, appeared contrite, and stayed out of her father's way.

Forgoing the Williamses' Christmas ball was a sacrifice, but with nothing new to wear, it wasn't much to miss. But then, the Williamses' ball never was as fun as the Gordon's New Year's Eve ball.

With any luck, her father would calm down by then. Elizabeth couldn't help but wonder if she would have received any punishment had the ink not spilled on Father's precious report. As if the governor even cared about what trifling matter her father pontificated about this time.

She pulled her wrap tighter against the cold wind seeping in the window, hoping the stench of camphor would soon dissipate. Being stuck in her room all week was penance indeed.

—✠—

"Reverend Gideon Frost."

Gideon stared at his ordination certificate, tempted to add it to the sermon notes fueling the meager fire. He should have continued as his father's apprentice and become a shoemaker. Too bad his brother Aaron had taken over the shop upon Father's death, leaving no room for him in the one-man business. *What arrogance to believe I had been called as a preacher of the word.*

Five years ago, his calling to minister and help people had fueled his every desire. So long ago, Gideon felt, as if he looked back on a different person.

With the conclusion of the war and the first American printing of the English language Bible, new denominations had sprouted and thrived. Under the Massachusetts Parish Church system, most churches remained Congregationalist. New sects were allowed in the community by vote as parish churches, and a few obtained that status, but those that did so thrived on tax contributions.

A traveling preacher from one of the new denominations had inspired Gideon to join him after a particularly poignant meeting. Gideon paced the room, recalling—for the hundredth time that month—that meeting. He wished he still felt the fire.

The notes to his last sermon burned to gray ashes. Gray as the low clouds. Gray as his life.

Once, his faith had guided his every action, dictated his every thought. A faith he only pretended to maintain now. He still believed in God, but reconciling his feelings with his readings in Holy Writ and theological treatises left him with more questions than answers. Questions that gnawed at his heart. How could he shepherd a flock if he couldn't discern the truth of God for himself?

He buried his head in his hands. His tears had long dried up, replaced only with a gray emptiness.

If only Ruth hadn't died, he would not be questioning his faith.

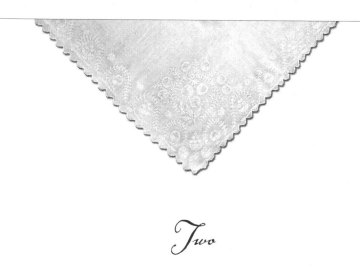

Two

FATHER'S VISE GRIP ON ELIZABETH'S elbow propelled her out of the church, across the street, and into the house. Only when he let go did Elizabeth dare reply to his whispered accusations. "I did not ogle a married man!"

"Do not lie to me. You were staring at Mr. Wilson when I came to sit down. Then you kept trying to look at him through the entirety of Reverend Woods's sermon." Ebenezer's face grew red, his thick gray eyebrows accentuating his frown.

Elizabeth turned her back to her father and removed her cloak. She gave her mother the tiniest of conspiratorial eye rolls. What would it take to calm Father down this time? She turned to face him and plastered on a well-practiced innocent face. "I did not stare at him. I only admired his wife's new dress." Turning to her mother, she continued. "Did you see her hat? And the lace—some of Mrs. Wilson's best work. Who knew Lucy Simms would ever turn out so fine? Almost pretty, wasn't she?"

Rebecca nodded in agreement. "I was shocked to see—"

"Mrs. Garrett, we are not speaking of clothing or how Mrs. Lucy Wilson has improved." Ebenezer put a particular emphasis on Lucy Simms Wilson's last name. "We are discussing our daughter's behavior toward Mr. Wilson—a married man whom my daughter continues to throw herself at, embarrassing us all." He allowed his coat and hat to be taken by the houseboy before stepping into the parlor.

"Father, I did not throw myself at him today. I told you, I learned my lesson. I would never have pursued him had I realized he was actually married. The circumstances were so peculiar, and they never courted after his return." Elizabeth bowed her head in a way she hoped showed remorse.

"Yes, dear, she's been most contrite. She's hardly complained about the ugly dress you forced her to wear today. Why, she is the laughingstock of all the girls. Who else wore a high-collared, decades-old dress on Christmas Eve? I shall never live the shame down." Rebecca fanned herself and flopped into her favorite chair.

Elizabeth tugged at the sleeve of the mud-brown wool frock she'd worn to church. She'd chosen it over the gray one because the cloth had lost most of the camphor stench.

"Never live it down! A dress? You'll never live it down?" The windows vibrated with his bellowing. Elizabeth winced. Last week's fight all over again—Father acting a magistrate instead of a father, deciding her actions were different than she intended. Couldn't Abner Sidewall, the town drunk, start a fight or swear at the reverend and give Father something else to do?

Elizabeth held out the skirt of the dress. "Father, this is a severe punishment. I mean, this dress is—"

Thump! Ebenezer slammed his walking stick on the floor, causing his wife and daughter to jump. "No more! You are going to be retrenched if it is the last thing I do! Not only in frivolities but in manners. Child, you've missed the entire point. It is not just last week's behavior. The pattern of your life must be turned and reformed. Pruned from the wild tree into something...something useful."

Retrenched? Wasn't that the phrase Grandmother Patience Garrett used when someone needed dire reform? Did Father think her as bad as all that?

"Can't this wait a few days?" Rebecca Garrett placed her hand on her husband's arm. "Today is Christmas E—"

"Absolutely not!" Ebenezer cut his wife off with a roar, his face flamed with indignation. "Did you not see your daughter making eyes at Samuel Wilson before the service started? And she thinks this is about a dress! Last week in the middle of the street she threw herself at the same man, her bosom bared for the entire world to see." He punctuated his remarks with thrusts of his cane.

Elizabeth shrank into the corner. Her father never hit women or anyone else she knew of, but the way he was wielding his cane, she began to worry.

"Elizabeth, darling, go check on dinner while I handle your father." Rebecca waved Elizabeth out of the room.

Though Elizabeth thought it impossible, her father's face grew redder, the veins at his temples pulsing. "No! You will not leave. And I will not be handled." Thump! The walking stick connected with the floor again. Elizabeth froze in the doorway. "Mrs. Garrett, you've failed our daughter, and I am taking over. You've raised a strumpet." He turned to Elizabeth. "I will have no more of your wanton ways."

Rebecca stepped closer to her husband. "But, dearest—"

"Don't you dearest me. You told me you would handle her behavior years ago when we first heard allegations of her browbeating the other girls at school. When Mr. Whittier blamed Elizabeth for spreading the malicious gossip that almost ended his daughter's engagement, you told me you had her under control. When she ruined Miss What's-her-name's dress at the Christmas ball two years ago, you claimed it was an accident. When she became the most notorious flirt north of Boston, you said it was necessary. Then she pursued a married man, half dressed in the middle of the street in front of the parsonage, no less. Samuel Wilson ended any hint of courtship weeks before marrying Lucy. Your daughter's excuses in those matters only point to her slatternly manner. Woman, I say no more! Your daughter is beyond the pale!"

"But—"

"I will not suffer her to continue to make a fool of me." Thump, thump! Ebenezer spun to face his daughter before thumping his walking stick a third time. "You are forbidden to leave your room until I find some relation to take you in for the duration of your retrenchment."

"Even for Christmas?" Elizabeth asked, wide-eyed.

"Especially for Christmas! And any gift your mother bought will be returned or sold as I am sure it will be more foppery. What you shall receive is one of those little Aitken Bibles. Now go!" Ebenezer raised his cane and pointed it up the stairs.

The walking stick shook, her father barely controlling his rage. Fearful that trying to cajole him now would only bring more reprisals, she scurried to her room to prepare for a later battle.

—… ✗ …—

Gideon buried his head in his hands, attempting to pray, but no words came. Nothing came. Consuming numbness swirled about him.

The morning's service had ended in disaster. How was it possible to ruin the Christmas message? The sermon he'd planned, forgotten in his melancholy, had been replaced by rambling thoughts. Instead of being full of hope and rejoicing, it had become a requiem. The faces of his parishioners had stared back at him, questioning. Gideon had stumbled to find his place, but it was pointless to pretend he found joy in the sermon. The doubts he struggled to hide from his congregation had overshadowed the angel's declarations of joy. Even the older women's faces had fallen from expectant to bewildered as he'd endeavored to rein in his thoughts and follow his notes. By the time he'd mumbled his amen and called for a benedictory song, anger had replaced confusion on many a face.

Would the church elders come today and inform him of his dismissal, or would they be kind and wait until after Christmas? Two weeks ago, the chair of the selection committee had informed him they were considering seeking a replacement pastor for the little flock, and a letter lay drafted and ready to mail to the seminary from which he'd graduated. But they'd voted to give him another chance. Gideon was positive the letter would be sent posthaste.

Last year's Yuletide sermon had been sublime, his first in Greenwich's little white church. In the front row, his wife's face had been radiant, as Mary's must have been centuries ago. Ruth's rounded form had inspired his homily as he focused on the thoughts of a young Mary shunned, turned from the inn, and then hosting shepherds and kings. The impending birth of his child had acted as the catalyst for feelings of Christmas more poignant than he imagined possible. Rejoicing had been natural, comfortable, and expected, and the congregation had rejoiced with him. It was the best of all Christmases.

Another minister had preached the Easter sermon while he'd prayed at Ruth's bedside. His infant son already lay in the cemetery adjoining the churchyard. The prayers he'd uttered had failed to penetrate the ceiling of their little cottage or were ignored completely.

Left on his own, he listened to platitudes he once gave freely. How empty. How meaningless. Dare he offer guidance to his congregation when he'd lost all confidence in the Divinity that had once guided him? His fellow clergymen gave unsatisfying answers to his questions. The Bible seemed to contradict itself. No wonder disagreement of the various denominations became contentious at times. Had God willed his wife and son to die? Was this a learning experience, as some claimed? Or punishment for his arrogance in believing he had been called to lead others?

At first his congregants had shown patience with his grief, but as young widows had wooed him with meals and the mothers of marriageable daughters cornered him on each Sabbath afternoon over dinner, it became apparent they felt he should cease mourning. Death from childbirth was common enough—at least a tenth of his male parishioners lost a wife or two. Gossips claimed old Mr. Whittaker had married three women in all.

Gideon tossed a log onto the fire. No point in letting the meager flames die. He didn't need someone checking on him because smoke didn't rise from the chimney. He didn't wish to see anyone. When the room grew dim with the setting sun and only a few embers remained, he banked the fire and moved to his bed, his limbs stiff from sitting so long.

He should try to pray again.

⇢ ✳ ⇠

"It isn't fair," Elizabeth complained to the empty room. She worked off her gloves and threw them at the mirror.

Looking at her reflection, she wondered again why such an ugly gown existed. Grandmother Garrett should have been named Prudence instead of Patience. Her dresses lacked style and were most likely made from the cloth sold at bargain prices because others refused to buy such drab colors. The brown wool-and-linen dress boasted no adornment whatsoever. Not even a fancy button. The collar, five inches above the neckline of her favorite crimson gown, felt like a noose around her throat. The high-collared shift, something an old farmer's wife would wear to keep warm in the winter, scratched her chin every time she dipped her head. The muddy brown did nothing for her complexion, robbing her face of color and making her blue eyes appear as pale as if they'd been laundered too many times.

She yanked out the pins holding her hair in the unflattering bun father insisted she wear, and her flaxen locks tumbled down to her waist.

Elizabeth picked up her brush, then set it down. She studied her reflection from each side. The Puritan-style bun may be as unfashionable as the dress, but it added curl to her straight hair. Glorious. Long, soft waves of gold now tumbled down her back, and she admired the way the light played off her blonde tresses. Maybe the bun would come in handy, after all. She gathered her hair back up in one hand and allowed it to fall. Mother said men adored long hair. If she arranged for it to uncoil on cue, the action would be a perfect flirtation.

For the next half hour, Elizabeth experimented with various ways to pin the bun so it would fall on demand, but without success.

A knock on the door ended her explorations. The door opened and the maid, balancing a tray, entered. "Pardon, miss. The magistrate said to serve your meals up here." The girl set the cloth covered tray on the dressing table and retreated.

Elizabeth wrinkled her nose. The smells coming from under the cloth were not the delectable ones rising from the kitchen below. Roast duck, baked squash, spice cake, and plum pudding had teased her nose and stomach since before church. The tray on the table promised none of those. Gingerly, she lifted the corner of the cloth. Coarse brown bread, pease porridge, and cheese. Even the servants fared better today.

This ghastly repast would not do. She hefted the tray and marched out the door, but when she was halfway down the stairs, her father appeared at the foyer.

Arms crossed, he glared at her. "Where are you going?"

Elizabeth lifted her chin. "To the kitchen."

"The maid will be glad to know you saved her the errand." Ebenezer took the tray from her. "Now back to your room."

"But I am hungry." Elizabeth tried to pass her father.

Ebenezer lifted the cloth covering the tray, "Obviously not hungry enough to eat the food you were brought."

She wrinkled her nose and snorted. "That isn't food. It is slop."

"This slop, as you call it, is the very food that keeps the Commonwealth going. I was raised on it. And it is the only type of food you will get until you learn to be grateful for your bounties."

"Never!"

"You may wish to reconsider your choice of words, child. I shall see that another tray is sent up tomorrow. Nothing like a bit of hunger to help one be thankful." Ebenezer turned his back on her and walked toward the kitchen.

Elizabeth stomped her foot on the stairs and followed the smell of roast duck.

"Back to your room. Or must I lock you in?" Ebenezer set the tray on a side table and took a step toward her, his face turning the shade of a ripe holly berry.

She raced back to her room before he made good on locking her door or saw the tears she fought to hide.

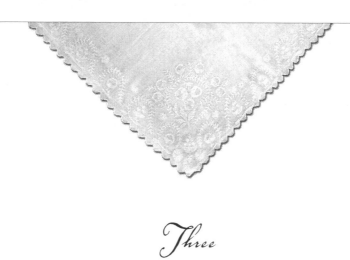

Three

A LIGHT RAPPING BROKE EBENEZER'S concentration. He stopped writing and glared at the door. His wife believed she was the exception when he said to stay out of his study. No wonder his daughter lacked discretion.

"Dearest, I know what to do with our daughter. May I come in?"

Ebenezer stifled a groan. The sweetness in his wife's voice reminded him that too many sweets caused stomachaches and even headaches. Better to get whatever she had in mind over with than to suffer all day. He covered the letter with a blotter and gestured for his wife to come in and take a chair.

"My sister Lydia is so lonely and longs for a companion, and her husband has all the best connections. I think we should send Elizabeth to live with her. There are many advan—"

Ebenezer cut her off before he had to listen to all the virtues of his wife's silly sister. "I agree. Sending Elizabeth to an aunt's may be the best way to teach her the essentials lacking in her education. In fact, I am composing a letter to her aunt this very moment."

"You agree?" Rebecca's brow furrowed. The poor woman, unprepared for his easy capitulation, seemed to be at a blessed loss for words.

"Yes. I think her aunt would work wonders with her." Ebenezer's grin should have warned his wife all was not as she assumed.

"Oh, well…in that case, may Elizabeth come down for Christmas dinner? Reverend Woods and his wife are coming, and with Nathaniel's arrival last night, there will be only five at the table." The fluttering of Rebecca's hands betrayed her nervousness.

"I already told you, she will stay in her room, and she shall continue to until the day she departs."

"But, dearest—"

"Mrs. Garrett!" Ebenezer straightened in his seat. "I will not be crossed in this. I don't care whether President Adams is coming for dinner or the room is unbalanced. If it bothers you so much, ask Cook or that little mouse of a maid to dine with us. Elizabeth stays in her room. Now leave me."

Ebenezer shuffled papers in front of him, pretending to read them. Rebecca opened and closed her mouth several times, but not a sound escaped. At length, she left the study.

Careful not to make a noise, Ebenezer circled his desk and checked the hallway. He shut the door and turned the key. Wiping his brow, he returned to his desk. If his wife read the drying paper next to his blotter, she would have realized the aunt he'd referred to wasn't his vapid sister-in-law. No, Elizabeth had received enough coddling in her life. The last thing she needed was to live in Brookline with her own maid and suitors plied on her at every turn. Elizabeth required something entirely different.

He returned to the desk and picked up the newly composed letter. This aunt would be perfect. He signed the letter with a flourish and dusted the fine paper with a bit of salt. After folding the missive with care, he dabbed sealing wax on the open edge. Ebenezer reached for his seal but stopped. This was not official correspondence. He removed his father's signet ring from his smallest finger and used it instead.

Turning the letter over, he wrote, "Mrs. Mindwell Richards, East Stoughton, Massachusetts."

⊷ ❇ ⊶

The ninth chime of the mantel clock faded as a knock sounded on the door—the first sound on his door since someone had left a plate of food on his doorstep for Christmas dinner yesterday. This visit would not be as enjoyable as that of the lukewarm roast goose, congealed gravy, and pickled beets.

Before reaching for the knob, Gideon straightened his coat and vest. As suspected, the three men of the selection committee stood on his porch, their faces grim.

He let them in and indicated they should sit at the table. Mr. Thomas shook his head and remained standing. "We will not be long." The other two men nodded their agreement. "We notified the seminary, and they will be sending a new candidate this week. We expect you to be ready to leave on Friday's stage." Mr. Thomas consulted a paper in his hand. "Reverend Ingram indicated you would be welcome to stay in the dormitory while you look for a different assignment. Do you require assistance in packing? Some of the women folk will come clean on Friday after you leave."

Four days. They must have sent their message off to the seminary before his disastrous Christmas message. They weren't giving him an opportunity to bid farewell to the congregation or say his good-byes to friends. Looking at the three men in front of him, he wondered if he even possessed any friends to whom he could give his adieus. Gideon realized they were waiting for a response.

"No, I will not need help packing, nor do I require a ticket for the coach, as I have Jordan to ride. My books and clothes will not take long to put in a trunk, which can be sent by freight or stage." The house and its furnishings, other than the cradle tucked in the attic, belonged to the church and would be passed on to the next minister.

Gideon shifted his weight and waited for a response. Mr. Thomas looked to the other two men, then reached for the door. Gideon beat him to it and opened the door wide. None of the men looked him in the eye as they shook his hand and left, taking any warmth the day had kindled with them.

Gideon mounted the narrow stairway. Packing his single trunk would not take long. And with no sermon to prepare, there would be little to do for the rest of the week. Perhaps he would leave earlier.

Crack, crack, crack.

Each swing of the ax sent splinters flying. Gideon blinked back tears. He had no desire to miss because he could not see clearly.

Whack, whack, whack.

Again and again he swung the ax, destroying months of his work. He couldn't take the never-used cradle with him. It wouldn't fit in his trunk. Nor could he leave the unused piece behind to an undetermined fate.

"Reverend! Reverend!" The shouting interrupted his swing, and he lowered the ax.

"What are you doing, son?" Only one person had called him son. Mr. Whittaker. The old man shuffled closer, leaning on his cane.

"Now, why did you go and do that? Turned all your hard work into kindling," the octogenarian said as he bent over and retrieved a sliver. "Not even big enough to start a fire." He let the piece fall between his fingers to the ground. "Come, son, it's too cold out for my old bones."

Gideon turned toward his house and wiped his tears, hoping the old man hadn't seen them. He felt Mr. Whittaker's cane rap against his leg. The old man wielded his cane the same way Gideon had used a sword in his youth.

"Not at your place, son. You probably don't have a decent fire in there. My little Martha left my meal over the fire, and there is plenty to share. Someday you'll have a granddaughter like my Martha."

Gideon leaned the ax against the back door and grabbed his discarded coat, all the while biting his tongue. He would never be a grandfather. His only chance for a posterity had died months ago. He followed the old man across the path and into the next yard.

Two fires still burned in the enormous kitchen fireplace, making the kitchen much warmer than Gideon's home had been since the last of summer fled. Something delicious simmered in the pot hanging over the larger fire. The scent of still-warm bread lingered in the air. Gideon closed his eyes and breathed in the homey aroma. He missed the scent of a busy kitchen. Ruth's kitchen.

Mr. Whittaker interrupted his thoughts. "Will you grab a couple of those bowls down and fill them?" he asked as he slipped into a chair at the table. "Get the teapot and cups, too."

Gideon set the requested items on the table and took a seat.

Mr. Whittaker mercifully kept up the one-sided conversation. Gideon found he was unable to speak, afraid that emotions he'd rather keep private would seep out.

"Ah, I left England behind to fight for independence, but I never quite gave up my love of a good cup of tea." The old man stirred his cup and inhaled the steam. "Nearly killed me when my wife signed the pact to protest the tea tax with the other women back in '70—or was it '71? Then the war. All those years without tea." He shook his head and took a sip. "I like chocolate well enough, and tolerate coffee, but on days like today I need my tea. Reminds me of my Ruthie."

Gideon's body froze at the name, the tea in his mouth moving neither down nor out. He stilled his hand before he could spill his tea and forced his throat to relax and let the liquid pass. He didn't dare ask the question he was almost sure the old man was begging him to.

Silence filled the room.

"You want to ask, but you can't say her name, can you?"

Gideon stared into his empty teacup.

"Son, how many children do you think I have?"

"Six?"

The old man slapped his leg and roared with laughter. "Not by half. If you count my boys who died in the last war, eight of my children lived to maturity. Ten did not. Two died along with their mothers in childbirth." Mr. Whittaker punctuated his words with little jabs of his spoon.

Gideon set his cup down and stared at the man.

"Surprised you, didn't I? I suspect you knew my wife, whom we buried last spring, was not my first, since everyone still called her Widow Black, though we had been married for more than ten years."

Gideon nodded. He'd heard tell of two other wives who'd preceded the widow.

The old man sipped his tea. "Most folks around here know of her and two of my other wives. Mostly because all my living children are theirs. Few people know about Hannah or my Ruthie." Mr. Whittaker paused and drank his tea, then refilled his cup.

"I lost everything when I lost my Ruthie coming over nearly sixty years ago. I wandered the streets of Boston wishing I were dead, and half felt it. Of course, I never worked a day in my life until we left England. Raised to be an earl, I went to the best schools, but I knew nothing about life or death. And precious little about love, though I fancied I did."

Gideon clamped his jaw as to not spew the soup in his mouth. Old Mr. Whittaker an earl? Of all the outlandish rumors he'd heard in his position, this wasn't one of them.

"Appreciate you keeping that information to yourself. Don't want anyone thinking I'm a loyalist. Not even my grandchildren know. Martha, my third wife, my granddaughter's namesake, figured no one need know about my past as I became a new man who found God. Never did tell my Sally or Widow Black. Too many years passed, and some unlucky fool now holds the title in my stead. Here's to that poor man." He raised his teacup in salute.

They both ate in silence for the next few minutes.

"Didn't call you over here to tell you of my aristocratic lines. When I saw you destroying your son's cradle, the same one you built with such love last spring, I thought I needed to tell you the story of my Ruthie and Hannah. Because, Preacher, it would be a shame if you made the same mistakes this old man did. I think you are bright enough to learn from them. How old are you—thirty-five?"

"Twenty-six."

Mr. Whittaker shook his head. "Twenty-six and you act like you are older than I am, waiting for the good Lord to take you home." He pushed back his chair. "Dust yourself off and come to the parlor. The chairs are more comfortable. Martha can deal with a spot o' dust."

Two stuffed chairs, both worn smooth from frequent use, flanked the fireplace. The older gentleman took the chair farthest from the window and indicated for Gideon to take the other. Gideon settled into the seat and noticed that Mr. Whittaker held something in his hands.

"Here, son, these will help you as I tell my story." Gideon leaned forward and took the three miniatures from Mr. Whittaker. One, obviously more worn and aged, stood out from the others.

"The one you are looking at is my Ruthie, painted from memory. The dark-haired woman would be Hannah, and the fair one is my Martha. I didn't paint the others."

Gideon nodded. The young woman in his congregation did resemble the older Martha in the last frame.

"My Ruthie was the most beautiful creature I ever saw. I was smitten. But I was an earl's son, and she a mere tenant's daughter." He paused as if searching for the correct words. "Well, it wasn't done." Mr. Whittaker gazed into the fire, a smile on his lips. "I pled with my father to allow me to marry her, but my father laughed at me. Told me to bed her if I must but to find a girl of my own rank. I regret to say I took part of his advice. Tearfully, Ruthie told me of our child and begged me to help her. My father yelled at me for hours, and I yelled back. We came to blows. I left the house, never to return.

"Two days later we sailed for Boston. As I had little money, our accommodations were far from grand. Though we hadn't wed before sailing, we registered as husband and wife in the ship's manifest due to her condition. I was convinced that once we landed in Boston, we would solemnize our vows." Mr. Whittaker pulled a handkerchief from his pocket and wiped at his eyes.

"The trip was terrible—stale food, constant storms. My poor Ruthie contracted a horrendous illness. All I could do was hold her close. Two days before we made port, my Ruthie awoke." Mr. Whittaker paused and loudly blew his nose. "So much blood. That night I wrapped the baby and Ruthie in a bit of sail and slid them overboard."

"I sent word to Ruthie's parents of her death. Eventually my father learned of it and sent me missive after missive, begging me to return to England to take my rightful place. I never responded. If only he'd let me marry her, she would have lived—or so I told myself. "

The old man paused and lifted his face heavenward. "We don't control death, or much else, son."

Though I wish we could. It hurts so much! Gideon kept his thoughts private, knowing the conversation still had a ways to go before it wound to its conclusion.

"I wandered about Boston, finally running out of money. Hannah's father ran a shipping company and hired me as a clerk. A kind man, he often sent meals by way of a houseboy or some other servant and allowed me a cot in his warehouse.

"On a few occasions, I ate at his home with his wife and children. His oldest daughter, Hannah, would smile shyly at me while her younger sisters giggled. Soon Hannah took to delivering my meals. She recognized my despondency and in her innocence tried to console me." Suddenly, Mr. Whittaker brought his fist down on the arm of his chair, causing Gideon to jump.

"I prayed for God to forgive me, but being a stupid, self-absorbed man, I took all the consolation she offered and more. Her father found us. We wed soon after.

"Not yet sixteen, Hannah possessed wisdom beyond her years. She always knew I loved another, yet she gave and gave and gave of her love. In time, I came to respect and admire her for her tenacity. With each son she bore, my wounds healed a bit more. Then the oldest caught measles, and by the end of the week my entire little family lay underground in the churchyard. Too late I realized I loved Hannah. She never knew.

"I spent many hours head in hands in the churchyard, until the curate dragged me to his home. He taught me truths from the Bible I never heard preached in my youth.

"Not long after, I met Martha as she was spinning flax into linen at a competition in Boston where she and her feisty friend Mina bantered back and forth and laughed frequently. I wanted laughter in my life. Martha and I went for walks on the Common. Soon I convinced her to marry me. I told her everything, and she forgave all. We were together more than twenty years when she passed." Mr. Whittaker stood and poked at the fire, his words settling with the flames.

"I am sure you've heard of Sally, the spinster I married out of mutual need, as Martha left me several young children. Poor Sally—neither of us figured at her age she would ever carry my child. She actually carried two, but she did not live to hold her second."

Gideon shifted uncomfortably. Gideon was intrigued by the story, but he didn't want Mr. Whittaker to regret being candid with him. "You did not need to confess—"

Mr. Whittaker waved Gideon off. "I know you loved your Ruth and that losing her and the child feels as if God has torn away a bit of your soul. But don't make the same mistakes I made with Hannah. You are not yet thirty. You will marry again, have children again. It's what a man and woman are made for—to be parents. You will again long for a wife and for fatherhood. You must let your Ruth go and allow yourself to find love again. I've loved five, the memory of one never diminishing another. Trust that your wife and son are with God, as you've preached, and find a new path for your life, son."

They sat watching the flames dance in the fireplace. Mr. Whittaker took a deep breath. "I know they are sending you back to the seminary. I offer you another option. Martha's friend Mina is now widowed. She needs help keeping her little farm running. I could recommend you to her employ."

Farming? Gideon knew the basics. His father had only owned two acres—just enough to support a milk cow and supplement his shoe-making business.

Mr. Whittaker crossed to a writing desk and wrote something on a scrap of paper. "I don't know what your seminary will do with you, but now you have another option."

Stuffing the paper into Gideon's hand, Mr. Whittaker ushered him out the back door.

As Gideon crossed the yard, he realized he hadn't uttered ten words the entire conversation. In the moonlight, he saw the slivered remains of the cradle. Perhaps he shouldn't have destroyed it. He reached down and picked up a piece about the size of his palm. The double hearts and flowers he'd carved for the head of the cradle to represent his love and family remained intact. Since he owned no miniature of his Ruth, he would clean up the edges and keep it as a token of remembrance.

He entered the little house, set the wood on the table, and looked at the paper Mr. Whittaker had given him.

Mina Richards, East Stoughton

Where was East Stoughton?

Four

GIDEON SAT IN THE STRAIGHT-BACKED chair, the only seating available in the austere office. The gray light filtering through the lone window did little to brighten the bare walls, and the massive desk in front of him lay devoid of anything but a single stack of papers. The ticking of the clock on the wall was the only sound. In the fifteen minutes since the clerk had ushered him into the office, the sounds of the clock had grown louder and the seat harder. Waiting became a new type of penance.

Just as the clock hands reached their uppermost position, the door opened and a portly man dressed in black entered the room.

Gideon stood. "Reverend Ingram."

"Sit, sit," Clive Ingram said as he shuffled around the desk and sat in the chair. He picked up the top paper from the stack and perused it for a moment.

"Well." He lifted another sheet.

"Well, well." He read a third. Only one remained on the desk. "Well, well, well."

The distinct impression that things were far from well flooded Gideon. Reverend Ingram picked up the last paper and scanned it before setting the entire stack back on his desk and straightening them on the top and right side.

"Well, you quite thoroughly angered the little flock we gave you out in—" the reverend picked up the top paper—"Greenwich. Only one of the selection board members wrote in your defense. The rest feel that although you were most promising a year ago, since the death of your wife you've ceased to nurture your congregation. What say you?"

Gideon bowed his head, unable to look up as he answered. "There is little to say other than what they wrote. I am a failure."

"Do you want to be?"

Gideon's head shot up. "Pardon?"

"Do you want to be a failure?"

"No." To his own ears, the answer sounded uncertain. Would leaving the church make him a failure, or did it mean another path lay ahead?

Reverend Ingram raised his brow. "Maybe I should ask the question this way: Do you want to be a minister?"

Gideon gave the smallest of shrugs. "I have not been able to feel my calling or the Holy Spirit as I once did since—" The silence finished what he could not. "Doubts emerge as I search the sect's doctrines and the Bible. They don't always match."

"No, they don't. I would say you were not preaching material at all if you did not see the inconsistencies. Any preacher worth his salt studies and understands the problems. No denomination is perfect; all fail in some way or another. We must preach God's word the best we can and ignore the parts man cannot discern. Doubting has ruined more than one man."

"But—"

"Not all things can be answered by an appeal to the Bible. Scholars spend their entire lives studying and answering questions. You may rely on their writings when you are lost."

This answer may have comforted Gideon three years ago when he'd studied here, but after his loss, it left him feeling highly dissatisfied. Some of these scholarly ideas were at odds with what he believed about God's permanence.

The reverend continued. "Most of us have moments of doubt and weakness. A few, like you, let their doubts fester until those doubts steal their peace. Some questioning the ministry return and stay for months, attending classes to find answers. Others choose to be assistants to our established clergy, ministering to the flocks without the need to preach for a time. Does either of these options fit your needs?"

Gideon contemplated, not sure if either suited him.

"There is always leaving the clergy." Reverend Ingram delivered this with such disdain, Gideon hesitated.

"May I take the night to contemplate my decision?"

"Of course. I know you need time to pray for guidance." Gideon felt the correction in the reverend's answer. "The dormitory is almost empty as most of the students are visiting family until mid-January. Ask Norton to show you an unoccupied cell. You are welcome to stay there for now. If you choose to remain, we will arrange for other accommodations." He opened a desk drawer and pulled out a paper.

"This is a list of the clergymen who've requested assistance. It may aid you in your choice. Until tomorrow, then." Reverend Ingram opened another drawer and began searching its contents, effectively dismissing Gideon.

⟶ ❋ ⟵

Old Mr. Norton was as old as the drafty building housing the seminary. Gideon followed his stooped form up the stairway. A couple of lights shone from the three-walled cells lining either side of the central hallway. A few privacy curtains were pulled shut, while others stood open. Old Norton hobbled along, the lantern bobbing in hand, checking each of the little cells as he passed. He halted at the fifth.

"This one seems empty enough. Not even a blanket. Do you have one in your trunk?"

Gideon slid his trunk off his shoulder. Ruth's wedding quilt lay at the bottom. He did not want to use it here—too many private memories stirred at the sight of her handiwork. "Only my wife's wedding quilt."

Old Norton studied him. "I'm sure your quilt is too fine to use in these dusty dorms. You will find some old woolen blankets on the shelves in the lower hall. I trust you remember your way around?"

Gideon nodded in response.

Old Norton set the lantern on the little table next to the outside wall. "Rules and schedules are still the same. The reverend is forgoing night service this week. Prayers at six o'clock sharp each morning in the chapel. Best wear an extra pair of socks—only four others are here besides Reverend Ingram and us this week, so the chapel is colder than normal, if that's possible."

Not likely. As a student, Gideon had joined in the competitions to freeze water on the stone floor in the time it took Reverend Ingram to finish his morning service.

Old Norton turned to go, then paused. "Oh, and meals are served in the kitchen this week. Check in the morning, and I'll give you a duty. No point in running a full roster with everyone on holiday."

Gideon listened to Old Norton's uneven steps retreat down the hallway. He glanced to the other end where light spilled from the cells. Doubtless the occupants had heard every word. They would pass this way soon enough; no reason to go introduce himself. They'd probably already learned of the preacher who'd been fired after his Christmas sermon and would want to satisfy their curiosity.

He shivered. The dorms were almost as cold as the chapel. Some of the students joked, saying Reverend Ingram had gotten his denominations confused when he'd opened the seminary in the abandoned school and mistaken students for monks under a vow of poverty. The buildings certainly supported this idea. Gideon would need a blanket around his shoulders even to sit at the desk.

He stepped into the hall only to step immediately back into his cubical. As he knew it would, the water pitcher stood empty. A film of ice would cover the water's surface in the morning, but he would need to wash and shave before the morning devotional. He'd best fetch water now.

Returning, he found two men leaning against the wall posts next to his room. Gideon nodded as he passed them and entered his cell. After setting down his burdens, he turned and extended his hand. "Gideon Frost."

The taller man shook his hand. "Ethan Dover."

The other one stepped forward. "Mark Fletcher. Is it true? Were you terminated on Christmas?"

Ethan glared at the shorter man.

Gideon let out a sharp laugh. "Never let it be said that only the women in our congregations carry tales. No, the day after. But yes, my Christmas Eve sermon was the last feather on the horse's back."

Mark opened his mouth to speak, but Ethan silenced him with a glare. "Do you need anything?"

Gideon shook his head, hoping they would leave.

"Mrs. Norton has been leaving pies and puddings in the kitchen for us over the break. We were going down to see what we can find. Do you want to come?"

Gideon made a show of inspecting his cell. "Not tonight. I need to arrange things." The excuse was lame as they all knew it would take only a few minutes to make the bed and pull out a fresh shirt for tomorrow. But both men took the hint and moved to the stairway. Old Norton had indicated four students in residence—two more to meet. Gideon ran his hand through his hair, wondering how little he could get away with unpacking. He put his hand in his pocket and pulled out the paper the reverend had handed him in the office. The third item down caught his eye.

East Stoughton.

Gideon stared at the paper. A coincidence? His answer couldn't come that easily.

He unpacked his Bible and a change of clothing. As he moved about, his eye kept going back to the paper on the desk.

Why did East Stoughton keep tugging at him?

With his breakfast dishes cleaned and put away to Mrs. Norton's satisfaction, Gideon made his way to the offices in the school building.

As Gideon entered, Reverend Ingram looked up from the worn volume of sermons he was reading. "Come in, Gideon. I didn't expect you so soon."

"East Stoughton."

"Hmm?"

"What is in East Stoughton?"

"Not much. It's a little farming community fifteen miles south of Boston. They started building a church there a couple years ago. The outside is almost done, but the inside is far from it. Unofficially, it acts as the parish church, as Stoughton proper has one or two churches filled to capacity and the traveling distance is a bit far for some of the older people, but since the area is not incorporated, there are no funds." The reverend shrugged. A recognized parish church would receive monetary support from the town as per the Constitution of the Commonwealth. "The congregation is so spread out Reverend Porter can't get to everything. Especially with a wife and four children and another on the way. He needs help visiting the far-flung members."

Gideon processed the information. He'd assumed it would be an older man who needed help, not a young father.

"Frankly, I don't see you wanting that post. For being so close to Boston, it is isolated. It's pretty small, nothing like a real town, although they just built a new school. Someone saw a bear a few years back. I don't know if East Stoughton is the best situation for you."

Gideon nodded. The reverend began searching the drawers in his desk before he found a sheet of paper and scanned it.

"As I suspected, there is no income with this position, though it offers room and board. Have you considered the posts in Boston or the one in Shrewsbury?"

Gideon shook his head. "Thank you for the information. I shall continue to pray." Gideon left the room knowing his answer would be the same. He hoped Mrs. Richards still needed help. He would be in East Stoughton by the end of the week.

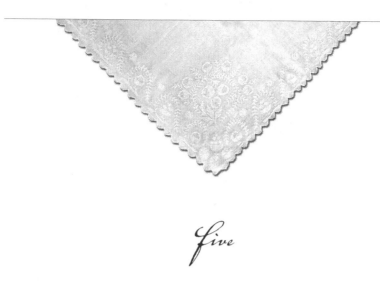

five

ELIZABETH TRACED PATTERNS IN THE ice crystals on the windowpane. Snow fell, and like a layer of new paint, it blanketed the older snow, gray with chimney smoke. More snow meant the trip to her aunt's would be delayed. Again. For three miserable weeks she had remained in her room. Father supplied task after task to keep her hands from being idle and becoming tools for the devil. Elizabeth rolled her eyes.

She'd mended every bit of clothing in the house in the past two weeks, earning her the maid's gratitude. She'd packed her trunk, the only one allowed her, twice. Father had checked everything she'd placed in the trunk and confiscated her favorite embroidered silk stockings, declaring she did not need such things. Mother protested, but Elizabeth meekly submitted to her father, knowing she would see the stockings again if mother had anything to do with it. And she read the only book available to her, the Bible.

Using the time to her advantage, she took to proving her father wrong. Nowhere in her new Bible could she find a verse about idle hands being the devil's playthings. And Reverend Woods had confirmed her assertions with a note, pointing out that the spirit of the quote was implied in several passages. This annoyed her father, who figured that if she had time to bother the reverend with missives, she could write a daily summary of her Bible reading. Today he'd assigned Psalms 16. Three sheets of paper full of words she knew he would want to read now lay on the table waiting for the maid to deliver them.

So far she managed to earn a reprieve from the bland meals the maid brought to her the first ten days of her imprisonment. She now enjoyed the same food served to the rest of the family, in her room. Father refused to allow her to even return her own tray to the kitchen.

She hoped to get back a few of her favorite gowns, particularly the crimson one. The few dresses she had kept had been modified, with three inches of fabric added to the necklines. She did the work herself. Fortunately Father did not recognize finished sewing from basting and didn't check her seams. It would take less than an hour to return the dresses to their former state once she reached her aunt's home. None of the remaining clothes was suitable for an evening party, but she'd hidden some money away. Not enough to purchase a dress from one of the Boston dressmakers, but more than enough to buy the cloth to make one herself.

Elizabeth grinned. Her one talent was sewing. Did the other girls really think such perfectly fitted dresses came from Boston? The crimson gown's low neckline? Modified so expertly her mother hadn't realized the change and insisted on purchasing a set of previously rejected stays? She'd never bothered to return the daring neckline to its original position. After all, fashion was changing.

Tired of watching the snow, she turned from the window to the mirror and practiced dropping her hair as she had every day since Christmas Eve. She casually tucked an imaginary stray hair into the matronly bun she wore. She detected no evidence of the pin she'd removed as she dropped her hand to her side. For several moments, she pretended to chat with someone. With the tiniest shake of her head, her hair tumbled down her back. Quickly, she gathered the curled tresses, pretending to be mortified. The remaining pins almost always stuck in the same place, making them easy to locate. She pinned the bun up in record time and gave the mirror the nod. If that move didn't entice some young man, then he was beyond enticing by even Lady Godiva. If a gentleman stood close enough, she could "inadvertently" brush his arm or hand with her long locks. Someday she might thank her father for forcing her to wear a dowdy bun. Now, if she could try it out on a man and not in her imagination. Would his eyes grow wide? Would he stutter? Surely Aunt Lydia's friends would have sons.

It had taken Elizabeth years to learn how to manipulate her mother, but Aunt Lydia presented no challenge whatsoever. The woman was far too trusting. Perhaps if any of her cousins had lived beyond infancy, her aunt would be the wiser. Uncle Joshua likely only cared if Elizabeth made a match benefitting his business. It was all too perfect. She would catch a wealthy husband and leave this small town forever. How had mother orchestrated such a coup?

If only she could get out of this room! If she didn't leave it soon, she would go mad and start talking to herself like Father.

Had she ever liked the horrid vine-and-rose flowered wallpaper?

The magistrate shuffled through his correspondence. He set aside the letter with an official seal and his newspaper to read later, and glanced at the two letters for his wife. No doubt from her witless sister.

The naive women thought he was sending Elizabeth to Brookline. He almost laughed aloud at their stupidity. Letting them plot a fictitious future full of balls, outings, and suitors served his purpose well enough, and it kept Rebecca out of his office and freed him of most of her nagging. Last night, he relinquished a pair of Elizabeth's silk stockings to get her to stop pestering him for a few more days while he awaited an answer from his aunt.

"Does she not comprehend I am serious when I talk of Elizabeth's retrenchment? Of course, it's my own fault for having such a silly wife," Ebenezer muttered as he opened the letters. Blinded by his ambition, he'd married Rebecca in a move to guarantee his career and had won a handsome wife in the bargain. He'd vowed Elizabeth would not grow up empty-headed and had given her schooling and such. But he'd overlooked her character, taking for granted that she would be naturally compliant and agreeable.

Elizabeth could speak intelligently on any topic but had adopted her mother's belief that all a woman needed to secure her future was to be beautiful. Why hadn't he put a stop to the behaviors years ago? Elizabeth had never known want nor hardship and subsequently had never developed kindness and compassion. Everything she did, from delivering food to the poor to writing essays in school, reflected a self-serving motive.

He may be the finest magistrate in district history, but he'd failed as a father. Now one last chance to help his daughter become the honorable woman he knew she should be presented itself. Yet even his solution pointed to his failures. He must now rely on someone else to teach the life lessons Elizabeth should have learned at his hand.

If only his aunt would agree. No reply had come in the last three weeks. "What if the old woman is dead? What will I do then?"

Ebenezer turned his attention to the official looking missives on his desk. Several hours later, he opened the Boston Gazette to study the news. He shook the pages to unfurl them, and a dirty paper fell to the floor.

He stooped to pick up the mud-covered, folded sheet. The written directions were blurred, but the return direction remained clear: "Mrs. M. Richards, East Stoughton."

His answer had arrived.

The little Bible she'd been balancing on her head dropped to the floor as the door flew open with a bang.

"Hurry! Your father says you are to leave the morning after next. We must pack."

"Pack? I've packed and repacked. Father inspected every corner of my trunk and locked it. He has the key." Elizabeth pointed to the trunk in the corner. Old and worn, the case was not one of the larger ones they used to travel to Boston each spring. "There is nothing left to pack and no place to tuck it."

Rebecca pressed her fingers to her lips and peeked into the hallway before shutting the door. She crossed the room to Elizabeth's side.

"Have you forgotten your silk stockings or your crimson gown? Or"—Rebecca gave a small grin—"your Christmas gown?"

"Father ordered those dresses sold."

Rebecca rolled her eyes. "No, he said to sell them—if I could. I reassure you I cannot sell them."

Mother knew how to twist father's words to her every advantage. Too bad he never recognized what an incredible mind she possessed or he would understand criminals far better. Elizabeth was instantly intrigued.

"If you look in the stack of linens the maid delivered, you will find the new gown between the sheets."

Elizabeth scrutinized the pile of linens. Father required her to change her own bedding, but she hadn't yet bothered with the process. In the pale light filtering through the window, it took her a moment to find the dress. Once she picked it out, she wondered how she'd missed the beautiful cloth. The fabric was of the palest blue, and unlike the dingy-yellow, coarse fabric of the sheets, the dress was soft and smooth. She fingered the fabric and knew instantly that it was silk. She lifted the dress out of the pile and began to unfold it.

"No, don't. It took us hours to fold the dress so that it fit. Lydia's maid will be muttering under her breath for a week at the ironing, but it will be worth all the trouble. It is the latest fashion after those Paris plates you saw this fall." Rebecca took the folded garment from Elizabeth.

"But, Mother, Father has the key, and the trunk is already packed to the brim. However will we get it inside?"

"Elizabeth, please. Just trust me. Now, if you open your wardrobe, at the back you shall find your crimson gown."

Bending down, Elizabeth peered into the nearly empty wardrobe, then reached to the back of the shelf. Finding nothing, she turned a questioning glance to her mother.

"No, in the bottom, wrapped in brown paper." Rebecca pointed to the location.

Elizabeth dropped to her hands and knees in search of the package. The floor of the wardrobe was littered with dirt, an old stocking, and dead bugs. Elizabeth cringed as she searched for the parcel. She let out a breath she hadn't realized she'd been holding when she felt paper in the back corner.

"Careful with that. We folded the gown to the exact dimensions of the trunk so it will fit under the false bottom. It took the maid four times to get it right."

"False bottom?"

"Exactly. Your father picked the oldest and ugliest trunk without considering to whom it belonged. It was my great-grandfather's unique trunk." The pride shone in Rebecca's face.

"The one who fled England disguised as his wife's sister?"

"The very one. Great-grandfather purchased the false-bottom trunk to conceal his writings and a change of clothing. Men's clothing."

Elizabeth nodded. One of her grandmother's favorite tales told again and again—her grandfather had tricked his pursuers by dressing as a woman and sailing to Boston so he could preach the Bible the way he wanted. Try as she might, Elizabeth failed to picture any man dressing as a woman and not being noticed. She'd heard stories of a few women who'd dressed as men during the Revolution and fought with no one noticing. Both ideas were equally inane by her way of thinking, but the false bottom came in handy regardless of origin.

Rebecca pulled a key from her pocket, pinching it between her fingers.

"Mother, how did you get the key?"

"This key is different from the one your father has. Help me scoot the trunk away from the wall."

Rebecca inserted the key into the lock and turned it to the left. The top of the trunk popped open. Elizabeth took a step forward. Rebecca put her hand up to stop her. "Now this is the trick—to not remove the key but turn it a complete revolution."

A small pop accompanied the falling forward of the trunk's front panel. Rebecca caught it and lowered it to the floor. A three-finger-width space appeared at the bottom of the trunk.

"Quick, hand me your crimson gown." Rebecca slipped the package into the narrow space. It fit perfectly. From her pocket, she extracted a handkerchief. Elizabeth recognized her favorite silk stockings peeking out from the corner. Rebecca tucked the cotton square in the compartment that now held the wrapped gown.

Elizabeth watched in awe as her mother pulled a beaded purse from the same pocket. "It isn't much, but you should be able to purchase a hat and some new boots." The bag was also tucked into the hiding spot.

"Remember, do not remove the key when this part is open."

"Why?"

"Why? What a silly question." Rebecca wore a perplexed look. "I have no idea why. I did it this way because my father told me to. Don't ask questions. Just do it exactly this way. To close the secret compartment, lift the panel and hold it in place, then turn the key back until you hear the click. You can now remove the key and access the top of the trunk as usual."

"Why didn't father's key do this?"

"Because it isn't the notched key. Enough questions. Hand me the other dress. If we tuck it between your petticoats, your father is unlikely to notice if he does check again." Amazingly, Rebecca rearranged the stuffed contents of the trunk, fit the silk dress in, and closed and locked the lid.

"Keep this key safe. See the notch at the end? That is how you tell the two keys apart." Rebecca held the key up for Elizabeth's inspection, then placed the key in the palm of her hand.

Rebecca checked her reflection in the mirror. "I'd best go before your father returns from Reverend Woods's house."

She kissed Elizabeth lightly on the cheek and flitted from the room.

Elizabeth pondered the key in her hand. Indeed, Father stood to learn much from the criminal mind of his wife.

⊷ ※ ⊷

The third step down creaked loudly enough to create an echo, startling Elizabeth back a step. The last time she descended the stairway was Christmas Eve, twenty-four days ago. Even the church house remained off-limits. She paused and stepped back onto the squeaky riser.

The noise wasn't any louder than before; she'd simply forgotten to walk on the left side. A silly thing to forget, but it bothered her. What else would she not remember?

Nathaniel leaned against the dining-room door, a glass of amber liquid in his hand. He raised his drink at her in a mock salute. "The prisoner is paroled." He took a sip as she finished her descent. Transferring the glass to his other hand, he offered Elizabeth his arm. "Come, let's sit. Father hasn't yet returned, and Mother is haranguing Cook over some minor detail."

They crossed to the parlor. Elizabeth sat on the edge of a chair, her back rigid, her ankles crossed. Nathaniel slumped onto the couch.

"Relax, Lizzy, it's just us. Your last evening at home. You can drop the royal-princess act."

Elizabeth leaned back and dropped her shoulders. "When did you arrive?"

"Late last night. The coach ran late due to a broken wheel, so I slipped into the house."

"Why didn't you come visit me this morning?"

Nathaniel arched his brow. "I was unaware the prisoner was allowed visitors."

Elizabeth shifted in her chair. "Since when has a rule stopped you?"

"Oh, Lizzy, you can't be serious?" Nathaniel threw his head back and laughed.

No point in responding, so she glared as she stood and circled the room, dragging her hand over each piece of furniture. "Do you miss home when you are working with our uncle?"

"This place? Not much. It is, as you say, 'rather dull.' I missed you, though. Few women have your intellect. I don't care what Mother's told you, men don't prefer stupid girls. Well, the stupid men do, but most of the successful men I meet married intelligent women."

Elizabeth cocked her head and studied her brother. "Is that what you are doing? Looking for some studious maiden wearing spectacles?"

She continued around the room adjusting the various vases and figures littered about.

"She doesn't need them."

Elizabeth spun around so fast she almost dropped the vase she was holding. "Who is she?" Elizabeth set the vase back on the mantel and advanced on her brother. Nathaniel scooted over and patted the couch next to him.

"Who said I had a woman in mind?"

Elizabeth sat beside him and tugged on his sleeve. "You did just now, and that expression you wear is far too innocent. Who is the fortunate soul? Where does she live? You must tell me."

"Why should I tell you anything?"

"Please?" Elizabeth hugged his arm.

Nathaniel tapped his finger on his chin. "Very well, then. Her name is Cecilia, and she lives in Philadelphia. I am hoping to convince our uncle to find someone else to travel all over for him and let me oversee his business there."

"Is it as serious as all that? Have you asked for her hand yet?"

"No, not yet, not until I know what type of life I would be giving her." Nathaniel drained the last of the liquid in his glass and set it on the table.

"So you would live there?"

"I think so. Cecilia is quite fond of Philadelphia, and I have no reason to set up business here."

"You would leave me?"

"You are the one who is leaving. The chances you'd come back are rather nonexistent. You'll meet some farmer down in East Stoughton, get married, and have a whole farming family."

Elizabeth jumped up. "A farmer! You must be joking. I am going to Brookline to my aunt."

"Aunt Lydia? Where did you get that idea? Can you imagine Father sending you there when he is intent on your reformation? He told me this morning you were to go to his aunt's in Stoughton."

Elizabeth balled her hands into fists and turned to leave.

Nathaniel grabbed her arm. "Stop. If you go storming in there and upset mother, your last supper in this home will be ruined. Be calm, and we can discuss this."

She tried to shake her brother off but without success. "Let me go."

"Not until you listen to me. Now sit back down. Father will be here at any moment. If he sees us fighting, he will send us both to our rooms."

Elizabeth rolled her eyes but complied. "Fine. So what is this about East Stoughton? I'm positive Father said I am to go to my aunt's."

"I am sure he did; he simply never said which aunt."

"But the only aunt I know is Lydia."

"You were young when you met her, but I believe Grandmother's sister, Aunt Mindwell Richards, visited when Grandfather died."

"Mindwell?" Elizabeth shivered, a sister of her grandmother would be horrid. Grandmother Garrett only ever wore black and quoted the Bible at least ten times in every conversation. A sister named Mindwell would be doubly bad.

"Father said she is widowed now but still keeps the farm. She needs help, and you've been volunteered. Father is sure she can reform you."

"Me? On a farm?" Elizabeth stifled a laugh.

"That's what you would have gotten had you caught Samuel Wilson. He washed up at Harvard. He will never be a doctor. Though not many doctors are better off than the poor farmers who pay them in eggs."

"Where is East Stoughton?"

"East of Stoughton." He grinned and raised his empty glass in another mock salute.

Elizabeth batted her brother's arm. "Nate," she said in a warning tone.

"Someplace south of Boston, maybe fifteen or so miles. Farms and forests, fewer people than here but not much different. Someone spotted a bear there a couple of years ago. Or was it a wolf?" Nathaniel tapped his chin. "Bear, I am almost certain."

"You are teasing me. There would not be bears so close to Boston."

"Never been there myself, but Father said it is still quite wild. Though my guess is that since the war, it has become more settled. I don't think he's visited our aunt in years. I'm sure you will find a few men there. They are building a church and a new school, so there must be some businesses."

"Aunt Mindwell? Farmers? Bears?" Elizabeth stared out of the window, repeating the words. The front door slammed. "Father."

Nathaniel shook her gently. "Lizzy, you will survive and conquer. You always do." He put his arm around her and gave her a squeeze. "You'll be well enough off. Don't let the cat out of the bag until Father does."

"I'll keep the secret, but only for Mother's sake, not yours."

Nathaniel stood and offered his arm. "Supper?"

Mother had asked Cook to prepare several of Elizabeth's favorites for supper, but Elizabeth only picked at her food. Nathaniel's revelation had turned her stomach to stone. She couldn't even force the molasses-baked squash down.

How could Father have deceived Mother so? Mother had mentioned Aunt Lydia no less than seven times since they'd sat down to supper. Elizabeth had bitten her cheek more times than she could count, having come close to setting Mother straight about her destination. Her last night or not, the temptation to yell at her father over his deception and the overwhelming injustices of this past month was great.

Nathaniel must have sensed her feelings, as he kept frowning at her and shaking his head whenever she opened her mouth to speak.

Elizabeth spooned another bite of squash into her mouth, trying to shut out her mother's voice. A pointless exercise, she was almost relieved when her father interrupted.

"Stop. Enough of this nonsense! There will be no balls or outings. Elizabeth is going to be reformed, not pampered."

"But Lydia—"

"But Lydia nothing. I said she was going to her aunt's, not your simpering sister's. Lydia couldn't reform her parlor curtains let alone a headstrong girl."

"But I assumed—"

"Yes, you did, and I have heard enough of your plans to know I was correct to contact my Aunt Mindwell Richards."

Rebecca dropped her spoon and sent it clattering to the floor. "Aunt Richards? Is she still alive?"

"Of course, she is alive."

"But I thought—"

"Mrs. Garrett, enough of your thoughts. Now, you are going to listen to mine. We will leave at first light, and we will travel to your sister's, as both Nathaniel and I have business with Joshua. If the weather holds, we can be there for a late supper. Then the next day, I will take Elizabeth to East Stoughton. There she will be expected to help keep house and cook."

"Father, how could you? I am not a servant!"

Even Nathaniel jumped when Ebenezer's fist hit the table. "Did you learn nothing in school? This is not England. You are equal, not better, not worse. It's time you understand this and stop putting on airs."

Rebecca had recovered enough to protest. "A farm? Cleaning? Cooking? She has never done any of that."

"Whose fault is that? Did your own mother not teach you such skills? I know of myself she did. Your meals were some of the best I had, but you've failed your daughter by teaching her only how to stitch fancy clothing. You have left her with no choice but to marry a wealthy man for his money."

"What is wrong with that?"

"Mrs. Garrett!" Ebenezer's voice rang with warning.

Nathaniel locked gazes with his sister.

Comprehension dawned. Father had married Mother in hopes of becoming his father-in-law's successor. This was why he treated their mother with such disdain—he had fallen for a pretty face and a future job. Elizabeth didn't want to be married to a man who could not abide the sight or sound of her. Was she of use to do anything else? Tears filled her eyes, and the image of Nathaniel started to blur.

"May I be excused?" Elizabeth did not wait for an answer before retreating to her room.

—≺· ✳ ·≻—

Elizabeth flopped onto the bed in Aunt Lydia's guest room. The sun had set hours ago. She'd spent most of the day either sleeping or pretending sleep as her brother and father had discussed everything from the president's policies to business prospects. Even in the cool January morning, the enclosed carriage had become stiflingly warm before they'd reached Reading, where they'd changed horses. Nathaniel had attempted to start a conversation more than once. Her father had reprimanded her for sulking.

Elizabeth did not give voice to her questions. How could she ask him if her suspicions were correct about his marriage and her future?

She paced the luxurious room. The downside of sleeping all day was that now she couldn't. Aunt Lydia had offered to console her over a cup of the finest chocolate, but Elizabeth had no desire to listen to her Aunt bemoan her fate. Lydia would repeat the same three sentences over and over, all focused on her own loss of a companion. After a late supper, Elizabeth realized living with Aunt Lydia would have been a torture all its own.

Beyond her great-aunt Mindwell's name and where she lived, Elizabeth knew little of the circumstances she would soon find herself in. She tried to recall anything she may have heard about her aunt. Grandmother Garrett had several sisters. Elizabeth had never paid attention to the stories she'd told. Only one comment came clearly to her mind—something about Mindwell being the most misnamed sister, considering Grandmother was named Patience and her other sisters Charity, Virtue, Prudence, and Empathy. Elizabeth was not sure how to interpret that information.

Grandmother Garrett had urged Elizabeth to hurry almost as often as she quoted the Bible. Patience seemed to be a virtue she lacked. The old woman had passed before Elizabeth's ninth birthday, so the memory of grandmother's impatience didn't mean much. By her way of thinking, each of the names was hideous.

Great-grandfather, a Puritan minister, believed children should live up to their names. Given the amount of time her Grandmother had spent scolding and quoting scripture, he'd passed something on, but it certainly wasn't the virtue of patience. So what would Aunt Mindwell be like? Or should she call her Aunt Richards?

Uncle Joshua confirmed Nathaniel's description of East Stoughton. His words echoed in her mind: "It is astounding such a backward place still exists so close to Boston and all of its conveniences."

A picture of a cabin surrounded by woods filled her mind. Elizabeth paced the room as her imaginings grew—a stooped old woman dressed in black with a black-lace cap, knitting on the porch; bears howling in the woods and the old woman shrieking. Elizabeth jumped.

When she realized the sound she'd heard was the cats fighting in the alley, Elizabeth sank onto the fainting couch, her heart beating fast. Best not to imagine things.

For a moment, earlier in the day, she contemplated running away. But with no way to support herself, she knew the plan was foolishness. Her only option was to go to Aunt Mindwell and bide her time. How long could the old lady live, anyway? A few well-written letters might convince Father of her reformation. She would return home before spring reached full bloom, midsummer at latest. Maybe Mother would plead her case. When Nathaniel wed, she would go to Philadelphia and stay with him. Cecilia's friends may have brothers. In the meantime, she must plan carefully. She discarded the thought of trying to get Aunt Mindwell to want to send her home. The chances of her father finding something even worse for her were too high.

The clock in the hall chimed midnight.

Six

THE GOLDEN HUES IN THE quilt Mrs. Richards had placed on the bed gave the gabled bedroom a cheery feel, though the room was sparsely furnished and less than her spoiled grandniece was likely used to. Gideon thought it a wasted effort.

A creak of the floorboards alerted Gideon to the entrance of Mrs. Richards, who kept insisting he call her Mina. He stood aside and waited for her instructions.

"Place the rug by the bed." A rather unnecessary direction as no other space large enough for the small rug existed. Gideon unrolled the rug and laid it in the indicated spot, adjusting the edge a bit to the left to cover an area where the floorboards were still uneven despite the repairs he'd finished earlier that week.

Mina placed her hands on her hips and studied the room. "Well, what do you think?"

"I hope she appreciates the trouble you've gone to."

"Oh, she won't. At least not at first. You forget, you are a rare gem. So many of your generation are too self-centered." Mrs. Richards reached up to pat Gideon's arm. He towered almost two heads above her stooped frame.

Mina tottered down the narrow stairway, Gideon following, his head bent so as to not bump it on a beam. Again. He wished she would use her cane. In the two weeks he'd worked for her, he noted the cane spent more time in the corner than in her hand. When it did occupy her hand, she was using it to reach something overhead rather than to support her aging body. He mentioned his concern once, only to find another use for her cane. The whack to his shin hadn't hurt much, but the strength behind the reprimanding rap had caught him off guard.

"Would you like some dinner? Might be the last good cooking you eat for a while."

Gideon raised a brow. Mrs. Richards's talent in the kitchen rivaled his own mother's.

"I'm going to give up cooking for a while. I fully expect there won't be anything edible for at least a week." Mina chuckled as she spooned a savory smelling stew into a bowl.

"If you own to so little faith in your niece's help, then why is she coming?"

Mina set the bowl on the table and reached for the bread, but Gideon beat her to the loaf and sliced a piece for both of them.

Mina accepted the slice and shook her head. "You spoil me, young man."

He pulled out a chair for her and waited for her to sit before gathering the last of the meal and joining her for a prayer. He ate several bites before continuing his questioning. "You didn't answer my question. Why did you agree to her living here? You clearly believe she will be of little help."

"Because God isn't sending her here so she can help me. He wants her here so I can help her."

Gideon set his spoon in his bowl.

Mina continued. "Preacher Boy, haven't you learned yet that things are not always as they seem, especially when God sticks His oar in the water?"

She studied him for a moment before shaking her head and continuing to eat.

He tried to shrug off the nickname. She called him Preacher Boy occasionally as she'd discerned the real reason for his presence in what she insisted on calling Curtis Corners instead of East Stoughton.

And what did she mean about God sticking His oar in?

For all the old woman's oddities, it was her relationship with God that puzzled him the most. She talked about Him as a friend when she discussed her daily reading and her prayers at meal times felt different.

He finished his meal and cleared both of their dishes.

"Leave the soup over the fire. I expect my nephew and grandniece anytime now, and I am sure they will be hungry." There was a bitter tone to her voice.

Gideon wondered if her eating an early dinner had anything to do with the impending company.

"I'd best be heading out. Reverend Porter asked me to look in on a couple of his parishioners down Brockton way this afternoon. I'll be back before sundown to do the chores."

"Did he give you good directions this time?" Mina laughed. The last set of directions indicated a right turn where a left should be taken. It was a wonder Gideon returned before finding the seashore.

Gideon handed over a folded piece of paper.

Mina scanned it and harrumphed. "Good enough, but mind you, don't eat any of the Widow Snow's pickled beets. You'll likely get a bellyache before you're halfway back. And wear your scarf today. Just because there is no snow on the ground, doesn't mean it isn't cold." She handed the paper back to him.

A grin quivered at the left side of his mouth as he put on his greatcoat. He didn't dare give the smile full bloom lest Mrs. Richards guess he grinned at her mothering him. He escaped out the back door.

Brown. Brown. Gray.

The scenery did little to help Elizabeth's mood. Woods full of skeleton trees and muddy fields attested to the recently melted snow. Rock outcroppings popped up now and again to break the monotony. Farmhouses occasionally dotted the road, eventually giving way to a close-knit grouping that included a store, and a church, or school.

Her father hadn't spoken for the past five miles. Elizabeth was glad of that. She could not endure another lecture with her fate so near. If she heard one more time how much of a disappointment she was or how wanton her behavior had become, she would leap from the buggy and walk. To where she knew not, but walk she would. Without Nathaniel as a buffer, her father's conversation had focused only on one subject—her failures.

South of Randolph they passed a church, which despite showing signs of weathering, did not look quite finished. Not long after, the houses bunched together again. At a fork in the road, her father headed west.

"Ah, we must be here. See the new school?"

Startled at her father's voice, Elizabeth followed his pointed finger to the red brick building. Why, the building couldn't be more than two years old! What type of place was this and so close to Boston! Not even a proper town. Elizabeth gripped the seat and closed her eyes. If only Mother were here, she would turn Father around.

The horses stopped in front of a small white gabled house with green shutters. At least it was not a log cabin—better than she hoped. Two tall trees stood in the yard. The corner of a red barn peeked out just beyond the house. Other well-kept houses dotted the street, giving her hope of some society.

Elizabeth waited for her father to give her a hand before descending from her seat. The wind tugged at the hood of her cloak. As she grabbed the soft wool with her free hand, a man on horseback trotted around the house as she stepped away from the carriage.

Oh, he was tall! Elizabeth discerned little of his face from beneath his wide-brimmed hat. She thought his nose might be a bit crooked and his eyes dark. He barely spared a glance their way.

How rude. Elizabeth couldn't recall the last time she'd been snubbed by a man—other than Samuel. Perhaps the ugly brown dress and cloak gave him no reason to look twice. Regardless, he rode down the lane. An excellent rider. It would be a shame if he were married.

Seeming not to have noticed, her father started up the walkway without her.

Elizabeth hurried to catch up.

A slightly crook-backed woman wearing a linen bonnet of unusual design opened the door to the house. Elizabeth thought the head covering quite flattering, devoid though it was of the usual ruffle. She needed to experiment with the pattern as she was sure she would be expected to wear one.

"Aunt Mindwell?"

Elizabeth's brow furrowed at the uncertainty in her father's voice.

"Ebenezer, come in before you freeze. You too, child." Elizabeth straightened her back. *I am not a child.*

The door closed behind them. Her father stood in the hall as if waiting for something.

"Ebenezer, if you are waiting for someone to take your coat, you will be standing there until it's time to leave. As for you," the old women peered up at Elizabeth. "Take your cloak into the kitchen. Use the hooks by the back door." A raised cane pointed the way. Elizabeth hurried to comply, sensing if she didn't, the cane might find another use.

The kitchen, though barely larger than her bedroom at home, was warm and cozy. Elizabeth's stomach rumbled at the smell of something savory coming from the pot hanging over the fireplace. A slice of toasted bread was all she'd forced down this morning before leaving Aunt Lydia's. That had been hours ago. Her innards rumbled. She obediently hung her cloak next to a faded shawl and returned to find her father and aunt sitting in a sunlit parlor.

Glaring at one another.

Elizabeth looked from one to the other, wondering if she should return to the kitchen. She turned to leave when her aunt broke eye contact with her father and turned her gaze on Elizabeth. "Stay, child."

Elizabeth slid into a straight-backed chair as far from her aunt and Father as possible. A thick packet of papers lay on her aunt's lap, the corners of what appeared to be bank notes sticking out, but from across the room, Elizabeth couldn't be sure.

"You really expected to hand me this," Aunt Mindwell lifted the stack of papers, "and your daughter, and leave in the same hour? I know my sister raised you better than to act in such a cowardly manner."

Silence filled the room. Outside, two boys ran past, their playful shouts reverberating off the windows. Still, her father did not reply.

"Very well, fetch her trunk and be gone."

"Perhaps your man?" Ebenezer trailed off. He seemed scared. Impossible.

"There is no man. I employ a helper half day. He is not here at present. I am sure you can bring it in yourself."

Aunt Mindwell stood and crossed to the window. "If you leave within the hour, you should reach Brookline, or wherever, long before the storm hits."

Elizabeth studied the cloudless sky through the window. Her aunt must be mistaken. Her father slunk out of the room. She'd never seen him cower before anyone before. Not even the men he sentenced to prison who flung insults as they were carted away made him flinch. Who was this woman?

Elizabeth rose to follow suit.

"Sit down, child." The command was firm but gentle. "We will discuss other matters later, but let us get one thing clear now. I am called Mina, or Aunt Mina, if you prefer. The first time you call me Mindwell or Richards, you will sleep in the barn. The second time, you will find yourself on the first stage north."

Elizabeth nodded.

"What is wrong, can't you speak?"

"Yes, Aunt Mind—um, Aunt Mina." Elizabeth thought she saw the reflection of a smile in the window glass.

"Close enough for now. Oh no! Careful." Elizabeth followed her aunt's gaze to the street. They watched mutely as her father slid her trunk off the boot of the carriage and into a mud puddle.

"I do hope that old trunk is well built, or you will be starting in on the laundry sooner than expected."

Elizabeth worried about the secret compartment in the base of the trunk. Her dress would be ruined if the mud seeped into the small space. She leaped from her chair and ran out the front door to give her father a hand.

The wind whipped her skirts about her as she ran down the path. Her father did not attempt to move the trunk from where it fell. Instead, he proceeded to untie the horses. By the time Elizabeth reached the trunk, her father had climbed upon the seat.

"Father!"

Ebenezer flicked the reins, and the horses began to move.

"Father!"

The only response to her yelling was a dismissive wave as the carriage headed up the street.

Elizabeth grasped one handle and tried to pull, but her boot slipped in the mud and she fell on her backside. Dampness crept through her petticoats.

"No!" she yelled into the wind and the vacant lane. She stood and tugged again on the trunk and succeeded moving it several inches. Three more violent jerks moved the trunk out of the mud and onto the browned grass. She circled to the other side and started to push the trunk, but her dainty half boot failed to grip the ground and she fell to her knees. Tears formed at the corners of her eyes as she tried to stand.

A shadow fell over the trunk. "Come inside before you catch a cold. Gideon can bring it in when he gets back if one of my neighbors doesn't come to lend a hand first." Elizabeth found herself being herded back into the house. They didn't stop until they stood in the kitchen. An odd clicking sound filled the room. It took Elizabeth a moment to realize it was her teeth chattering. Her aunt handed her a blanket.

"Sit, child, and have some soup and a bit of tea. Best get you warmed up."

The soup helped the chattering, and the warm cup of tea thawed her fingers. Her face was too cold to let the tears fall. Why did Father leave without a good-bye or fare-thee-well? Or helping with her trunk?

Mina set a bowl in front of Elizabeth. "I think we both planned on starting this off a bit differently."

Elizabeth dug in, then stopped, suddenly remembering the manners her mother had drilled into her. "Oh, you are not eating. How rude of me."

"Don't worry, I ate earlier. I think we'd best get you cleaned up. Your dress is going to need a good soaking. Do you have…" Mina let the sentence hang. "Let me guess, all your clothes are packed in the trunk in my front yard."

Elizabeth nodded.

Mina began to chuckle. Elizabeth started to giggle. Mina wiped at her eyes. "I am sorry, dear, but it is so ridiculous. You can't unload your things in the street, and I am sure I don't own a single thing that would fit you without showing half your leg. Oh, but my dressing gown may!" Mina hopped up with what Elizabeth thought was surprising speed for a woman of such advanced age.

Elizabeth had never heated water for her bath before. Her impatience had resulted in a rather shallow and tepid affair, but it was sufficient to wash the mud from her limbs. Aunt Mina produced a clean shift. Considering that her great-aunt stood two or three inches shorter than Grandmother, the shift was longer than Elizabeth expected. Coupled with some warm woolen socks, thick petticoats, and Mina's bed robe, Elizabeth felt much better, even if she appeared barely dressed.

Mina instructed Elizabeth on the best method for ridding her clothing of the mud stains. Another chore Elizabeth never expected to do.

"No, child, you must put your back into the scrubbing. Dirt doesn't come off clothing by placing it in water any more than the mud comes off you without your scrubbing with a cloth."

Hands buried in the hot water, Elizabeth considered telling the old woman what she thought about the indignity of washing her own clothes. But without any accessible clothing, she dared not push the matter. She couldn't be sure her aunt wouldn't send her home in her muddy clothing. Why was Father so afraid of Aunt Mina? It wasn't her size. Elizabeth towered four full inches over her aunt.

Elizabeth inspected the hem of the petticoat she was washing. It remained the color of weak tea, not the pure color of new snow her maid always managed. How much more would she need to scrub? Before she immersed the garment in the water again, Aunt Mina's bony fingers took hold of it.

"Not a bad start. Too bad it will not be sunny tomorrow, drying this in the sun would do wonders, as would bluing. But you don't have time for either today."

Elizabeth studied her red hands and wondered what bluing would do to them. The combination of lye and ash soap in the scalding water threatened to do permanent damage to her skin. She scrubbed again. Oh, her shoulder! She started to reach for the aching spot but realized her hands were dripping wet and plunged them back into the washtub only to narrowly miss splashing water on herself.

Aunt Mina peered around Elizabeth's side. "That is as clean as you are going to get your clothes today. Better finish up with the rest of your things, or we won't have time to make any supper."

Make supper? Didn't Aunt Mina employ a cook? Surely she didn't expect me to cook, too? Elizabeth started on her stockings.

"Don't rub those too hard. It would be better if they soaked for a day. Stockings do have a way of stretching in all the wrong places. If they do, instead of catching a glimpse of your delicate ankle, some young buck will think you have more wrinkles on them than I do on my face." Mina laughed.

Elizabeth scowled. How was she ever to figure out the old lady if she acted prim one moment and bawdy the next? It wasn't her fault the dressing gown was too short.

By the time Elizabeth finished washing, she thought her shoulder might never recover.

"You'll need to rinse everything out now. If lye soap stays on your shift, it will itch like poison ivy."

Elizabeth closed her eyes. Why didn't her aunt have a pump inside the house? She slipped on a pair of too-large boots and shrugged into her cloak.

"Empty the tub first, in the spot I showed you, or the whole yard will look like a pig wallowed in it."

Since the washtub was too heavy to lift, Elizabeth filled a bucket with the dirty water and trudged for the door. Her arms ached. She began to see the advantage of doing laundry in a washhouse or out of doors.

Reformation? Who needed that? At this rate, she would wake up dead in the morning.

Seven

THE WIND CRAWLED BETWEEN GIDEON's buttons and slithered beneath his scarf, biting his skin wherever it touched him. Gray-blue clouds gathered in the east, marching toward the south shore, ready to lay siege and reclaim the ground in the name of winter.

Gideon gave Jordan a nudge, and the horse picked up his pace as if he too sensed the need for haste. Jordan was the best mount he'd ever owned, despite the pun of a name Ruth had given him. "As long as you own this horse, I will know my Gideon is crossing safely on Jordan." Few of his parishioners caught the joke, but most of his fellow clergy chuckled as soon as they put the names together. Gideon wondered about the few who merely frowned.

Snowflakes fluttered around his head as he turned down the lane to Mrs. Richards's home. Mina—he needed to think of her by her chosen name in private, too, or slip again and give her reason to use her cane on his shins. White haze blurred his vision as the snow began to fall in earnest. Something lay in Mina's front yard. He squinted. A large box? A crate? He drew closer. A muddy trunk. He should not have left Mina to face her nephew and grandniece alone.

He dismounted Jordan and studied the old thing. No point in leaving it out in the snow. Hefting the trunk, he started around to the back, Jordan following. He dare not track mud through the front door.

As he rounded the house, a woman exited the back door dragging a bucket. Then she hobbled to the corner of the house and dumped its contents into the French drain. The girl from this morning turned and headed for the pump. In Mrs. R—Mina's dressing gown and his barn boots, he wouldn't mistake her for a mere girl again.

He watched her pump the water in little jerky movements, as if she'd never pumped water before. She must be used to an old-fashioned bucket dip well. Halfway back to the house, she lifted her gaze from the ground and locked eyes with him, then let out a screech and dropped the bucket, the water splashing the front of her clothes before he could say hello. Before he knew it, she'd dashed into the house, slamming the door behind her.

With his hands full of the muddy trunk, Gideon stared at the closed door. He did the only thing he thought of and bellowed, "Mina!"

Mina crossed the room and opened the door to her bewildered helper.

"How good of you to fetch the trunk."

"Where would you like this?"

Mina glanced at the stairs where her niece had retreated and considered the trunk for a moment.

"Set it there by the door. With so much mud, best leave it here until we can clean it up."

Gideon set the trunk where Mina indicated, then looked from Mina to the stairs and back to the trunk.

"That is your 'little' niece? She is older than I expected."

Mina grinned. "Yes, that is Elizabeth. Knowing how thin the walls in this house are, I will only say my meeting with my nephew was more disappointing than anticipated. But my niece is a pleasant surprise, and I believe this situation may be beneficial to both of us."

Gideon surveyed the messy kitchen. Puddles of dirty water spotted the floor. The half-empty washtub and basket of wet clothing gave him cause to doubt Mrs. R—Mina's optimism. He opened his mouth to speak but thought better of the idea.

Mina patted his arm, grabbed a rag from the bin, and started to wipe up the mess. "You'd best hurry and get the chores done. I bet two feet of snow will fall before morning."

Gideon went to the spot where he kept his older boots, but instead of his boots, he found two very muddy women's half boots. Even covered with the drying brown dirt, he discerned their fine craftsmanship. Probably from one of the more expensive Boston shoemakers. Not many men honed their talents to the skill required for such work.

"Where are my—" No point in finishing the sentence as he remembered whose feet were wearing his boots only moments ago.

"Oh, dear. I think I heard her trip out of them on the way up the stairs," Mina said as she continued wiping at the puddles.

Gideon walked to the stairway, relieved to find both boots. One must have fallen off on her first step. The other made the entire assent and lay on the top stair. He hurried to grab the top one lest he encounter her again. As he bent to retrieve the boot, the unmistakable sound of a woman sobbing reached his ear.

Not wanting to deal with either woman, Gideon rushed out to the barn. On his way, he spied the abandoned bucket, filled it, and set it on the porch before going to unsaddle Jordan.

Heavy footfalls sounded on the stairs. Too loud for Aunt Mindw—Mina. That man! Burying her face in the pillow, Elizabeth tried to stifle her sobs. The footfalls retreated. Perhaps he had not heard her.

She did not want to see him ever again. He should have made his presence known, not stood staring at her while she pumped water in her aunt's dressing gown. How unbelievably rude.

Of course, slamming the door in his face while he carried her trunk was rude as well, but he'd scared her.

She sat up and wiped her eyes. Crying was silly. Well, usually, but crying out all the things she couldn't put into words actually helped.

She crossed to the washstand and rinsed her tears away, the icy water stinging her cheeks. Typically she would have balked, but the cool water soothed her reddened face. In the small mirror, she tidied her hair. Good thing she'd used plenty of hairpins to put her hair up this morning. If it had tumbled down in all the mud…She shuddered. As cold as the house was, drying her hair would take forever.

Movement outside the window drew her attention. The man was walking into the barn. At least she thought it was him. The falling snow made it difficult to tell. He must have left the trunk downstairs, as no thump of the heavy trunk being set down had echoed on the landing. Perhaps if she hurried down, she could dress before he returned to the house.

She pressed her hand to her chest. The key! The ribbon holding the key was missing. Elizabeth closed her eyes and tried to concentrate. She'd tied the key on before she left Aunt Lydia's. She'd checked twice before leaving. When she'd hung up her cloak in the kitchen, the key had lain warm against her skin. She'd tugged on the ribbon to be certain. However, when she had stripped down for her bath, she didn't remember untying the ribbon. Why hadn't she realized it then? Perhaps because her chattering teeth had rendered the thought impossible.

The key must have fallen off when she'd wrestled with the trunk out in the yard. Elizabeth sank onto the bed. It would be impossible to find now with the snow coating the ground and the evening light fading. She felt again for the key. Nothing.

Her stays. Maybe the key had become caught in them. The stays lay on the kitchen sideboard, having escaped the muddy fate of the rest of her clothing. The man had been in the kitchen! Had he seen her stays too? How long could she avoid him? He must be around often if she saw him both coming and going.

Elizabeth hurried down the stairs, listening carefully to make sure only Mina was in the house. She stopped short when she entered the kitchen and found her aunt on her hands and knees, cleaning the floor.

"Aunt Mind-a." She hurried to correct herself. Her aunt looked up. "I, uh, you shouldn't, uh."

Mina used the chair back to pull herself up, then rubbed her knees. "Yes, I think you're right. But you ran out on me."

"I, uh, there was this man, and I—" Elizabeth waved her arms uselessly for a moment. What was it about her little aunt that scared her so much?

"And you slammed the door before he could bring in your trunk."

"Oh no, I hadn't meant to."

"Oh yes. Lucky for you Gideon is a preacher and is used to folks doing funny things."

"Preacher?" Elizabeth's voice came out as a strangled squeak. "The preacher saw me dressed like this? I can never—"

"You can, and you will. First let's get you properly dressed, before he finishes in the barn. Then you can apologize and thank him for rescuing your trunk."

"I lost the key outside when I tried to bring in the trunk."

Mina studied her quizzically and pulled a key out of her pocket. "Your father left it for you." She handed Elizabeth a key attached to a short ribbon. Elizabeth took the offered key. The underside was smooth, missing the special notch.

"Don't stand there. Get some other clothing out."

"It's the wrong—never—This will do." Elizabeth allowed the sentence to fade into a mumble.

Elizabeth unbuckled the leather straps and shoved the key into the lock. She tried to turn the key the special way. As Mother said, it refused to turn. She turned it the other way and opened the top. Her fingers searched for some other way to open the other compartment. What if mud had leaked into the hidden space?

"Is something wrong, child?"

Elizabeth shook her head, then nodded. "There is another compartment this key doesn't open. It is at the bottom, and I am afraid the mud—" Elizabeth shrugged.

Mina raised her brows.

Elizabeth bit her lip, knowing she'd said too much.

— ※ —

Gideon debated leaving Jordan in the Richards's barn for the night. The Porters' barn was no more than a shed, and the addition of his horse would crowd the structure. On the other hand, he didn't relish walking a half mile in the snow in the growing darkness. The snow fell steadily. If the wind picked up, he might lose his way. He didn't like leaving Mina alone, either. Yet staying in the house with the not-so-little niece would be frowned upon by the congregation—and the niece.

He wasn't leaving Mina alone. She had her niece, even if she didn't know how to pump water. Gideon reminded himself not to judge. There could be another explanation. The woman may be injured. That would explain the wrapper she wore. Whatever the reason, he'd better pump some more in case the pump froze tonight. Leaving the barn, he checked the knots on the guide rope to the house. He didn't want to leave Mina without a way to find the barn in case the storm turned into a blizzard.

Passing the woodpile, he grabbed an extra armful. Already the snow lay as deep as his ankles. He used his foot to knock on the door.

Mina opened the door before his foot connected a second time. Gideon pivoted so as to not kick Mina. Somewhere in the house a door closed with more force than necessary. Gideon unloaded the wood into the woodbox.

"Looks like we are going to get a deep one tonight. I'll fill up your water buckets before I leave for Porters'. Anything else you need?" Gideon rubbed his hands together.

"You sure you can make it all the way to the parsonage? If the wind picks up, you won't be able to see your hand in front of your face."

"It is clear enough. I'm going to take Jordan, so I should arrive before anything changes."

Mina nodded. "Best get going. I've seen it drop a foot of snow in less than three hours before. I don't want you caught in the worst of the storm."

Gideon grabbed the water bucket and hurried out to the pump. He returned and dumped the bucket into the large pot, then repeated the process twice.

On his last trip, he grabbed more logs, just in case. The door opened wide, and instead of Mina, her niece held it. He hurried in and set down his burden.

"That should keep you through most of tomorrow if need be." He turned to the niece. "I don't suppose you know how to milk a cow or feed livestock."

Elizabeth bristled. "No, I don't." She lifted her chin the slightest bit.

Gideon turned back to Mina. "If I can't return in the morning, make sure you take your niece with you to the barn. She can figure most of the chores out, but don't you overdo." Gideon jammed his cap on his head and left the room before either woman responded.

Elizabeth looked at her aunt and shrugged.

"You can talk to him tomorrow. Finish rinsing your clothes while I find us some supper."

Eight

MINA STRETCHED OUT ON THE fringed bed. The dream of her late husband, Henry, slowly faded. The colder the morning, the more she missed him. Every morning for forty-four years, she'd awoken warm at his side, which she hadn't appreciated in mid-August. This second winter without him made her long for the sweltering summer mornings she'd once complained about. The flannel-wrapped bricks she'd placed at the foot of the bed had lost their heat hours ago. Maybe she would invest in a warming pan. Widow Snow claimed the pan was far superior to heated bricks. Although it seemed like a waste of money when a brick or rock would do the job and not cost a single penny. She did not relish getting out of bed and was certain her niece was not used to early mornings, but what if Elizabeth arose first and tried to build up the fire?

Assuming Elizabeth had missed that part of her education, too, Mina leapt from the bed and pulled on her wrapper. The kitchen remained dark and empty. She sighed with relief to see the copper curfew tucked in the corner, protecting the hot coals.

Washing, cooking, and cleaning—how had her nephew's wife ignored the education of his daughter? What was this world coming to? Her poor sister would roll over in her grave if she knew her granddaughter had turned out to be a spoiled sluggard.

Like all her sisters, Patience had been misnamed. She would never have let things get to this point. Thinking Patience was overreacting,

Mina had laughed at her sister all those years ago when she'd worried her granddaughter was being spoiled beyond repair. Perhaps a chance remained to correct the course, but it would all depend on Elizabeth. Her niece must want to change.

And to do that, Elizabeth needed to wake up.

⧗ ✳ ⧗

Thump. Thump. Thump.

Elizabeth rolled over on her soft feather bed. Why didn't the maid come in already? Frost clung to the window, and her breath hung in the air. She needed her can of hot water.

Thump. Thump. Thump.

No flowered wallpaper. Slanted walls. Ugh. She was not at home. No maid. At least not for her. Aunt Mina got one yesterday—her.

Thump. Thump. The knocking continued from the floor below. Yet another use her aunt had found for the intricately carved cane.

"Coming!" Anything to get the pounding to stop. Pain shot through her shoulder as she sat up, the abused muscles in her back tightening. Retrenchment? More like a slow, painful death. Her foot recoiled into the covers when she tried to stick it out. Brrrr. If the work didn't kill her, the cold would.

Thump. Thump. Thump.

"I said I'm coming!" Elizabeth hopped out of bed. If her aunt was anything like her grandmother, having to call a third time would mean a painful punishment. Aunt Mindwell was not big enough to box Elizabeth's ears, but the cane could inflict some harm.

The gray wool dress she'd worn last night after opening her trunk remained her only option as the rest of her clothes still sat in the trunk in the kitchen. Before slipping the hideous and itchy garment on, she pulled on the thick stockings and petticoats kept warm under her quilts. She ran down stairs without rebraiding her hair.

"Tomorrow I expect you to be down here by six thirty to start the fire. I will teach you how to build up the fire for the day, then you can make breakfast for us."

Before sunrise? Elizabeth opened her mouth to object, but her stomach rumbled and she changed her mind. The alternative might be going without food. "What shall I make?"

"What can you make?"

She bit her lip before answering. "Nothing, but when I was little, I did help Cook mix batters."

"Let us start with something simple—frying yesterday's bread and boiling a couple of eggs. You can also start to cook the beans I soaked overnight for our dinner. Gideon takes the noon meal with me, so I make plenty. Extras work for supper." Mina sat on the bench at the table and proceeded to direct Elizabeth's every move.

Aunt Mina claimed the two pieces of bread less black than the others and scraped them over the slop bucket. Elizabeth scraped her toast, but the fact that her pieces had caught fire rendered them unsalvageable. Still, she picked the pieces apart, hoping to find enough to keep her stomach from rumbling. Mina had not trusted her to heat her morning cup of chocolate, so she filled up on Mina's chocolate and the boiled egg. Elizabeth figured one could do little to ruin a boiled egg.

She was wrong. Obtaining a particular shade of green, the egg tasted worse than it appeared.

Mina studied the clock—nearly nine, and Gideon remained absent. The snow still fell lightly, more than a foot and a half having accumulated. Watching Elizabeth's attempts to iron the clothes she'd washed yesterday gave Mina second thoughts about keeping her promise to Gideon not to tend to the animals alone.

The girl was a menace. Twice she'd burned her hand because she forgot the cloth pad to hold the handle. Fortunately, there was the snow, readily available to cool the burn. Mina winced as Elizabeth reached for an iron without her rag again. Just in time, Elizabeth snatched her hand away and grabbed the cloth. Now if she could keep from totally ruining her clothes. Thankfully, the burned spot likely wouldn't show on the drab-brown dress, and no one would see the petticoats.

Mina returned to her spinning. The thread slipped, her fingers not as agile as they had once been. But she enjoyed the hum of the wheel. Fewer people spun at home now. Mina considered giving up spinning and weaving more than once as purchasing cloth became easier. Maybe next year. This year she would teach Elizabeth.

"Ouch!"

Mina caught her niece sucking her finger. Another burn and only a quarter hour had passed since the last one. And still no Gideon.

"Child, enough ironing, I think. Set the irons to cool on the edge of the hearth. We need to check on the animals."

As Mina pulled an old greatcoat from the peg, she worried. *Oh, Henry, I hope I am up to this task.*

Only forty-six strokes and Elizabeth's arms were shaking too much to brush the other fifty-four. Why was Aunt Mindwell making her do such menial labor? It was perfectly humiliating. Supper consisted of burned beans. The same beans were not quite done at dinner. Aunt Mina either had no sense of taste or pretended nothing was amiss and ate. Elizabeth's stomach rumbled, whether in protest of the food she'd consumed or in hunger for anything edible. Even pease porridge would be welcome now, providing someone else cooked it.

Little chance circumstances would improve. Tonight they set out what her aunt called a bread start. If she ruined the bread, would her aunt keep forcing her to perform work she was not raised to do? Mother had raised her to run a household and oversee servants, not be one. A thousand complaints went through her head, but none crossed her lips. Not even when the goat kicked the milk bucket. Not that it contained much milk—the goat hadn't given up its milk easily. Her aunt took up the milking only to have Mr.—or Reverend, which was unclear—Frost walk into the barn. His censorious glare was accentuated by the grim line of his mouth. He shooed them out of the barn and left before dinner, which was part of his pay.

⊶ ❈ ⊷

Gideon sat at his desk in front of his open Bible, the words blurring on the page. What was Mina thinking? Her incompetent niece would kill them both by starvation or poorly cooked meat before the month was out. If he hadn't arrived when he did this morning, a serious accident might have occurred, more than the spilled milk someone had let seep into the straw lining the stall. And that someone was probably the reason Mina had been milking when he'd stepped into the barn. He'd wasted no time in escorting both women back to the house.

He'd skipped dinner when Mina had warned him off with a head shake and a grimace. With several families to check on, he found food elsewhere.

Worst of all, the niece was more than commonly beautiful. He'd berated himself last night for noticing her at all. It was against all he'd promised himself after Ruth died, to take note of another woman for anything other than her kind heart, which he wondered if the girl even possessed. He'd caught the rebellious look and proud lift of her chin in the barn. He'd met girls like her before. If Mina thought she could reform her niece, he'd better help her by praying for a miracle.

Maybe God would answer a prayer for Mina. Miracles might work for someone else. His own prayers had remained unanswered for months. He needed direction. Did he remember enough of the trade his father had taught him to be a success? He would write his brother in the morning about having his tools sent down. Or maybe he would go visit him.

Gideon pulled out a piece of paper and uncorked the ink bottle. A letter would do.

⊶ ❈ ⊷

Elizabeth lit a second candle, an extravagance she wasn't sure her aunt would approve of but necessitated by the dimness of the room. She would blow it out as soon as she finished her letter.

Dear Mother,

I am well. It has snowed here but has mostly melted away. I think it must melt faster this far south. Aunt Mindwell's house reminds me of Ford's cottage. Not large enough to host a party, but more than I expected. She does not employ any servants and never has, other than someone to help with the farming. There is a man who comes and cares for the animals and does the heavy work. As near as I can tell, he is a reverend but is in some disgrace with his church. I can share naught of his disgrace as it is a carefully guarded secret. All I know is he was formerly posted at a church in the western part of the state. At first, I thought he left a wife there, but I have learned he is a widower. I do not understand why some woman hasn't gotten him to propose. Despite his crooked nose, he is rather handsome and not yet thirty. Even if he is doomed to be poor, he would be a catch for someone. He lives with Reverend Porter and helps him with the congregation, as it is rather widespread, consisting of more than the fifty or so families in the area Aunt calls Curtis Corners.

It would probably shock you to learn that Aunt has made me her cook. It is likely to be as disastrous as you expect. I kept hoping if I failed to cook well she would relent at my learning, but after more than a week of inedible meals, I have put my mind only to learning this one skill well. I made a perfect Johnny cake yesterday, and today's bread is not hard and flat. Mr. Frost, her employee, ate with us today at dinner.

It is shocking. We eat in the kitchen as she has no dining room. The room that should be the dining room has a huge weaving loom in it, and we must eat with the help.

Aunt Mina, she doesn't like the name Mindwell, has determined now to teach me to spin and eventually to weave. I wonder why, with modern factories being built every day making such excellent fabrics, she would want to do something so laborious.

She has started me on a drop spindle, which is aptly named as I seem to drop it to the floor often. It usually rolls under the chair and breaks the thread.

Speaking of under the chair, she made me mop last week! And wash laundry. It took two full days. I don't think she understands the whole retrenchment idea Father lectures on. I am not to be reformed but remolded into a maid.

Be at ease on my account, as I am constantly on my best behavior, so I can return home to you.

Your loving daughter,

Elizabeth

Nine

Elizabeth stretched. She pulled her bed gown and stockings out from under the quilt and put them on. There was no need to put on her dress until after they ate, as a fire would have to be kindled. Elizabeth hurried down the stairs and discovered red coals under the curfew. She had properly banked the fire—a thrilling sight after yesterday's mishap. In no time the fire was burning brightly and the water boiling.

Last week, on account of the storm and resulting ice, Sunday services had been canceled. Elizabeth passed several uncomfortable hours reading Bible passages aloud to her aunt in the parlor while her aunt rocked and rocked. Spinning and sewing were both forbidden Sabbath activities. Elizabeth longed to meet someone besides her aunt and the stoic Mr. Gideon Frost. The postmaster didn't count.

Elizabeth sliced some bread. This loaf was not as disastrous as her first batch but was still better suited to milk toast than normal eating. It would make a sufficient breakfast.

Mina entered the room, also clad in her bed gown. She said nothing about the rags tied into Elizabeth's hair but did raise her brows as she fingered one. It wasn't like Elizabeth planned on an elaborate hairstyle, just something to accentuate the single bun she'd worn the past several weeks.

Mina set about making her daily chocolate. Though she required Elizabeth to do all the other cooking, making chocolate remained off-limits. Elizabeth wasn't fond of the bitter concoction, but Aunt Mina's was more tolerable than most as she added a measure of sugar to the syrup.

Outside, the barn door creaked. Elizabeth looked out the window, hoping the half curtain hid her from view. Between the rags tied in her hair and her dressing gown, being seen by Mr. Frost was something she'd rather avoid. His silent presence at the table each day gave her plenty of time to study him. Handsome, sad, and brooding. It wasn't hard to guess the source of his sadness, widower as he was.

Aunt Mina must have guessed the reason for her focus on the barn. "He likes to do his Sabbath chores early. He will leave the milk on the porch, along with any eggs."

Elizabeth's shoulders relaxed. She'd wanted to impress him today and show him she wasn't the dowdy niece of his employer. She was, after all, the "prettiest thing on the North Shore." His late wife must have been uncommonly beautiful as he paid Elizabeth no more attention than he did his burned beans. Today would be a good day to try her falling bun on a man. She pictured his deep-brown eyes widening in appreciation.

"Walk? But it is more than a mile!"

Mina shook her head and prayed for patience. "Yes, meaning it is too close to worry about hitching the horse to the buggy. The sun is shining, and the roads are dry. Hurry up, now."

"But my slippers ..." The protest died on Elizabeth's lips. One glance at her aunt's sturdy boots, and she knew the answer. She slumped onto the bench, pulled off her slippers, and replaced them with her half boots. Still too fancy for walking a mile.

"We must see to getting you a sturdier pair. Remind me to take you to the cobbler's on Tuesday."

Elizabeth groaned inwardly. The last thing she wanted was a pair of ugly, serviceable boots like her aunt's. But she would need them to keep her half boots and slippers from being ruined hanging laundry, gathering eggs, or walking to who knew where.

She straightened her blue skirt. Though far from her favorite crimson gown trapped in the keyless trunk bottom, the deep-blue dress was the favorite of those she'd kept. Last night she'd unpicked the fabric she'd added at her father's insistence. It did not match anyway, being a solid color against the block-print bodice. The collar on this dress had a fashionable yet prudent line. The embroidered fichu she wore was made of thick cotton, a practical concession to the weather since it was heavier than the silk and lace ones she favored. She smiled a bit as she pictured Gideon seeing her dressed fashionably rather than in the old clothes she wore around the house. Should she loosen the fichu? She hadn't decided yet. It had taken forever to get the newer set of stays in place without the help of a maid, but she knew her figure was shown to its best advantage that way.

Elizabeth finished tying her boots and put on her cloak, fastening the silver frog, then she held the door open for her aunt. Time to meet the residents of this little hamlet.

Mina's knee throbbed as she walked up the hill next to her niece. She should have taken the buggy. Not that she would admit it. More likely than not, they could get a ride home with one of the Brockton farm families. She'd planned on taking the buggy until Elizabeth had come downstairs dressed in her modified gown. The gown, though not as brazen as the one her nephew had described, was enough to prompt her to teach Elizabeth a lesson. A lesson Mina soon regretted, even if Elizabeth's gown was gathering dust as she hoped it would.

In one of Boston's churches in the wealthier parts of town, the dress would be one of dozens similar. Here it would stand out both in fabric and cut. A bit of dust and mud on the dress would be a kindness to her niece. Other than Gideon, only two unattached males attended on a regular basis; one a simpleton and the other a lecherous beast of a man. She thought to caution her niece about him but worried that warning her would only send her straight into his arms. Better she keep a watchful eye instead. Her fichu better not become loosened too much, or Mina would take a needle to the dresses herself.

A memory of Henry's flushed and attentive face flitted through her mind. After a particularly vigorous dance, he'd picked up her white-work fichu, which had fallen to the floor as they'd slipped into a secluded corner. She'd bent to retrieve the fallen fabric, but as planned, he'd beaten her to it. That single act had guaranteed the proposal only a day later. Not until their Becca was of age did Mina realize that if her father had seen her actions or the look on Henry's face, she would have been wed that very night. Mina couldn't help but wonder if Ebenezer realized how like Elizabeth she had once been.

Still, Elizabeth needed guidance. There were times for desperate measures and times to behave in a proper manner. Elizabeth needed to learn the difference. Henry had been on the verge of proposing for weeks before she'd dropped her fichu. He'd just needed a boost to get over his shyness.

The rumble of a passing wagon jarred Mina out of her reminiscing just as the wheel found a puddle, splashing both her and her niece.

"Sorry, Mrs. Richards!" yelled the farmer's wife.

Elizabeth snorted in disgust but did not comment.

"Three," Mina muttered under her breath. She'd made a game of counting how many times she caught her niece minding her tongue each day. So far she'd reached sixteen before Elizabeth made some comment, which she immediately apologized for. Mina longed to tell her she was not like her sister Patience, Elizabeth's grandmother. Mina had never boxed a child's ears, even when her son set the hayfield on fire. But for now, Elizabeth's fear of an imaginary punishment kept her in check. The ruse would serve its purpose until fear of punishment was replaced with a desire to behave.

The church was far more pleasant to look at from the exterior than the interior. There were no stained-glass windows or finely carved wood to trace with her eyes as the minister droned on. Rough, backless benches left her with nothing to lean on. Only four of the pews shone with a waxy polish. The others appeared unfinished. They sat in the back, the benches surrounding them remaining empty as the congregants huddled together in two groups on either side of the aisle for warmth near the front of the room.

Two births, a death, and a pair of newlyweds were announced. But the diversion of the newly married couple standing to show off their wedding finery was denied by this pastor. It seemed the newlyweds were also separated by the aisle, with the men on the left side and women on the right. Her favorite part of church service since childhood was watching the bride and groom stand during the sermon and turn slowly so all could admire their finest clothing. She often pictured what she would wear on her wedding day. She envisioned how her eardrops would sparkle in the light streaming through the windows. Her husband would wear a handsome new coat in the latest fashion.

Here, the minister made an announcement, but the bride and groom only smiled from either side of the room. They didn't even seem to be wearing their finest and didn't stand.

Not fair! Twice in the past two months she had been denied the opportunity to gawk at a newly married couple and be diverted from the sermon. The first had been the cause of this punishment. If Samuel and his wife had only stood during the service, father would not have caught her staring at them. Lucy reportedly married Samuel wearing her shift and hadn't come to the meetinghouse for a month after her nuptials. Perhaps she'd been too embarrassed to stand to allow others to admire their wedding attire, as was the custom in most area churches. However, Lucy's new dress rivaled her own, its lace exquisite. Elizabeth snorted at the thought. Quickly she brought her handkerchief to her nose, hoping all would mistake her laugh for a sneeze.

Aunt Mina's stern look gave Elizabeth cause to listen to the sermon again.

"Repentance." The minister delivered the word in a flat voice.

That one word sent her mind wandering again.

—※—

Gideon observed the congregation from where he sat behind the podium. Mina's face slowly relaxed, the tightness around her eyes softening as the sermon lengthened. Clearly she was in pain. What had she been thinking to walk to church? He set the buggy out so Mina could hitch the horse to it like he did every week.

Miss Garrett must have made a mess of things again. He made a note to check on the horse. How such an ill-equipped woman roamed the earth was beyond comprehension. He pictured her working the horse into a frenzy trying to harness it to the buggy and keep her dress clean at the same time. He would need to make sure someone offered Mina a ride home. As for Miss-I-Need-to-Show-Off-My-Lovely-Blue-Dress, she could walk home. The only woman in the congregation who'd completely removed her cloak would have no problem with the cold. Most women opened their cloaks but did not remove them against the chill of the room.

Not that he noticed the dress or how it suited her much better than the gray and brown ones she'd worn since her arrival. It was harder to think of her as a girl, or child, as Mina kept calling her, in the blue dress. Miss Garrett was all woman, on the outside at least.

Realizing he was staring, he moved his attention to the other side of the aisle. Two older men nodded in sleep, and the sermon was only half over. He knew exactly how much of the homily remained as Reverend Porter had practiced on him thrice this week.

Mr. Jones didn't bother to pretend to listen to the sermon, his eyes following his new bride. What a shame the practice of sitting as families was not followed by Reverend Porter. Mrs. Curtis wrestled her young twins alone. Shame indeed. He would suggest the change to the reverend. The room would be quieter if the fathers and older brothers could help with the younger children—including the reverend's own son. Two-year-old Eustace Porter had escaped his mother's hold again.

Theodor Butler caught his eye. The man was definitely not paying attention. Instead, he was gawking at Elizabeth. He needed to warn Mina. More than one of the congregants had brought complaints against Mr. Butler. The young maid of the storekeeper had named him the father of her babe and claimed she was forced. No charges had been brought before the church elders or magistrate, as a servant was not in a position to be believed. Few won against one of the richest men in town. The babe went to a foundling home, and the maid was permitted to continue her work, as her employer gave no credence to the tale.

Ah, Reverend Porter had reached the main point of the sermon and would finish at any moment. Gideon turned his mind to the song he would lead the congregation in to complete the service.

Elizabeth pulled on her cloak but didn't close it, though the tiny stove did little to keep the room warm. She toyed with her fichu while watching Gideon survey the congregation. She failed to catch his eye other than for a brief second when his brow wrinkled, hardly the admiring gaze she expected. She continued to study him as the sermon droned on. He narrowed his eyes, something seeming to have disturbed him.

When she looked across the aisle in hopes of discovering what her humorless friend saw, she found a man who watched her with a crooked grin. His eyes looked not on her face but on the hand playing with her fichu. A shiver ran up her spine, and she dropped her hand and looked away. Something in the man's gaze left her feeling scared—it was almost as if he didn't need her to lower the fichu to know exactly what lay hidden underneath. Elizabeth tried to focus on the minister. Repentance was for sinners. Different church, same sermon.

During the benedictory hymn, Elizabeth chanced a second look at the man. He openly stared at her. The grin he gave her did not reach his eyes. Once, through the kitchen window, she had seen a feral dog stalking her father's favorite hound. Elizabeth now understood how Apollo must have felt facing the wild dog. She looked away quickly, certain she did not want to encourage him.

Elizabeth followed Mina down the aisle to shake both Reverend Porter's and Gideon's hands. She adjusted her cloak so Gideon could appreciate the dress. She glanced down to see that the fichu covered everything. A display like she had given Samuel would not be appreciated in the church. And as a widower, she doubted Mr. Frost would be as impressed. Sadly, it was too public a place to try her hair. But Gideon would be by this afternoon.

As Aunt Mina shook Gideon's hand, he bent low to say something in her ear. Aunt Mina glanced into the churchyard and nodded. Elizabeth wondered what passed between them but found herself face-to-face with Reverend Porter and unable to recall what he'd just asked her.

"I beg your pardon?"

"I asked how you liked our little town. But it is good to see you watching over your aunt."

Elizabeth nodded to let him think her distraction was due to concern for her aunt. "It appears to be nice, and the snow melts a bit faster than on the North Shore."

"That is right. You are from the North Shore. I shall visit you this week. Have Mrs. Richards send me word by Mr. Frost as to when would be convenient for an afternoon visit. I am free on Wednesday."

Meaning you will visit on Wednesday whether or not it is convenient. "Yes, sir."

She moved on to Gideon, stretching out her hand and looking up at him, her lashes fluttering only once. Gideon did not take her hand, so she dropped it.

"Miss Garrett, I would save your flirtations for those you are genuinely interested in. It is unwise to be seen as a flirt." Gideon's gaze moved beyond her to a spot in the churchyard.

Elizabeth followed his glance and saw the man from earlier.

"Heed my warning. Good day."

Elizabeth hurried down the stairs, her dismissal completed. Mina waited.

"The Stewards have offered us a ride home." Mina took her arm and led her to the wagon that had splashed them earlier.

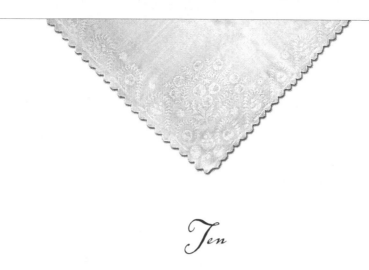

Ten

AFTER A LIGHT DINNER, AUNT Mina excused herself for a nap. Mr.
Frost did not come to dinner after church. Instead, he rode his horse
on by as Elizabeth watched out the parlor window. The Howell
family had invited him to share their Sunday meal. It took Elizabeth
a moment to place the family. She failed until her aunt reminded her
of meeting Joanna outside the church. The mousy girl reminded her
of Lucy and was one of a handful of eligible girls in the congregation.
Obviously she'd set her cap for the preacher's assistant.

Elizabeth added a trickle of hot water from the kettle to the basin
in the dry sink. The advantage of Mr. Frost's absence was she only
need clean two sets of dinnerware. Perhaps she would take a nap after
she tidied up. Her muscles didn't ache as they had last Sunday, but
the early morning hours she kept took a toll. If Aunt kept these types
of hours her entire life, it was a wonder she was still alive at her age.

The dishes dried and put away, Elizabeth poured the dirty water
into a bucket. Best empty it now so Aunt Mina did not need to
remind her later. Before he left, Father neglected to tell her that her
aunt would be writing a weekly report of her behavior, a fact her aunt
had mentioned only moments ago. Thank goodness she abandoned
her plan to flirt more with Mr. Frost at church. She would need to
be careful with her flirtations.

Before hefting the bucket outdoors, Elizabeth looked over the
kitchen once more. Nothing needed an extra wipe of the cloth, so she

headed out to the drain without putting on her cloak. She emptied the bucket carefully so as to not drip on her blue dress.

The sound of Jordan's trot reached her in time to smooth the wrinkles from her dress before horse and rider came around the house.

Mr. Frost nodded his head before dismounting. Elizabeth's hand flew to her bun. Did she dare? No one else would see them behind the house. She palmed one of her pins. Now to get him in conversation.

"Mr. Frost, Aunt Mina asked me to set aside some of the apple pudding. Would you like to come in?"

"One of Mina's?"

Elizabeth did not miss the hopeful sound in his question. "No, but she did supervise, and it turned out so much better than my bread."

Gideon led Jordan to the barn. "Very well. I need to talk with Mrs. Richards. I'll be in momentarily."

He disappeared before Elizabeth could tell him Aunt Mina slept. Just as well. She doubted he would come in if he knew her aunt wasn't there to act as a chaperone.

Now to plan. She studied the kitchen from the doorway. If she stood at the sideboard and pretended to be startled when he opened the door, she would be framed by the afternoon light coming through the window. Not close enough to have him "accidentally" feel her hair, but the light from the window would show it to its best advantage.

Elizabeth set the bucket in its place and stepped to the sideboard.

"Jordan, I'm making a mistake. I hope she doesn't see it as encouragement. You know I wouldn't go in without Mrs. Richards being present." Gideon removed the saddle from Jordan's back. "This may cure my fondness of apples. A week ago I would have told you it was impossible to ruin beans, but even the sow refused to eat them. If it wasn't for the cheese and dried fruit Mrs. Richards slips to me, I might be starving."

Gideon wouldn't go in at all, but he needed to warn Mina about Mr. Butler further than the "Keep her away from Mr. Butler," he'd whispered as she left the church. The man might come calling, and he doubted Elizabeth would refuse him. The best outcome was a marriage wherein Mr. Butler continued his philandering ways beyond his wife's notice. But with Elizabeth's flirtations, he feared Mr. Butler might take liberties Elizabeth didn't intend to offer, despite the fact her father's profession put her somewhat in a different plane than the girls he usually seduced.

With Jordan settled in the stall, Gideon found no other reason to delay further. Only Elizabeth was visible through the kitchen window. Mina must be in the front parlor. He let himself in the back door.

Elizabeth squealed and whirled around, her hair tumbling down her back as her bun fell with the sudden movement. The movement appeared practiced, and his eyes narrowed. Could a woman plan for her hair to fall? The ineffective movements she made to fix her hair showed off her hair rather than set it in order, solidifying Gideon's suspicions.

He stayed near the door, not wanting to encourage other flirtations she might have in mind. "Miss Garrett, I suggest you retire to your room and repair yourself." His harsh words echoed in the kitchen.

Elizabeth's face fell, and her hands stilled, but she made no attempt to leave the room.

Gideon used his best preacher voice to address her. "I warned you to be cautious with your flirtations this morning. Some men would believe such an obviously planned disaster as an invitation, not a flirtation. Why you choose to try such a game with me is beyond comprehension. I suggest you save such trickery to use on your husband once you are wed, as he is the only one who should appreciate your lovely tresses."

Elizabeth's face turned as red as the apples in the pudding he would not be eating. No words escaped her open mouth before she closed it. Her hands dropped to her sides, and her gaze fell to the floor.

"Hurry and repair the damage before your aunt comes in." Gideon folded his arms and gave her what he hoped was a very solemn face. It must have been because as Elizabeth flew up the stairs, the quiet click of her door his only answer.

With long strides, Gideon walked to the parlor. Mina was not there. Her bedroom door was closed. That explained part of Elizabeth's boldness. Mina must be napping. A door opened above, and Gideon sprinted for the back door. His talk with Mina could wait.

⟶ ✕ ⟵

The back door shut just as Elizabeth reached the bottom step. Completely rebuffed. Instead of admiration, disgust had marred the features of Mr. Frost's face as she'd let her hair fall. Worse, he'd recognized the deliberate flirtation. *What if he tells Aunt Mina?*

She crossed to the back door and opened it. Gideon was leading Jordan out of the barn. "Mr. Frost!" She raised a hand to hail him as he moved to mount his horse.

Gideon mounted, but he stilled Jordan to stand in place and waited as Elizabeth approached.

"Mr. Frost, I want to apologize for my behavior. I should have been more circumspect in my conduct. I don't know what I was thinking to behave in such a manner."

"I believe you know exactly what you were thinking, and I happened to be a convenient target for your flirtations. I believe you have had too much time to do as you please for too long and wasted it on things of no consequence. I implore you to cease not only for your own sake but for your aunt's as well."

Elizabeth crossed her arms and tilted her chin up. "Are you trying to tell me, Mr. Preacher, that my soul is in mortal danger?"

"Nothing of the sort. I am trying to tell you as a friend that your actions could be easily misconstrued by the wrong man and that the consequences might be dire. I would not wish that upon you or your aunt."

"A friend?" What an odd notion. The word did not apply to men.

"I consider myself not only Mina's employee but a friend as well. I thought we were also headed into a friendship, but I will not be used in your little entertainments. Friends behave honestly one with another. So yes, I have been honest today and therefore acted as your friend."

Jordan pranced his impatience.

Elizabeth took a step back, her brow furrowed. "Why would you want to be my friend?"

Gideon stilled Jordan again. "Miss Garrett, I find friendship with many people enhances my life. As yet, I have no reason to deny a chance for friendship."

"Even after today?"

"Even after today. I hold high hopes that you will find your way and moderate your behavior."

Elizabeth took another step back and lowered her face.

Gideon tipped his hat. "Good day, Miss Garrett. Tell your aunt I shall return about suppertime." He gave Jordan the command to move.

Elizabeth stood frozen in place as they rounded the house. Friend? What a peculiar notion for a man to wish to be a friend to a woman. When Aunt Mina woke, Elizabeth realized she had forgotten to ask Gideon not to tell her about the incident.

⸺ �֎ ⸺

Elizabeth set the soup on the table in front of Aunt Mina's plate. It smelled edible, but aromas could be deceiving. The flat bread she'd baked on the hearth looked passable. Aunt called it ashcake. But since she'd made it on the hot bricks instead of in the ashes, the little cakes had picked up few ashes. It was not light and airy like the biscuits Cook made in the pan at home, but it wasn't hard like the brickish bread she'd made Monday last. Aunt Mina told her the little cakes could be baked directly on the ashes of an open fire and was, therefore, an important recipe to know.

Elizabeth doubted she would ever need to cook on a fire out of doors. A cold gust hit her back as Gideon entered the kitchen. She didn't turn to face him. Instead, she bit her lip and willed him not to tell her aunt of this afternoon's folly.

"Mrs. Richards, Miss Garrett."

Aunt Mina tapped his chair with her cane. "About time. This supper promises to be the best meal of the week."

Elizabeth took her seat at the table.

Aunt Mina addressed Gideon. "Preacher Boy, it's your turn."

The prayer was given, and first bites taken, followed by second and third. Elizabeth exhaled a long breath. She had done it. The meal didn't garner any excuses to be abandoned after a bite or two.

Aunt Mina smiled. "I think, child, we shall not starve after all."

Elizabeth looked to Gideon, who shoved another bite of the ashcake into his mouth. He nodded.

Something welled up deep inside of Elizabeth. She hadn't failed. Suddenly ravenous, she finished her food, ignoring the conversation as she planned her next meal.

Her aunt's words cut through her musings. "Gideon, would you like some apple pudding?"

"Yes, please."

Elizabeth cleared the table and brought out the pudding, passable only because her aunt had hovered over her the entire process.

When the dishes were ready to be washed, Aunt Mina extended her hand. "Preacher Boy, will you help an old woman to the parlor? I seem to have mislaid my cane."

Elizabeth studied her aunt. The cane had been in her hand before the meal started—the mysterious disappearance likely an excuse to talk with Mr. Frost alone. Unsure that it was proper to pray the almost-minister didn't reveal her afternoon's indiscretion, she hoped very hard. As she washed the dishes, the muted voices in the other room rose and fell. Her temptation to eavesdrop was quelled by the knowledge that silence in the kitchen would lead to sure discovery.

She placed the last bowl in the cupboard as Gideon came into the room. "I came to empty the slop bucket and dishwater for you."

"Thank you, Gid—Mr. Frost."

"With your aunt calling us by our first names and nicknames, it's hard to think of each other more formally, isn't it?"

Elizabeth nodded and wiped up the drips of water that fell into the dry sink.

Gideon shifted his weight. "Would you mind very much if we were on a first-name basis, at least around the house?"

Elizabeth hoped no shock showed on her face as she turned to address him. "It would be easier, but you are a minister. I don't know that it would be proper."

The corners of Gideon's mouth turned down. "You know I am not really a minister anymore, right?" He didn't wait for an answer. "I was, and I may be again. But for now I help out where Mr. Porter asks, as a volunteer. So it is not improper on account of my position in the clergy."

"Is that why Aunt sometimes calls you Preacher Boy?"

"Most likely. I think she does it to remind me I need to choose what I will do come midsummer. She has some opinions on the matter." Gideon gave a wry smile and lifted both the dirty water and slop buckets. "Will you get the door?"

Elizabeth hurried to comply.

As Gideon passed her, he said in a low voice. "Come out on the porch for a moment."

Elizabeth grabbed a knit shawl off the hook and followed him out the door.

As soon as the door shut, Gideon inclined his head, indicating she should follow him. He dumped the water bucket, then turned toward the pigsty. Elizabeth hurried to keep up with his long strides.

"I didn't tell Mina about this afternoon."

"Oh, thank you, I prom—"

Gideon held up a hand to stop her. "I don't want you to make promises you don't intend to keep. But I do think you should tell Mina yourself."

"Tell Aunt Mina? What if she sends me away? Father will find something far worse. I know it."

"Do you really think she will send you away?"

Elizabeth bit her bottom lip and thought for a moment before shrugging her shoulders. "I am not sure. My grandmother would have. But Aunt Mina—"

"I believe she can give you a woman's perspective on your behavior and perhaps guide you so that in the future when you are genuinely interested in a man, you can better express yourself."

Tears threatened, but she blinked them back before answering. "I won't do it again, but I don't…I can't…I just can't tell her."

"Elizabeth," his voice was firm, "if you really desire to reform yourself, you need to face your foibles and learn from them. Your aunt wants to help you."

"Are you sure she won't send me away?"

"I don't think she will. And if she threatens to, I'll intervene."

Confess? It was too hard. More challenging than learning how to cook. She looked away from him. He would make an excellent preacher. Her heart almost wanted to follow his advice. Was this what friendship was like?

"You'd better go in. Mina will wonder where you went." He handed her the empty buckets.

Elizabeth walked toward the back door but stopped at the sound of his voice. "Difficult things help us become better people. It might be hard now, but it will only be harder tomorrow."

A tear fell down her cheek. She didn't reply but continued to the door.

Aunt Mina stood near the fire when she entered the kitchen. Elizabeth set down the buckets and brushed the tears from her face, hoping her aunt hadn't noticed. No such luck.

"Why the tears? Sit by the fire and tell me."

Gideon was right. Aunt Mina did not send her home.

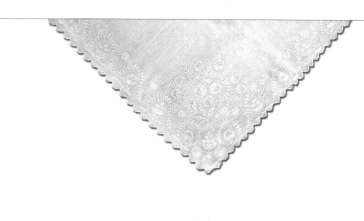

Eleven

ELIZABETH CRUMPLED THE PAPER. MOTHER'S hand had penned the words, but it was as if Father had dictated every word. Father had not bothered to write, had not apologized for dumping her trunk in the mud, or even muttered a good-bye when he'd left her here. Now he dictated mother's letters. Not a single bit of gossip, not even a mention of deaths and births broke up the lecture laid to paper. *Why doesn't Father just correspond with me himself?*

She paced her little room, but it was so confining. As she passed the window, she spied a small ridge beyond the fields where the ice-blue sky rose high above the bare trees. The spot beckoned to her.

Elizabeth rushed down the stairs and grabbed her cloak "I'll be back soon!" The door slammed behind her.

Choosing the road running in the general direction of the ridge, she searched for the spot. Emotions she'd tried to hide began to force their way out of her eyes. She wiped at them as the ridge blurred.

The road curved to go around the hill. Carefully, she picked her way across the fallow field. The ground was soft but not particularly muddy. As she neared the ridge, the ground rose in a gentle slope. The gray rocks at the top reached up like a citadel wall. A dozen trees, stiff as soldiers, stood guard. Their uniforms, once green and vibrant, now littered the ground. The cracks in the stones were barely discernible from the mud. A rock wall indicated the border of the field and kept the trees from invading. Ten feet inside the wall and surrounded by furrowed earth sat a lone boulder, belonging to neither the ridge nor the field.

Elizabeth walked around the stone worn smooth by time and weather. She tried to climb on top from the south side, then from the north. On her third attempt, she decided to forgo being lady-like. Hiking up her skirt, she scrambled up the west side and sat looking downhill.

In the distance, she saw the houses in little Curtis Corner belting out cook smoke, wagons riding by, and a few boys waving to each other as they left the school. Aunt Mina's house looked smaller than it did when she swept it. Cleaning the house made it ever so much larger. No wonder the poor maids her mother employed looked so tired.

Elizabeth reached into her pocket and pulled out her mother's letter. The tone was harsh and alienating, like a sentence her father handed down to a criminal. As she reread the letter, she realized it wouldn't matter what she did. Her father seemed determined that she could never change enough for him.

Standing on the boulder, she faced the rocky ridge and yelled into the wind. "Ebenezer Garrett, you don't know me, and you do not control me. You say it is impossible for me to improve. You do not know me. I will prove you wrong!" She shook her fist and uttered a primal scream, raw with emotion.

Never had she allowed herself to scream in such a manner. A tightness inside loosened.

She yelled again. "Do you hear me, Father? I will prove you wrong!"

Gideon tightened his scarf. What had the fool girl been thinking to run out of the house like that? Mina's worried expression drove him faster. Elizabeth had left over an hour ago. Heavy clouds had moved in from the coast. She'd given no indication of where she was going. He doubted she was making any social calls as she rarely spoke to anyone after Sunday meetings.

Mina said she'd run out the back door, so he followed her footprints around the house and back out to the lane, but there was no sign of her.

He returned to saddle Jordan. While he doubted Mina's fears of panthers or bears would come to fruition, Elizabeth wandering into the forest and getting herself lost was a very real possibility. He'd met few women possessing a decent sense of direction. Most women, like his Ruth, couldn't find east at sunrise.

He headed northwest along the lane searching for more of Elizabeth's footprints. As he got to the edge of town, he thought about turning around and going back, but movement in the far field caught his eye and he urged Jordan on across the field.

The movement became a form, and the form became a person, and the person was yelling.

Elizabeth shook her fist at the ridge, the wind catching her words and carrying them to him. "You are wrong! Do you hear me? Sitting up there, judging me?" Elizabeth raged at the rock wall as the wind whipped her cloak around her. She tossed her head back, the cloak's hood slipping, the wind ripping her hair free.

She opened her fist, revealing a crumpled paper, and ripped it end to end. "This is what I think of your letter. You never knew me! You never cared until I threatened your reputation. You are wrong. Wrong! Do you hear me?"

"Rather well."

Elizabeth spun toward him and lost her footing. Gideon reached for her, but on horseback, he was not close enough to catch more than the fluttering cloak, and she landed in a heap in the center of the boulder, her hair tumbling around her and obscuring her face.

Gideon pulled his hand back, letting the cloak fall to cover her ankles.

She swiped the hair out of her face, her blinking turning into a glare. A trail of tears lined her face, heavy enough to have preceded the fall. They were not a result of injury. Color flamed her face as she opened her mouth.

Gideon thought it better to speak before a shrewish remark escaped her lips. "Mina is worried. A storm is coming." The wind confirmed his words by gusting and sending Elizabeth's hair into her face and open mouth.

As she sputtered and grabbed at her hair, the wind ripped the papers she held from her hand and carried them to the ridge wall. She wrapped her hair around one hand and stuffed it in her hood. "This wasn't deliberate. I didn't mean to—"

"I didn't think you did. Time to go back to Mina's."

Elizabeth scowled up at him. "You've delivered your message. Tell her I will be home shortly."

"Get on. Jordan can carry both of us."

"I will walk." Elizabeth searched the boulder.

From his perch atop his horse, Gideon saw she could not escape the boulder without hiking up her skirts.

He extended his hand. "Come, we can be back at Mina's in a few moments."

"The reverend and the strumpet? Go while you still have a reputation." Elizabeth used the cloak to wipe her eyes and laughed a bitter laugh.

Strumpet? What an odd thing to call herself. Elizabeth proved herself an accomplished flirt, but the behavior was far from that of a common streetwalker.

"Better hurry, Reverend, before my father finds out." Tears streamed down her face. "Go! Just go!"

Gideon furrowed his brow. He'd thought her a fool, but she was unsound. Poor Mina. Not only had they sent her a useless helper but one given to irrational behavior.

"No. Come, let us get to Mina's."

Elizabeth's gaze continued to roam over the boulder. "Please, I'll come straight away."

Gideon would have refused her again, but the fresh tears gave him pause. She didn't want to get down in front of him. He tipped his hat and nudged Jordan into a walk, his back to her.

He waited a moment, then turned to offer a ride, but she was running across the field toward Mina's barn, avoiding the road.

The fire in the tiny stove did its best to battle the cold of the attic. Gideon smoothed the papers on his desk. After spending an hour arguing with his conscience, he'd won, telling himself it was for Mina's sake, that he needed to protect her from her niece.

He'd read the torn and crumpled letter twice. The handwriting was soft and round, like a woman's. The signature belonged to Elizabeth's mother. Yet he could not believe a mother would write such a letter to her daughter. The word *strumpet* appeared not once but twice. No wonder the word had spilled from Elizabeth's lips at the boulder.

Even when his father discovered his sister in the barn loft with her now husband, his parents hadn't spoken so harshly. His nephew being born a mere five months after the marriage vows were completed testified that his sister's flirtations were well beyond Elizabeth's. From his seminary studies, he knew that as many as a third of the brides standing before him on their wedding day were increasing.

He'd thought to rescue the letter out of kindness, but the only kindness would be to burn it.

He revised his opinion of Elizabeth possibly being insane. She had been correct to find a private place to unleash her frustration and hurt. He vowed to be kinder to her, but he couldn't apologize without admitting he read the letter.

The flames of the warming stove licked at the pages of the letter before turning them into ash. He readied for bed, slipped into the narrow space, and wished, as he did each night, for Ruth to be tucked by his side.

As he lay there, the words of the letter came back to him. Would her father truly force her to marry some man with four children and send her to Ohio? He hoped for Elizabeth's sake she could at least find contentment in marriage, even if she couldn't have what he'd shared with Ruth.

Twelve

JOANNA HOWELL PROPPED OPEN THE window and set two mince pies to cool on the sill. Hiding behind the curtain, she watched for the tall minister and his powerful horse. Every Monday and Wednesday he left Widow Richards's home at half past ten and headed south toward Brockton.

Right on schedule, as his dark horse trotted down the lane, Joanna grabbed her shawl and hurried into the side yard. Despite the sunny morning, it was too soon for the laundry to be dry. She hoped Mr. Frost wouldn't know that she was only pretending to check the sheets.

"Good day, Miss Howell."

"Why, Mr. Frost, how do you do?"

"Just fine. Is your laundry already dry?"

Unwilling to lie to a man of the cloth, Joanna shook her head. "No, but I hoped all the same." She looked up at him and couldn't think of a thing to say.

Gideon tipped his hat and rode on.

— ❊ —

Elizabeth adjusted her basket and turned back up the street. It was the third time this week Miss Howell had managed to corner Gideon. First, after church when she'd helped a new mother with her children, then Monday, and now today while demonstrating her perfect domestic skills. Elizabeth could smell the spices of Joanna's cooling pies from Mina's front porch. No wonder Gideon had stopped.

How could she compete with perfection?

So annoying. Gideon only looked at her to find another reason to lecture her. Joanna was a mousy thing down to her dull brown hair. Prim and proper, like a minister's wife should be. At least she did not excel at flirting. Elizabeth doubted Gideon recognized Joanna's attempts at flirting. But then, Gideon was so dense he wouldn't recognize a good flirt as anything but another reason to lecture. He would never lecture Joanna, but he would give Elizabeth a lecture faster than soap bubbles popped if *she* ever tried the old check-the-laundry trick.

It might be fun to see if she could catch Gideon. If only the red gown weren't locked in the secret compartment.

Elizabeth's spindle skittered across the floor. Once again she'd broken the thread. Mina looked up from her spinning wheel in time to see Elizabeth crawl under the chair. But more than a half hour had passed since the last time Elizabeth had retrieved the aptly named drop spindle. Bit by bit, her niece was improving.

Mina schooled her features before Elizabeth stood and dusted off her skirts. It would not do to have her niece see her smiling at her unladylike behavior. Mina held out her hand for the spindle, then unwrapped several inches and slid the thread between her fingers.

"Much improved," Mina said as she wrapped the thread back around the spindle.

Elizabeth opened her mouth to comment but stopped, distracted by two boys fighting near the street. "Key? Did that boy say key?" Elizabeth sprinted out the door. Mina grabbed her wool shawl from the back of her chair before following.

"Give it back. I found it." The younger brother's blond curls bounced as he jumped up, trying to reach the prize in the older boy's hand.

"And I have it." The taller boy held his fist farther out of reach.

"Gimme the key!" Like an angry goat, the smaller boy rammed the larger in the stomach. The two went down and started throwing punches.

Elizabeth pulled the smaller boy off. She grabbed for the bigger boy's fist only to have his other fist complete a punch meant for the smaller boy, the blow connecting with Elizabeth's temple and sending her tumbling into the muddy street, where she landed facedown, just feet from Jordan and Gideon.

"George and Donald Purdy! Whatever are you fighting about?" Mina grabbed one boy by the collar. Gideon jumped off his horse, collared the other, and handed him off to Mina.

From the mud puddle, Elizabeth groaned as she started to rise. Dirty water dripped down her face and off her clothes. Gideon said nothing as he helped her to her feet and offered her his handkerchief. Elizabeth wiped her face and glared at the little boys.

The Purdy boys stood shamefaced before Mina. The taller one opened his fist and produced a key tied to a muddy piece of ribbon.

"My key." Elizabeth stepped to grab it, but Mina closed her hand around the offered key first.

"Run home boys and tell your mother what happened. I shall call on her tomorrow." The boys' eyes widened.

"Are you going to tell her I hit a girl?" George's voice squeaked, and his face paled.

Mina raised her brows and pointed down the street. The shorter boy ran off, George following behind bellowing threats at his younger brother.

Mina's gaze traveled from Elizabeth's head to her boots and she started to laugh. Elizabeth picked up her discarded shawl, holding it away from her soaked dress, and marched around the back of the house, her head held high.

Gideon followed Elizabeth with his eyes. When she disappeared, he turned to Mina.

Mina laughed harder.

Gideon bowed his head to hide a grin. Mina laid a hand on his arm. "Finish your visits. Give her time to clean up." She turned and walked back to the house.

—✺—

Elizabeth bent over the washtub and scrubbed her dress.

Aunt Mina joined her on the back porch. "Let it soak for a bit. The mud will come out easier."

"Soak?"

"Yes, soak. While you come in for a bit of dinner."

"But last time you had me scrub my clothes immediately."

"Last time was in January, and a storm was coming, and you were splashing all over my kitchen. This time it is sunny, and you are scrubbing on the porch."

Elizabeth stomped into the kitchen after her aunt and silently set about preparing for their meal. Food held no attraction. How could it after she'd been laughed at in front of the entire street? She'd only seen Gideon, but others could have been lurking behind their windows.

"Are you stomping around here because you are mad at yourself or at me?" Mina's question stopped Elizabeth midstride.

Why should she be mad at herself? She was the one who received a punch in the face and was pushed into the mud. And for what? Aunt Mina had laughed at her. A month. She'd lived here a whole month. Gideon treated her like a child, and her father sent lectures disguised as letters from mother. She'd learned to cook and clean, but for what? *To get laughed at!* And if she dare say a word, she would be tossed back to her parents' home, where she was not welcome.

Silently, Elizabeth ladled out the stew and cut the bread.

"I think it's time we expand your repertoire. The old brown hen would make us a good dinner tomorrow. I think I will teach you my mother's recipe for the high-crusted chicken pie."

Elizabeth bowed her head, not paying much attention to her aunt's blessing on the food.

"I'm sorry if my laughter seemed inappropriate. I couldn't help but laugh at the irony of losing and finding your key in the same way." Mina started to laugh again.

Elizabeth stirred her stew—so similar to the mud she'd washed off her dress. The corners of her mouth turned up. The situation *was* a tiny bit funny. The only two times in her life she had been drenched in mud was in her aunt's yard and over her trunk. Still not nearly as funny as Aunt Mina thought. She looked up and gave her aunt a half smile.

"You handled this time much better. Look how much you've learned in a month." Mina slid the key across the table. "You probably should open the secret compartment. If mud did seep in, you'll need this beautiful day to wash whatever you've hidden."

Elizabeth grabbed the key and rushed upstairs.

Elizabeth took the crimson gown off the line. Only a bit of mud had managed to seep into the secret compartment. The paper had protected the dress from staining, but the cloth had dried with the horrid stench of mildew. The silk stockings only needed airing out, but the foul odor clung to the dress. Aunt Mina had advised her to rinse it using apple-cider vinegar, then hang the gown in the breeze. Elizabeth held the skirt to her nose. The musty smell was gone. Who would have thought nasty smelling vinegar would erase the odor of mildew?

The skirt wasn't completely dry, but with the setting sun, it needed to come in. She pulled her work dress and petticoat off the line as well. Arms full, she hurriedly whirled into the house only to bump into something solid. Strong hands gripped her shoulders and steadied her as she stepped back.

Gideon.

"Sorry, I thought you heard me."

Elizabeth shook her head, becoming as tongue-tied as Joanna.

"I asked if you needed any help."

"Oh." Worse than Joanna, and her feet refused to move around him to the house.

If he possessed any manners, he would step out of the way. Instead, he raised his hand and brushed aside the hair she'd pinned to hide her bruised head. She felt the heat from his hand, though his fingers never came into contact with the swollen red patch on her temple.

He winced and dropped his hand. His mouth moved, but Elizabeth had no idea what he'd said. His near touch had paralyzed her brain. He frowned, took her by the arm, and led her into the house.

Elizabeth had regained her composure by the time they reached the back door, but Gideon did not release her until they were both inside.

"Thank you for your assistance, Mr. Frost." She nodded and hurried out of the kitchen. She heard Mina conversing with him as she scurried up the stairs.

She set the clothing on her bed and turned to the mirror, lifting a hand to touch the bruise. She must have been hit harder than she thought. She'd never acted like a ninny in a man's presence before and, handsome or not, Gideon Frost was the last man who, who ... He didn't even have his own church. His wife would be doomed to poverty. Plus, he still loved his dead wife—all adding up to an equation for a useless pursuit.

The two letters Mrs. Porter had handed Gideon upon his return to the house an hour earlier remained in his pocket throughout supper. Eating with the Porters was part of his board. At Reverend Porter's insistence, weekday suppers consisted of dinner's leavings and whatever food donations the parishioners gave the family. The fare was not much better than Elizabeth's attempts at cooking, and sometimes much, much worse. With Mrs. Porter nearing her confinement, one woman or another dropped off food almost daily. Tonight's supper featured a kidney pie rejected by some lucky family who undoubtedly ate something better for their evening meal.

Gideon detested kidney pie, even his mother's, and this pie was nothing like his mother's, having been cooked until the crust had become cinders. The Porter children squirmed and tried to feed theirs to the dog, which refused with a whine. The reverend downed his. Gideon wondered if the man had been blessed without a sense of taste. Poor Mrs. Porter picked at the food on her plate, all the while turning a deeper shade of green until she left the table.

While the reverend readied the children for bed, Gideon washed the dishes, making sure the remains of the pie made it into the slop. Taking no chances, he also emptied the bucket into the pigpen. When he returned, Mrs. Porter sat at the table, nursing a cup of tea.

"Bless you, Gideon. I don't think I could have smelled that for another moment."

Chatter of the children echoed from the floor above. Gideon shifted his weight from foot to foot. "Do you need anything?"

Mrs. Porter raised her teacup. "This is all I need tonight." She laid a hand on her rounded stomach. "Pray for Joanna to deliver tomorrow's supper again. She seems to provide quite often of late." Gideon didn't miss the speculative look in her eye. "And pray for this one to come soon. Then Matthew will go out and do more visits, and I can make sure only edible gifts end up on the supper table." She smiled.

Gideon stifled a laugh. "My Ruth used to do the same thing. When she returned the plate, she would tell the woman 'Not a scrap was left,' or 'Every bit was eaten.' Our neighbor, Mr. Whittaker, owned the best-fed pigs in town."

"My favorite is 'None of it went to waist. 'No one ever thinks I mean the homonym, as that would be so improper." A giggle rose from Mrs. Porter as the reverend walked into the room.

"Good to see you're in better spirits, dear. Perhaps now you can eat some of the pie."

The odd shade of green reappeared in Mrs. Porter's complexion. "I think not, dear. If you don't mind, I shall take myself to bed and leave the two of you to discuss this week's sermon." The reverend placed a chaste kiss on his wife's brow and helped her from the table.

It wasn't until Gideon sat down in the study that he realized it hadn't hurt to speak of Ruth.

⊷ ✳ ⊶

The clock chimed eleven times before Reverend Porter became satisfied with his Sunday sermon. Had Gideon expressed his thoughts, the conversation would have been much longer, as he didn't agree with the interpretation of the particular doctrine, believing it countered some of Peter's writings. But, as he learned his first week here, the reverend was not interested in the opinions of a "disgraced minister," so Gideon kept his mouth shut until he could take a candle and retreat to his room.

Just over two feet wide, the box bed had never looked comfortable and felt even worse, but tonight Gideon was tired enough not to care. Paper crunched as he pulled off his clothes. The letters. He laid them on the table next to the candle. The top one bore the seal of the seminary, most likely from Reverend Ingram. The other was in his brother's hand. Gideon broke the seal.

> *Gideon,*
>
> *I shall not pretend to be surprised that you are considering giving up the ministry. I think you had some doubts before Ruth's death. I located the tools you wrote about. However, after inquiring about shipping, it was more than you'd indicated you could pay. I would invite you up, but we both know you are loath to come. It will not help when I tell you Miriam is with child and very ill. Perhaps if she did not look so much like her sister you would come, but—*
>
> *I am planning to go to Boston the fourth Thursday in March to collect a large order of leather. Perhaps we could meet at our sister's, and I will bring your tools. I know Constance longs to see you too. If this plan is acceptable, please write both Constance and me.*
>
> *Always,*
>
> *Aaron*
>
> *PS. Miriam sends her love.*
>
> *PPS. I am sending a few of the smaller tools and some leather. Look for them toward the end of this week.*

It was past time he visit his family. He'd avoided stopping at Constance's when he'd stayed at the seminary near New Year's. Perhaps by summer he would visit his brother and Miriam. She may look like Ruth, but her manner was less reserved. Mr. Whittaker was right. It was time to move on. Joanna was an excellent cook, and edible food could make up for dull conversation.

Thirteen

In late February, spring tried valiantly to make an appearance, but after a four-day battle, winter won out, using a bitter north wind bringing yet another half foot of snow.

As she did most mornings, Mina sat at her spinning wheel. Elizabeth sat at a smaller one nearby.

"I think we shall finish the last of this before the snow melts."

Elizabeth looked up. "Finish? I thought you said you had too much flax to finish this year."

"Too much to finish alone." Mina put emphasis on the last word. "You have a knack for spinning. Your grandmother never liked to spin. But she did weave well enough. By the end of the week, we can start threading the loom."

The tiniest of groans escaped Elizabeth's lips. Mina suppressed a smile. To be honest, the task deserved a groan or two.

"Why do you keep your loom up year-round?"

"Long ago, about the time the king imposed the tax on textiles, so '63 or there abouts, I took in weaving for other women. Not many people own large looms like the one my Henry built. I lost my little twins before they were named that winter and needed a distraction so he built it." Mina paused for a moment. By then Thomas and Henry Junior were old enough to follow Henry around the farm and helped as much as they hindered. My Becca, who was just off leading strings, would play in the corner. Weaving is like a dance. Once you get the rhythm of it, you don't need to focus on the steps. I was able to think and occasionally cry while still being useful. Weaving six months out of the year on a loom as large as the one Henry built meant it just wasn't practical to take it down. Even now, when I only weave for about a month, it is just easier to leave it."

"I didn't realize you bore five children."

"Six, if you count George, but he didn't live out the day. I outlived them all, and my only grandchild. Becca died in childbirth. Her husband, William, died with Henry Junior, of dysentery. It killed so many of our soldiers. More of them died of illness than of the Red Coats' bayonets." Mina paused and looked out the window toward the small cemetery. At least Thomas died close enough to home to bury his body nearby. Henry Junior and William lay in graves surrounded by those of other soldiers, too far south for her to visit.

Elizabeth lowered her head over her spinning. "I'm sorry Aunt Mina. It must have been very hard for you to be so alone."

"It was not so bad, I had Henry by my side much longer than either of us expected, and I have good friends, and now I have you. Patience may not like it much, but I think I shall claim you as my granddaughter."

"Granddaughter?"

"Yes, if I had one, I would like her to be much like you."

"But, Aunt Mina, I am nothing but trouble."

"Posh. That is your father speaking. You're much improved over your arrival. I now look forward to your cooking, even on days when you try a new recipe." Mina let out a chuckle.

Elizabeth blushed.

"And you seem to have taken both mine and Gideon's advice to heart about your flirtations. Mina raised her brows. "Unless I haven't been apprised of something."

Elizabeth shook her head. "I haven't tried anything."

"But you have thought of it?"

The red on Elizabeth's cheeks deepened. "Just once or twice. I am avoiding Mr. Butler. So far I have remembered your council. I have been circumspect around other men."

"So far?"

"It is so hard not to be as I was. I want men to admire me."

Mina gave her niece a disapproving look.

"I know I shouldn't, but it makes me feel special when men pay attention to me. The first time I made a dinner everyone ate, it made me feel the same way."

"The roast chicken with the egg sauce recipe you found in your book was a momentous occasion. I am happy I thought of purchasing *The Frugal Housewife*, even if it was written in England. At least it was published in Philly."

Mina returned to her point. "Some day you will find the one man who is the only man you ever want to admire you every day until forever."

"I don't think that is likely. I made such a thorough fool of myself, no man on the North Shore will talk to me again, even with Father's money. And East Stoughton isn't brimming with bachelors."

Mina made a show of breathing in the smells coming from the kitchen. "I think it is almost dinnertime."

"Oh, I'd better go check my pies." Elizabeth hurried from the room.

Mina turned to the window. Gideon rode up the lane. Perhaps the man who would admire her niece wasn't too far away.

⇌ ✳ ⇌

The Steward family needed more help than he could provide over the next few days. Joanna Howell was the logical choice, but she'd tried to hide a bad cold from him yesterday when she'd flagged him down to get his opinion on one of *Fordyce's Sermons*. The last thing their house needed was illness.

Elizabeth was the only other woman he could think of to help the family. She hadn't burned food for more than two weeks, and her housekeeping skills now met Mina's standards. His biggest worry was how she would react to the Steward's humble circumstances. Had she matured enough to not comment on the cramped house and meager fare? Would the compassion she showed Mina transfer to others? He shook his head and sent a prayer heavenward as he unsaddled his horse.

If Mina and Elizabeth agreed, he would need to take Mina's buggy. He stepped in the kitchen, glad to see Elizabeth wore the ugly brown dress, a perfect choice for helping the Stewards.

Elizabeth reached into the oven and removed four loaves of bread. She didn't look up. "You are early. Dinner won't be ready until almost noon, which is an hour away."

"Where is Mina?"

"In the weaving room, sorting spools." Elizabeth set the bread on the table to cool. Amazing. Only four weeks ago her bread had looked and smelled like freshly kilned bricks. Today's bread could be favorably compared to any of the good housewives' loaves he'd tasted over the years. Perhaps Elizabeth was up to the task.

Gideon joined Mina in the weaving room. "Can you survive without Elizabeth for the next two or three days?"

Mina stopped sorting and pinned him with a look. "Why, may I ask?"

"It's the Stewards. The boys went and found poison ivy and managed to pass it on to the older two girls. Mrs. Steward's mother-in-law took the contaminated children to her house down in Bridgewater as she feared Deborah Steward would start her lying-in and didn't want the children around their mother and the baby." Gideon paused as Elizabeth entered the room. "The elder Mrs. Steward was correct, and Deborah delivered a fine baby girl early this morning. Midwife Jones doesn't want Deborah up yet due to her age and something else she wouldn't explain."

Gideon felt his face redden but forged ahead. "When David rode for the midwife last night, he took a tumble from his horse and injured his elbow and wrist. The midwife says it isn't broken, but she wrapped his wrist and put his arm in a sling. Midwife Jones can only stay for a couple more hours as Mrs. Clark will most likely need her services tonight and she wants to catch a quick nap. The Stewards need help at least for a couple of days until either Deborah can be up, or the older children are over their rashes, and her daughters and mother-in-law can return to help with the cooking."

"So who is at the house?" Elizabeth slipped farther into the room.

"David and Deborah and their two—now three—little girls. David can care for the little ones for the most part, but he is afraid both cooking and helping his wife will be too difficult. I told him I would come take care of the milking and barn chores he can't perform until the boys are back." Gideon looked from Mina to Elizabeth. "That is why they need Elizabeth's help."

"What would I do? I don't know much about babies."

"Deborah will take care of the baby, and David can help with the two little girls. They would need you to help cook and clean. Deborah may require some assistance too, but she can tell you what she needs." Gideon felt his face redden again. He turned away from Elizabeth. He should not be embarrassed. When she did not respond, he turned back to face her.

Elizabeth worried her lip. Gideon found her nervousness charming, so different from the defiant stand of only a fortnight ago. She needed encouragement. "I know you can do this. Two or three days at most."

"But my cooking—"

"Has much improved." Mina interrupted. "Deborah is likely to want simple foods. You've mastered many of those."

Elizabeth looked at her aunt. "What will you do if I am not here?"

"I dare say I will survive, child. If you take all but one of the loaves you just pulled out of the oven, there will be enough for me."

Elizabeth turned her gaze to Gideon's, her eyes still uncertain. "When should we leave?"

"As soon as you can pack a small bag of essentials." Gideon didn't know how to tell her to make sure they were plain ones.

Elizabeth started from the room, stopped, and turned. "Aunt Mina, do you have a valise or bag I can use?"

"In the other room upstairs there are one or two to choose from. And don't forget to take your needlework as you're likely to have some quiet hours between meals. Pack an extra apron with your work dress." Mina had just solved his problem about the type of clothing she should take.

Gideon and Mina watched as Elizabeth retreated from the room. Neither spoke until a door opened overhead.

"Don't worry Gideon, she will rise to the occasion and surprise all of us with her brilliance. It will do her good to see how the Stewards live." Mina gave him a knowing smile.

If only she can suppress her tongue. Gideon didn't express the doubt aloud. The Steward's modest home wasn't as large as Mina's, or as well built. At least five of the children would not be in residence, which was a blessing since the noise alone could overwhelm many a seasoned helper.

Elizabeth's light footfalls sounded from the stairway. Mina rose. "I best wrap some food to send with you. Having a new babe and all, they may need it."

An understatement, if he'd ever heard one. The Steward's cupboard stayed just shy of bare this time of year, though milk and eggs were generally available.

They met Elizabeth in the kitchen. Mina pulled out a basket and placed three loaves of the fresh bread wrapped in a towel beside a jar of gooseberry preserves. "Gideon, will you get some dried apples and the half ham from the cellar? Elizabeth, grab one of the bars of Baker's chocolate. Deborah will enjoy that. Oh, and take a couple cups of sugar, too."

Ten minutes later Gideon was helping Elizabeth into Mina's buggy, relieved she had not changed her dress and wore her plain cloak. His plan might work.

⋯✖⋯

Elizabeth had only been alone in a buggy with men she'd courted or attempted to court. She reminded herself that being in a buggy alone with Gideon was a necessity. She would not flirt with him—not that she wasn't tempted. On those rare occasions when Gideon smiled at her, like he had when he'd helped her into the buggy, her stomach flipped a little flip. She ignored it as much as possible, since, odd as it was, they were just friends.

She was filled with regret over the hair incident. The more she came to know Gideon, the more she wished she were worthy of his notice. Her "harmless" flirting had caused harm. Gideon would never take her seriously now. Sure, he would answer her questions and try to guide her and intervene when necessary, but it would always be as if she were a child and he her teacher. Sometimes a deep sadness came over his face. Elizabeth assumed it was because of his dead wife.

As for other men, there was little choice. Twice Mr. Butler had sought to corner her after church. Both times Gideon had intercepted him long enough for her to escape with Aunt Mina. But Mr. Butler's apparent annoyance was growing, as were his brazen appraisals. Even wrapped in her warmest cloak, a chill crawled over her whenever he looked her direction, as if she stood unclothed in his scrutiny. Mother was wrong—money would not cover all a man's ills. If it did, Elizabeth wouldn't fear Mr. Butler's attention.

Over the past week, Gideon had no reason to lecture her, giving her hope in her own reform. Could she make it through the next three days without doing something shocking? Or harming anything? What if she dropped the baby, or one of the little girls got too close to the fire? She crossed her ankles and hoped Gideon did not notice the way her legs shook. Good thing the road was bumpy.

Elizabeth took a deep breath and looked at the fields they passed. Here and there a slight tinge of green colored an otherwise brown landscape. What if she accidentally contracted poison ivy too? What did it look like? She bit her lip. She wanted to ask Gideon, but it seemed he preferred to ride in silence. More worries assailed her. What if she burned the food? Or undercooked it and made everyone ill? Why did Gideon and Aunt Mina think she could do this?

The buggy bounced in and out of a deep rut, and Gideon's hand flew in front of her like her mother's had when she was little. When Elizabeth turned to thank him, she found him studying her, and the words died on her lips.

"Are you worried?"

Elizabeth nodded.

"Don't be. Your cooking has improved, and the Stewards are used to plainer fare than even Mina. I should warn you that you may have to sleep on a pallet on the floor."

"The floor?"

"They live in a two-room cabin with a loft where the children sleep. I am only warning you so you don't complain."

Elizabeth's chin shot up. "Have you ever heard me complain? Mother says no one likes a complainer, so I don't."

"Not with your mouth, but sometimes your eyes tell their own tale."

Humph. Elizabeth did not deny she complained plenty, silently. How did he know? She would not give him the satisfaction of confirming it. "I am sure I will be comfortable wherever I sleep."

Gideon flicked the reins. "Then what is worrying you?"

"What does poison ivy look like? I would hate to get in it."

A chuckle sounded deep within Gideon's throat. "There won't be any near the house. The boys were probably playing in the woods. Poison ivy has clusters of three leaves. This early in the season it might be hard to tell which plant is the culprit or how the boys got into it. Stay close to the house and you won't need to worry." One of those rare grins lit his face.

He was making fun of her. She looked away.

His hand touched her sleeve. "Truly, I wouldn't have recommended you if I thought you couldn't do it."

The buggy lurched as they pulled into a muddy track in front of a dingy cabin. So did Elizabeth's heart.

⇥ ❋ ⇤

Gideon finished milking the first cow. David Steward stood nearby watching over his daughters as they played with the new barn kittens.

"I'll be honest, Frost, when you showed up here two days ago with Miss Garrett, I almost told you to take her back. I didn't think that spoiled little thing would do a lick of work. But she's been a godsend.

Helped my Deborah get washed up and did her hair some fancy way that has my woman grinning from ear to ear. Why, these two little ones have taken to her like they do to Christmas sweets."

Gideon poured the milk into the separator and moved to the next cow. He didn't express his own surprise. Not one burned meal in two days, and every time he saw Elizabeth, a genuine smile graced her face. Earlier that afternoon, he'd paused in his wood chopping when he heard her singing to the little girls as she hung the laundry.

David continued, his voice tight. "Did you know she stayed up late last night sewing us two new baby gowns from her own fabric? Embroidered some little flowers on the corner. My Deborah is beside herself. The hand-me-downs were in sorry shape after being used so many times, but Deborah insisted we use them and save the money for new shoes."

Gideon grunted a response, and the cow sidestepped, forcing him to focus on the milking rather than on Elizabeth's motives.

"I'm feeling pretty low about the opinion I formed of her the first time she came to church all fancy and showing off. I thought Mrs. Richards must be out of her mind to ask a niece like that to come live with her. I was none too nice to her the first day here, either. I could have put her up in the loft on the girls' bed, but I asked her to sleep on the floor near the hearth instead. Told her I might need her help in the night. She didn't complain. Was up before I was and made chocolate for my Deborah." David shook his head. "Chocolate. Deborah loves it, but we haven't purchased any in months."

"Miss Garrett is full of surprises." Gideon moved on to the last cow.

"My mother sent word. She should be bringing the older children home tomorrow afternoon. Sure been quiet around here without them. But it's been nice to have the time with my wife and baby. Deborah wants to name her Beth in honor of Miss Garrett." The little girls' giggles caught David's attention, and he turned to play with them.

Mina had been correct. Elizabeth had risen to the challenge and handled it wonderfully. Gideon wondered what her father would think if he could hear David Steward singing his daughter's praises.

Gideon finished the barn chores, poured off a quart of cream into a small crock Elizabeth had sent out, and carried it to the house.

He opened the door and held it for David, who trailed behind with a daughter in his good arm and the other clinging to his pant leg. His heart stopped beating for a moment as he stepped into the dimly lit cabin and was slow to restart as he took in the scene before him. The infant over her shoulder, Elizabeth swayed from side to side humming a quiet tune, her hair extending from her cap in a single long braid down her back.

She turned to him, brought a finger to her lips, then tilted her head to the quilt-covered doorway. Gideon read the words that formed on her lips. "Deborah is sleeping."

Gideon passed the information on to David, who'd finally reached the doorway.

⊷ ✳ ⊶

In the glow of the dying fire, Elizabeth removed her stays, then slipped back into her gray dress. Sleeping just feet away from Mr. Steward and knowing she might be called on in the night, she didn't like the idea of being caught in only her shift. As she'd discovered the first night, the stays were more uncomfortable than the wood floor. Mr. Steward and Deborah told her earlier that evening she could sleep in the loft on the older girls' tick, but Elizabeth had declined, wanting to be near if Deborah needed her again.

She heard the Stewards whispering and tried to block out their words, knowing they were not meant for her ears. Mr. Steward doted on his wife despite being surrounded with eight children in such a tiny house. He'd done his best to assist Deborah with the baby and the girls. More than once she'd heard him say "I love you" to his wife and daughters. After supper each night, he told the little girls a story. Tonight's was about the walls of Jericho tumbling down, complete with horn blasts, sending the little ones into fits of laughter.

Most surprising, he hadn't once yelled at anyone. And a couple of times she'd caught Mr. Steward and Deborah exchanging glances like the newlyweds in church. Married for at least sixteen years, and they still liked each other. More than liked—adored. Yet they owned nothing beyond the tiny farm that barely met their needs. The cabin was crowded and food was scarce. One advantage to a tiny home was it took almost no time at all to clean, and dust never had a chance to settle.

She closed her eyes and tried to imagine her parents behaving in such a loving manner. She couldn't. They owned a large house with a cook, two maids, and a stable boy. The food was abundant and space abounded. Everyone had a bedroom of their own, including the help. The Stewards had none of that. She couldn't imagine the crowd around the table when the other five children were home. But they were happy—and judging by the murmurs and giggles coming from beyond the blanketed doorway, very much enamored with each other.

If she ever found a man to marry, she hoped he would like her as much as Mr. Steward liked Deborah. It might be better to be poor and happy than to be like her mother. She needed Aunt Mina's advice.

Once again Gideon found himself sitting next to Elizabeth in her aunt's little buggy. She stifled a yawn, the dark circles under her eyes matching the story David shared. The baby had started crying in the wee hours. With Deborah confined to her bed, Elizabeth had walked miles around the table before the infant had finally quieted and slipped into slumber. By the time she'd returned to her pallet on the floor, the rooster was crowing.

Another yawn broke the silence as he drove. Elizabeth hadn't spoken since she'd flopped into the seat. He glanced over and caught her head bobbing. She straightened and looked around only to have her eyes grow heavy again.

Gideon would suggest to Mina that Elizabeth take a nap. If he suggested one to Elizabeth, he was afraid she would set out to prove she wasn't tired. Her stubborn streak was as wide as Boston Harbor, but he couldn't help but feel proud of her.

He wanted to write her father and fill him in on the details of the past three days. The letter he'd read a couple of weeks ago still raised his hackles. Couldn't Mr. Garrett see the intelligent and compassionate daughter he had? Yes, she was overly flirtatious, but Gideon reasoned that had more to do with her upbringing than being a proverbial bad seed. It wasn't his place to write Mr. Garrett, but he could encourage Mina to share some of the details.

A slight pressure on his right shoulder caused him to look down. Elizabeth slept, her head leaning into him. Gideon slowed the horse and avoided a rutted spot of road. He attributed the warmth that radiated inside him to his memories of Ruth. If he was going to marry again, Elizabeth was not a candidate. She would not be happy with the meager lifestyle he could provide either as a preacher or a cobbler. As soon as he picked up the rest of his tools, his first project would be to fashion a new pair of shoes for the youngest Steward boy. When he'd returned this morning with his siblings, he'd been wearing rags tied around his feet.

Elizabeth sighed and slid deeper into his side. Memories of Ruth mingled with the warmth of Elizabeth by his side. He flipped the reins to move the horse a bit faster, suddenly less worried about Elizabeth's need for sleep than the direction of his errant thoughts.

Elizabeth Garrett was the last woman he would ever consider entering into a relationship with.

Fourteen

JOANNA HOWELL DOESN'T DESERVE TO catch Gideon. She's as dull as ditch-water, and he'll never be happy with her. Just because she bakes bread without burning it, he thinks she is bride material. "Oh, Mister Frost, how kind of you to drop by." Of course, he didn't drop by. The ninny nearly accosted him in the street. She's hung the same sheet out every day this week, waiting for him to ride by. Bet she made a different pie each day, though.

So what if I haven't mastered pies. I helped at Stewards for three days and didn't burn a single thing. I made breakfast chocolate taste just like Aunt Mina's—not that Aunt Mina lets me prepare hers. But does he notice me at all or compliment me? No. What about all the time I helped at Stewards? Not a word of praise. But "Oh, Joanna is such a sweet girl" has peppered more conversations than I've seasoned with spice.

Elizabeth gave the bread dough another punch. Ever since Gideon had compared her bread at yesterday's dinner to the perfect loaf Miss Howell had given him last Monday, she'd wanted to punch something. Hadn't her bread improved markedly in one month from the stones she'd baked the first time?

Turn, punch, turn, punch. Elizabeth turned and punched the dough again and again, each punch more forceful than the last. Aunt Mina praised her. Gideon had—

Crash.

The bowl she was going to set the kneaded dough to rise in tumbled to the floor as she gave the dough an extra exuberant punch. Elizabeth wiped her hands on her apron and bent to retrieve the bowl, shard by shard.

The back door opened. Gideon. Could he never catch her doing something right?

"Not another one of Mina's bowls. You really must take more care."

Elizabeth rolled her eyes before standing back up and adding the broken pieces to the rubbish bin. "I assure you I did not break the bowl on purpose. And before you lecture me, I will buy Aunt Mina a new bowl next time we go into Stoughton." Elizabeth walked around Gideon to get the broom from its hook near the back door. *And the other one I broke was already cracked.*

"Might I suggest a wooden one next time?"

Elizabeth nodded. If she opened her mouth, she would say something she'd regret.

"The Howells asked that I dine with them at noon."

Wonder how long Joanna begged her mother for the invitation? Elizabeth nodded, afraid to stop herself from biting her tongue.

"Where is Mina?"

Elizabeth pointed to the weaving room.

Gideon strode past the last of the pottery fragments and into the weaving room. Snippets of conversation floated across the hall as Elizabeth swept. She tried to ignore them. The last thing she wanted to hear was how kind Joanna was or how talented.

She emptied the last of the shards into the bin and set the dough to rise in a different bowl, then she dusted the flour off her old brown dress. Uglier than ever. No wonder he gave her no more notice than she did what's-her-name, the maid back home. She wiped the bits of dough and flour from the table and into the slop bucket. Gideon hurried past her, the door shutting behind him. She glared at his retreating form through the window.

I may as well be a maid for all the good it does me. She bit her lip, trying to stifle the thought that formed, but it continued to grow. *What would he do if I wore the crimson gown?*

‒‒ ✳ ‒‒

Elizabeth squirmed on the wooden bench. Involuntarily, her hand raised to make sure her fichu was tucked into her bodice. She wished not for the first time that she'd worn her whitework one. Not only was it more opaque, it was also several inches longer. Her embroidered silk was not sufficiently long to crisscross over her chest without slipping.

When she had come downstairs this morning, Aunt Mina's brows had risen into her hairline, but she'd remained silent on the subject of Elizabeth's attire. Instead, she'd suggested they walk to church, as the day was mild for the first Sunday in March. By the time they arrived, not only was her dress covered in dust, but her slippers too—proving she should have worn her half boots and a less-conspicuous dress.

Gideon's short perusal left his mouth set in a hard line, his expression matching the disgusted one he'd worn when the goat had been ill in her stall. From his seat behind the podium, he avoided eye contact with her the entire sermon.

Not a single woman looked at her dress with longing in her eyes. Most seemed indifferent or, like Gideon, pointedly ignored her. Mrs. Howell sniffed and turned away, lifting her nose. Joanna followed her mother's lead. Mrs. Steward gave her only the briefest of smiles before turning down Elizabeth's offer to help with the younger girls, saying they would muss her fine dress.

The only person who gave her anything near an admiring look was Mr. Butler, choosing a seat directly across from her on the men's side of the aisle. He had been absent the last couple of weeks, and she hadn't calculated his reaction into her plan. A shiver traveled up her spine when she caught him eyeing her again.

She followed his gaze to her hand fiddling with the scarf. As she dropped her hand to her lap, her finger caught on a loose thread, pulling the fichu out of the low collar.

Mr. Butler's eyes took on a hungry look, the minister stuttered, and Gideon's face reddened. Elizabeth looked down to see the swell of her left breast exposed.

She grabbed for the slippery silk and caught the edge, only to have the other end loosen and reveal her entire chest. The cleavage she'd been so determined to use to entice Samuel with months ago she now rushed to hide.

Shame at her impropriety crushed down on her shoulders as if the sheer fabric were chain mail. Humiliation burned her cheeks. Her face must be a shade matching her bodice, which felt as if it had shrunk three dress sizes. Her throat constricted, and she couldn't swallow. Aunt Mina's hand rested on her leg, offering a calming reassurance, but Elizabeth spent the rest of the meeting with her head bowed, concentrating on a knot in the floorboard.

When the congregation stood for the final hymn, Elizabeth slipped from the building.

⊷ ❈ ⊶

A copse of trees north of the churchyard proved an adequate hiding place as the parishioners poured out of the church. Perhaps too adequate, as she caught pieces of conversation drifting out with the congregants.

"Poor Mina, to be saddled with such a niece."

"You know, she was dressed like one of those theater girls I saw in Boston. Not one of them better than she should be."

"The fabric was beautiful, but the low neckline—how did she keep them from popping right out?"

"Did you see Mr. Frost's face? He was mortified. And to think he has to work where she lives. So dreadful."

"Forget Mr. Frost. Did you see Mr. Butler? Mark my words, he will be after her like a fox in a henhouse. He won't quit until—"

Tears filled Elizabeth's eyes. She closed them and prayed for this nightmare to end. Would she ever learn?

Wagons and buggies rumbled over the packed earth, and children called their good-byes. A few more minutes and the churchyard would be empty. Then she would hurry home and burn the wretched dress.

Old leaves crunched as someone walked into the small wood. Her eyes flew open. Instead of finding Aunt Mina as she hoped, Mr. Butler stood not three feet away. Elizabeth's heart pounded. The churchyard lay silent. Should she run?

"Ah, my dear, I see you waited for me." He advanced a step, and Elizabeth flattened herself against a tree.

"Your aunt left with the Howells. She thought you already walked home." He rested one hand on the trunk above her shoulder. "She didn't see the bit of red flashing from behind this tree. Did you know in Spain they have bull fights and the matador waves a red cape to attract the bull?" He brought his other hand up and traced the line of the fichu with his finger.

Elizabeth tried to push him away but only succeeded in making the man's lecherous grin widen. "Leave me alone." The words were barely audible to her own ears.

"Alone? I think not." His hand moved lower, dipping his fingertips into the opening between the silk layers, brushing skin no man had ever dared touch. "As I suspected. Smoother than silk." He pulled the fichu from where it was tucked into the dress and replaced the cloth with further explorations.

Elizabeth hit his arm with all the force she used to beat Mina's rugs. He chuckled as he removed his hand from her bodice and brought it to her cheek.

"So you want to make me beg?" His lips came down fast and hard, and her head slammed into the trunk. The rough bark dug into her back. Her hat, caught between the tree and her aggressor, slid at an odd angle. Mr. Butler yanked it from her head, but the hat pin refused to relinquish its hold, taking a chunk of hair with it. Elizabeth's scream of protest became trapped inside her mouth and echoed through her head as he pinned her against the maple with the weight of his body and continued to press his mouth roughly over hers. Her hands, now caught between them, were of little use in fighting off his advances. She kicked and struggled, but he continued his assault. Demanding, degrading, and damning, the unrelenting kiss was unlike any she'd experienced. Revulsion filled her.

Fighting back with the only thing she had left, she bit down.

Mr. Butler reared back, blood pooling on his lip. "Why, you little—"

Slap! Elizabeth made quick use of her freed hand.

Expecting him to step back as a gentleman should, she did not anticipate the answering fist that connected with the side of her head. Pain radiated from the spot and obscured her vision, and she tried to take a breath and get the trees to stand still.

Pain sliced through her jaw as he roughly grabbed it and yanked her to face him. "No little doxy treats me that way." He pinned her against the tree again, the bark snagging her hair and biting into her back again. His mouth swallowed her protests as his hands tugged at her skirts.

She pummeled him with her free hand, but his explorations continued.

She clawed at his face, and when her finger found his eye socket, he reared back with a roar.

The fabric at her shoulder ripped, the bodice and sleeve separating where he gripped it.

"You!" One fist connected with her face, and something sharp dug into her cheek. The second punch caught her in the side, the force of the blow sending her to her knees. The scream trapped inside her finally broke free, followed by others. She could feel the twigs digging into her hands as she looked up and saw his leg rear back. She closed her eyes before the kick landed.

She heard the sound of the blow but felt nothing.

Then another blow and a grunt.

She opened her eyes and saw not two but four legs. She pulled herself up, clinging to the tree, and saw Gideon's fist connect with Mr. Butler's nose.

Blood splattered her dress.

Pushing her hair out of her face, Elizabeth gagged and ran into the empty churchyard on wobbly feet. She should retrieve her hat and fichu. It wasn't proper to walk down the street without them. The tears in her gown had left her shoulder and stays exposed. She crossed her arms in front of her, clutching her bodice together.

The sounds of the fighting carried from the trees. To forget the hat and run was the most sensible course, and so Elizabeth took it, hurrying out of the churchyard and away from the awful noise.

She would never wear the crimson gown again.

Father was right about her and the dress.

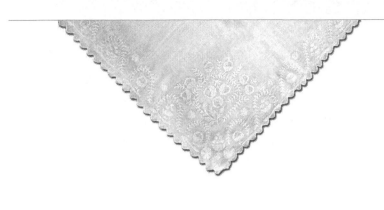

Fifteen

GIDEON RUBBED HIS MIDSECTION AS the hoofbeats of Mr. Butler's horse faded. He would have a nasty bruise. A bit of red caught his eye amid the twigs and moldering leaves.

Elizabeth's hat. He picked up the lopsided thing, not sure if it could be repaired. Several strands of hair clung to the hat pin. A few feet away, the once-snowy neck scarf lay in two dirty pieces. He stuffed the ruined fichu into his pocket to dispose of later.

Gideon searched the grove and churchyard. Where was she? He needed to make sure she got home safely. If Butler found her now, more than a dress would be ruined.

How long had she struggled with Butler before he'd heard her scream?

He ran his hand down his face, glad no fist had connected with it.

What would he tell the reverend? They had been counting on Mr. Butler's donation to help complete the building. Given the state of the lecher's nose, Gideon doubted the donation would be forthcoming. The blame would fall on him.

Was it possible to be dismissed from a lay position?

Gideon moved slowly across the churchyard. Butler's boot had connected more than once with his shins.

To the south, he spied a figure in a red dress hurrying down the road.

Gideon quickened his pace and caught up with her easily. "Your hat, I believe."

Elizabeth let out a little squeak, snatched the hat from his hand, and held it to her chest. Even with her head bowed, he saw a bruise forming. Her face hadn't fared as well as his own. She didn't look at him but increased her pace.

Gideon knew he must say something for Mina's sake, if not Elizabeth's. He took several long strides to catch up with her. Grabbing her elbow with more force than strictly necessary, he stopped her. "Just what happened?" The words came out guttural and low and harsher than he intended.

Elizabeth tried to shake off his hand. "Let me go. You are hurting me." She tried to twist her arm out of his grasp.

He loosened his grip but didn't let go. "Only if you talk to me."

Elizabeth spun to face him. "Unhand me, then." Tears mingled with the blood on her cheek. The bruises along her jawline and face seemed to grow as he watched. She kept one arm crossed in front of her, holding the ripped fabric in place, and shrugged him off with the hand holding the hat.

Gideon felt his face redden at the sight of her bare shoulder. He slipped off his coat and wrapped it around her, buttoning it under her chin.

Elizabeth's face reddened, from anger or embarrassment Gideon couldn't tell. Tears trailed unchecked down her cheeks. She clutched the rest of the coat closed and ducked her head to wipe her tears with her shoulder. "Thank you," she whispered.

Gideon stepped back. Something about the contact was slightly disorienting. A tendril of hair blew across her face, the rest of her fallen locks trapped beneath the coat. Gideon's hand itched to reach out and tuck the tendril behind her ear, but he fisted it to keep his hand firmly by his side. What was wrong with him? He was no better than Butler.

"Miss Garrett, what is the reason for dressing in such a manner?"

Elizabeth hung her head and gave no answer.

Gideon could not help but deliver the lecture he'd planned the moment Elizabeth had loosened her fichu during the service. "You

embarrassed your aunt, the reverend, and every God-fearing member
of the congregation. The only man not embarrassed is the one man you
should want nothing to do with, as you have discovered. How could
you embarrass Mina in such a manner? For her sake alone you should
have stayed within the confines of propriety. Was it not enough your
dress attracted the attention of every member of the congregation?
Did you not see even the children pointing? Not another woman in
the congregation has the money to purchase a dress like that. And to
show yourself as…as a…as a—Until this morning I thought I had
taken the full measure of your character. I thought your father too
harsh in his assessment. Now I am not so sure he was wrong."

Elizabeth's head shot up, anger flashing in her eyes. "What do you
know of my father's opinion of me?"

Gideon winced and stepped back. "Enough to know he would be
upset to see his daughter in such a state."

"Mr. Frost, what my father thinks is hardly any of your affair."
Elizabeth turned and continued to walk down the road to her gate,
somewhat unsteady.

Gideon caught up with her in two strides. "I agree. What your
father thinks is not the problem. The problem is your behavior, not
only in the churchyard but during the sermon. Virtuous women do
not undress during services."

Elizabeth stopped abruptly, using the sleeve of the coat to wipe her
face before turning to face him. "Undress? Disrobe? I did nothing
of the sort. My fichu slipped. It was an accident! And do you think
I invited Mr. Butler to take such liberties? No gentleman would ever—"

"Mr. Butler is not a gentleman."

"Then we are agreed on that point."

"I was referring to your removing your scarf during the sermon,
not your current state."

"I did not disrobe. I was trying to be covered and my hand slipped."
She lifted her chin.

"Slipped? No, your entire display this morning was for some other
purpose. You may not have intended for the scene in the churchyard,

but you did intend for some reaction. Why else would you wear a red dress to church?"

"I wore it because it was my favorite. And I—" Elizabeth hiccupped. "It doesn't really matter now, does it? I shall never wear the dress again. Not that it will matter to you, as I doubt Father will allow me to stay the week once he hears. He will never believe I didn't plan it all. He will blow it all out of proportion just like you are. I didn't mean for this to happen!"

Something in her voice stopped Gideon from responding. Sincerity? Remorse? Could he be wrong and the fichu slipped as she had said?

I will never rush to judgment. The words he'd penned during his seminary years after talking with an old sailor on the wharf came to mind. He'd broken his vow again.

The cool wind blew across the empty field, ruffling Gideon's shirt-sleeves. Several yards down the road, his coat kept Elizabeth warm. He followed after her lest Mr. Butler return. The harsh words he'd uttered begged for an apology. He hadn't asked if she was injured or offered his handkerchief to ease the bleeding. He was a cad.

Holding the coat, her dress, and the hat became almost impossible as the wind started to blow. Elizabeth dropped the hat and wiggled her arms into the sleeves of Gideon's coat, the fabric flapping beyond her fingertips. The coarse wool scraped against her shoulder where her dress no longer protected it. She heard Gideon behind her. She stepped on the center of the hat, giving it a twist and flattening the red flower before quickening her pace.

If only he would leave her alone. The momentary look of disgust on his face when she'd caught his eye during the sermon hurt as much as the lecture he'd just given her. Never had any man looked at her like that.

New tears threatened. She'd only wanted Gideon to see her as a woman. Not Mr. Butler. Certainly not him. The field before her blurred, and she stepped off the road and into a reasonably dry furrow.

"Where are you going?" Gideon's familiar hand gripped her elbow, but this time his grip was gentle and his voice inquiring, not accusatory.

Unable to answer, Elizabeth pointed to her boulder.

"I don't think that is a good idea. You shouldn't be out alone in case—and I shouldn't be alone with you. Mina will be worried. Let me escort you back to the house."

Elizabeth shrugged off Gideon's hand and took another step forward. Her foot sank into something unearth-like, and she stepped back. The farmer had fertilized the field. Her favorite fichu was gone, her best dress was torn beyond repair, and now her slipper was coated in manure. Mina had warned her against wearing the silk shoes. Ruined. Everything was ruined. She brought her hands to her face, or tried to, but the coat sleeves had her hands encased, and the wool fibers scraped against her cheeks. She shook the sleeves down to free her hands.

As soon as they were free, a handkerchief was set in them. She wiped her eyes before looking up at Gideon.

He held out his arm and nodded to the road. Elizabeth laid her hand on his arm and followed him back out of the field.

They walked in silence. Just as well. If he lectured again, she felt she might shatter like one of Aunt Mina's bowls. Each time her soiled slipper met the road, she listened to it echoing "Ruined, ruined, ruined." Not completely, but enough to cement her reputation in this little town, and it was all her fault.

When they came to the place where she'd discarded her hat, Gideon bent to pick it up.

They turned the corner, and the Purdy's house came into view, as did others. It seemed to Elizabeth that far too many people were resting on their porches after church this early in March. She extracted her hand from Gideon's arm.

"I should not have allowed you to escort me—your reputation. I am so sorry. I didn't mean—" Elizabeth bit her lip. One more word would set her tears to falling again. She concentrated on the dormer window of Aunt Mina's house. Gideon remained at her side, his fingers on the coat at her elbow giving her confidence.

He wasn't leaving her side. After the lecture he'd given her, he should have fled. Mr. Frost was the most confusing man. Perhaps if her head hurt less, she would understand.

Elizabeth walked to the back of the house, Gideon matching her step for step.

At the bottom stair, Elizabeth stepped out of her slipper. She had no desire to foul Aunt Mina's kitchen with it or scrub floors this afternoon. She kept her head down so as to not see Gideon's reaction to the impropriety of baring her foot. "I'll return your coat straight away." She hurried into the house.

Halfway up to her room, she heard Aunt Mina greeting Gideon. What she would give to never have to come back down the stairs.

Reverend Porter frowned. The conversation was not going as Gideon hoped. He wished he could pace as the reverend did.

"I could have you charged for any number of Lord's day violations, such as fighting with one of our wealthiest citizens. Only a half hour ago he was by pledging the rest of the funds we need to complete our building."

"Didn't you wonder about his face?"

The reverend paused. "I did ask, but he claimed his horse knocked him in the head—a burr caught under the saddle or some such." Waving his hand as if to dismiss the incident, he continued. "I am more concerned with Miss Garrett's actions. If the other girls follow her example, can you imagine what will happen to my little flock? I shall have to plan the sermon. I cannot condone her behavior."

"Her behavior? What of his? A few more minutes and I would not have been able to save her from him."

"But if she had dressed in a more appropriate way, you would not have needed to."

Gideon clenched his jaw to keep from raising his voice. "Are you blaming Butler's actions on Miss Garrett?"

"Did she not provide the temptation?"

The room grew stiflingly hot. Gideon needed out. Now. The temptation to hit something, namely the reverend, grew. "I see your point, but I do not agree. I think I had best take my leave for the afternoon." Not wanting to hear his answer, Gideon left the reverend's office intent on saddling Jordan. A good ride would clear his mind.

⸺ ✳ ⸺

Mina rocked in her chair near the window. The Bible sat in her lap, but she hadn't turned a page for more than half an hour. She needed wisdom. Gideon's brief description of his fight with Mr. Butler and his poor reaction afterward to Elizabeth caused her head and heart to ache.

After he'd finished his story, Elizabeth had reappeared, dressed in her gray dress, her hair back in its tight bun, staying only long enough to hand Gideon his coat and a muttered apology. Then she'd retreated to her room, where she remained.

Mina debated the merits of reporting today's incident to Ebenezer. When Elizabeth had descended the stairs in the red gown this morning, she'd been disappointed, but she had not foreseen the day's events. Regardless of what she wore to church, Elizabeth did not deserve the unwanted attentions of Mr. Butler. Of course, many would disagree with this view. She wouldn't be surprised if next week's sermon were entitled "A Virtuous Woman." She doubted Mr. Butler would be publicly censured. He never had been before. But Elizabeth was not a servant or a poor farmer's daughter; her father held both position and money. However, given Ebenezer's feelings toward Elizabeth and her need to reform, he would take Mr. Butler's side and force an apology or, worse, a marriage.

Mina shuddered at the thought. Pity Mr. Butler's wife, may it not be her dear Elizabeth. Perhaps it was best to leave this particular incident out of her next correspondence.

The shadows lengthened on the wall. Mina set the Bible aside and went to the cabinet to retrieve the witch hazel. She needed a closer look at Elizabeth's cuts and bruises.

Bones and stairs creaked as Mina made her way upstairs. Her knock at the door went unanswered. As Mina pushed the door open and peeked in, long shadows crept across the room. Elizabeth lay facedown on the bed, her shoulders shuddering as if she'd tried to stop crying for a while.

Mina sat on the bed in the space next to her and placed a hand on her shoulder. "Sit up, child. Let me see those bruises."

A ragged breath escaped Elizabeth's lips before she pushed herself up. Mina fought to keep a neutral expression. The left side of Elizabeth's face was swollen and purplish. Her eye peeked through a narrow slit. Dried blood surrounded a cut that must have come from the ring Mr. Butler usually wore.

"Open your mouth. Did he loosen any teeth?"

Elizabeth opened her mouth a fraction of an inch.

"Can you open it farther?"

Mina's brow furrowed at the mumbled no. She uncorked the witch hazel and poured some on a cloth. Gently she dabbed Elizabeth's face. "Where else do you hurt?"

Elizabeth held her palms up. The twigs and rocks had not cushioned her fall. Mina administered to half a dozen cuts.

"Any more?"

Elizabeth's face reddened where it wasn't already purple as she fumbled with the buttons near her collar and turned her back to her aunt.

Mina stifled a gasp as Elizabeth lowered the dress over her shoulders. Scratches covered Elizabeth's back. Mina leaned closer to examine them. "There are splinters in some of these. You will need to come down to the kitchen where I have better light." Mina shook her head as she lifted the dress back onto her niece's shoulders.

Elizabeth buttoned her dress before turning around. "Is Gideon…?"

"No, he is not here. When he comes, I shall have him bring us ice from the ice house." Mina softened her features in response to the terror in Elizabeth's eyes. "Don't you worry. I will not let him in."

Mina capped the witch hazel and stood. She did not relish going back down, knowing her hips would creak more than the stairs. Gripping the handrail, she descended one step at a time. When Elizabeth lingered in the bedroom, Mina turned back to call her and missed the next step.

Sixteen

THE TERRIBLE SOUNDS OF MINA'S fall echoed through the little house. Elizabeth ran from her room and dropped the papers she'd gathered when she saw Aunt Mina lying at the bottom of the stairs.

The scent of witch hazel drifted up from the broken bottle next to her aunt's still form. Elizabeth flew down the stairs, ignoring the feeble protests of her own bruises. "Aunt Mina! Aunt Mina!"

Blood oozed from a gash in her aunt's forehead. Elizabeth pressed the witch-hazel-soaked cloth to the wound to try to stop the bleeding.

"Help! Oh, help!" But there was no one to hear her feeble request. Not even God. Would God ever listen to her after today?

A horse neighed. Jordan!

Elizabeth patted the shoulder of her unconscious aunt and dashed out the kitchen door.

"Help!" Her volume increased at the cost of clarity. She threw open the barn door and yelled again.

Gideon took two strides to reach her and held her by the shoulders. "What's wrong? Is Butler here?"

"No!" It was hard to get the words out through her swollen mouth. She stepped out of his hold, grabbed his hand, and tried to pull him to the house, but he stood there as if confused.

"Aunt Mina fell!" she finally yelled, giving one more tug.

When Gideon realized what had happened, he began pulling her to the open kitchen door. Together they ran into the house. Mina's inert form remained at the bottom of the stairs. Gideon beat Elizabeth to her side.

Elizabeth started to kneel down when Gideon's hand shot out. "Glass!"

Shards of the witch-hazel bottle littered the floor. Seeing she couldn't get close to her aunt, Elizabeth did the next best thing. She grabbed the broom and cleaned up the mess. After all, cleaning was what Aunt Mina would have her do.

Gideon finished examining Mina. "I don't think anything is broken. I'm going to move her to her bed. Can you go get it ready?"

Elizabeth nodded and crossed the hall to her aunt's room, opening the door wide. She pulled back the quilts, then grabbed the towel from the washstand and laid it over the pillow. Aunt Mina looked so small in Gideon's arms.

"Light."

Elizabeth lit the lantern on the bedside table.

"Water and a clean cloth." Gideon's vocabulary shrank with the enormity of the situation.

"Docthor?" Elizabeth winced at the garbled word, but her mouth just would not work correctly.

Gideon gave her a long look before giving her a nod. "I'll go. No offense, but he might think you are the patient."

Elizabeth tried to smile at what she hoped was a joke. The smile felt lopsided.

"Hold this." He placed her hand where he held the bloody cloth. "I'll be back as soon as I can. If she wakes up, keep her in bed." Before hurrying out the door, Gideon gave her an awkward pat on the shoulder.

Elizabeth turned her attention to her aunt and hoped God would answer her prayers for Aunt Mina's sake.

⸻ ❋ ⸻

East Stoughton didn't have a doctor.

Gideon headed west along Page Street to Stoughton, hoping one of the doctors was at home. Jordan matched Gideon's need for haste, but it seemed as if Stoughton had moved several miles farther west. If he could have asked Jordan, the horse would have told him he'd set a new personal record for the three-mile run. When the houses began to appear closer together, relief filled Gideon.

The first doctor, Dr. Whiting, was not only home but was well acquainted with Mina Richards. Gideon waited only until Doctor Whiting climbed into his own carriage before retracing his way to Mina's.

Gideon wanted to run immediately into the house to see if Mina's condition had changed, but leaving Jordan in a lather would be irresponsible, so he gave the horse an extra handful of oats as the doctor pulled his carriage around by the barn.

As Doctor Whiting let himself in the back door, he called over his shoulder for Gideon to see to his animal.

Gideon prayed for Mina as he rubbed down the doctor's horse. Near the end, he added a plea for Elizabeth. Her bruises were far worse than he'd thought.

Entering the house, he found Elizabeth at the kitchen table with an untouched bowl of milk toast before her. Elizabeth looked up at him with her eyes full of tears.

"Mina?"

"She woke up." She swiveled to stare at the closed bedroom door.

Gideon let out a sigh and settled onto the bench on the opposite side of the table. Elizabeth turned back to him. She looked from her bowl to him before getting up and getting him a plate of bread and cheese and a bowl of the stew left from the earlier meal. She set it in front of him before returning to her seat.

"Does it hurt to talk?"

"Not much." Elizabeth stirred her milk toast but didn't eat it.

"May I pray?"

Elizabeth placed her hands in her lap and bowed her head. Gideon took the action as permission and prayed over the meal and for Mina's and Elizabeth's recoveries. Gideon heard her soft amen as he finished the prayer.

One bite of the meat in the stew revealed why Elizabeth wasn't eating it. He chewed steadily before asking her the questions he hadn't earlier. "How did Mina fall?"

"My fault."

"You pushed her?" Gideon fought to keep his voice steady.

"No! She came up to—with hazel." Elizabeth made a dabbing motion in front of her face, then opened her hand.

"Aunt Mina said to come down for…I wanted lethers." Elizabeth gestured to several crumpled papers at the corner of the table. Gideon raised his brows when he saw his name on one.

"She fell before—I should have—" Elizabeth's eyes filled with tears again.

Gideon wanted to reassure her it wasn't her fault. There was no guarantee Mina wouldn't have fallen if she had been closer. Of course, Mina shouldn't have been upstairs either. Not wanting to lie, he reached across the table and took her hand. He turned it palm up and examined the damage. None of the scrapes was deep. Elizabeth pulled her hand back.

"I'm sorry I didn't come faster." He swallowed to clear the growing lump in his throat.

Elizabeth shook her head and reached for the papers. She pulled one out and scanned it, then folded the paper three times before handing it to him. "Later, please."

Gideon tucked the letter inside his shirt pocket.

The door to Mina's room opened, and Doctor Whiting stepped out. They turned their attention toward him. "Mrs. Richards will mend faster if you can keep her resting for a few days. I have told her before to not go upstairs and to use her cane when walking." The doctor shook his head. He must have also known Mina was unlikely to listen to any advice. "She is going to have a good lump on her head. If you have any ice, it will help. Her ankle is also swollen. I'll check on it again to be sure it isn't broken."

Gideon spoke up. "I can get some from the Miller's ice house."

"Better bring some for Miss—"

"Gareth." Elizabeth's face reddened.

"Garrett," Gideon supplied.

"Yes. An application to Miss Garrett's jaw would be helpful." Doctor Whiting turned his full attention to Elizabeth. "Your aunt is quite insistent I look at you, too. She said there are several splinters in your back needing to be removed."

Elizabeth and the doctor stared at Gideon.

Doctor Whiting raised his brows. "Perhaps now would be a good time to go fetch some ice while I tend to Miss Garrett."

Gideon looked from one to the other, his face warming. A memory of the scratches he'd seen as he'd followed her down the street filled his mind. "I'll be back soon." He jammed his hat on his head and hurried out the door.

Elizabeth gave a little start as the door slammed.

The doctor went over to the door and latched it.

"I don't think Mr. Frost needs to walk in on us. Can you sit here with your back to the fire? It will give me the best light."

Elizabeth took a seat on the bench Doctor Whiting indicated. The doctor moved behind her, adjusting the location of the lamp. "If you can lower the dress over your shoulders." The doctor searched through his bag.

"Perfect." He reached over Elizabeth's shoulder to show her the little tweezers. "These should take care of those little splinters in no time."

The doctor talked nonstop as he removed five splinters. Elizabeth found the chatter soothing, especially when she needed to loosen her shift so he could reach the lowest one.

"There you go. All done."

Elizabeth recognized the smell of witch hazel as Doctor Whiting smoothed some on her back.

"Put yourself back together, and I'll take a look at your face." The doctor walked to the dry sink and made a point of wiping his hands while Elizabeth buttoned her dress.

"I'm ready."

The doctor turned to face her, then came over and sat on the bench with her. He adjusted the lamp and lifted her chin. "Open your mouth."

Elizabeth opened her mouth as far as she could, but it wasn't wide enough to let her tongue slip past her teeth.

"Any farther?"

Elizabeth shook her head.

"Sorry, this might hurt." Doctor Whiting stuck his finger in her mouth and pushed at her teeth.

Elizabeth felt two on the left move ever so slightly. The doctor pulled his finger out.

"A couple of them are loose. Eat soft foods for a day or two and none of Mina's taffy for at least two weeks. Does she still drink chocolate every morning?"

Elizabeth nodded.

"Tea?

"Never."

"Of course not. Too British for her. Have her share some with you. The milk and chocolate will be good for—" A knock on the back door interrupted the doctor. "Good, the ice."

Elizabeth heard the murmurs of conversation between the men at the door.

The doctor set the pail on the table.

"Wrap some of this in a cloth and hold it to your face."

Elizabeth grabbed a towel from a hook near the dry sink and did as he'd directed. Doctor Whiting took another towel and wrapped some more ice in it and beckoned Elizabeth to follow him into her aunt's room.

Mina stirred only slightly in her laudanum-induced sleep as the doctor held the ice to the back of her head. "Take my place," he said, motioning to Elizabeth.

Elizabeth did as asked. "The pillow will keep your aunt's ice in place. If she moves, try to get her back on it. When your ice starts to drip and melt, it will be time to remove both of your ice packets. Put the unmelted ice in the pail outside the back door. Ice before bed, then again first thing in the morning. I am leaving some laudanum for your aunt. A half spoonful should help her sleep."

The doctor studied Elizabeth for a few moments. Elizabeth squirmed under his gaze. "I'll check on your aunt tomorrow. Keep the ice on your face as long as you can."

Elizabeth heard the back door shut a few moments later.

"Oh, Aunt Mina. What have I done?"

⇥ ✳ ⇤

Doctor Whiting walked around his carriage. "I left the ice on the porch where the young lady can reach it. There should be enough for her to use tonight and in the morning. I'll check on them both tomorrow." The doctor set his bag on his seat, then took a step closer to Gideon. "The niece, Miss Garrett—do you know what happened to her?"

Gideon nodded.

"Was she raped?"

"Nearly." Reluctant to divulge too much, he kept his answer brief.

"Not by you, I assume."

"Never."

Doctor Whiting studied Gideon for a moment. "You are employed by Mrs. Richards?"

"Half days."

"Make an excuse to be here as much as you can for the next day or two. Miss Garrett isn't fit to be a nurse at the moment. I would prefer she rest as much as she can." With that, Doctor Whiting swung up onto his seat and told his horse it was time to go home.

Rubbing his hand down his face, Gideon watched the carriage disappear into the night. He would bunk in the barn for the night. Since he had no desire to face Reverend Porter again today, the barn seemed quite reasonable. Though a quilt would be nice.

He heard the door open and ice plunking into the bucket.

"Elizabeth?" Gideon hurried out of the barn.

"Gide—Mr. Frost?" She'd reverted to proper names. Now was probably not the best time to remind her they were friends.

Gideon stopped a few yards from the house where the rectangle of light from the door spilled out. "The doctor asked me to stay close, so I will be in the barn if you need me."

Elizabeth's shoulders dropped a fraction of an inch, and she took a deep breath. "People will talk."

"Once they learn of Mina's accident they won't." Gideon could not see Elizabeth's face with the light behind her, but he thought she nodded.

Elizabeth turned back into the house.

"May I borrow a quilt?" He did not receive an answer, but Elizabeth left the door open as she disappeared into the house.

He heard the steps creak as she rushed up the stairs. In a moment, she appeared in the doorway with two quilts in her arms.

Gideon's fingers brushed hers as he took them from her, and something old and familiar tingled around his heart at the contact. Gideon thrust the feeling out as fast as a burned biscuit. He barely registered the whispered "Good night" as the door shut.

Over the years, the Richards must have hired more than a few hands. At one point, someone added a lean-to on the back of the barn. Furnished with a narrow cot and a table that showed signs of multiple repairs, the tiny room suited his needs as long as he remembered to duck each morning so as to not hit his head on the sloped roof.

As he pulled off his coat, he heard the rustle of paper.

Elizabeth's letter.

He unfolded it, surprised to find her usual tidy script somewhat blotchy and illegible. He turned up the lamp to see it better.

Mr. Frost,

Please accept my sincerest gratitude for the help you rendered me in the churchyard. The words you spoke after were true, and I deserved a much sterner lecture and punishment. My father sent me here so I might be reformed or, as he says, retrenched. I am afraid I have proved my failure at that.

I knew this morning that I was slipping back into unwise behavior. ~~I did it because I~~ It doesn't matter why I wore my red dress. I knew better. Father said I would reach a bad end, and at least this time I have you to thank for my narrow escape.

I am sorry if I have damaged your reputation. I know I can no longer count you among my friends because a minister's reputation must be without stain and my friendship will surely stain it. You shall not have to bear my presence long as after I tell my father of today's events and my shameful behavior, I have little doubt he will take me away from here and try yet another way to mend my ways. He has threatened more than once to marry me to the next man who will take me west to Ohio or farther. Perhaps it would be best for everyone.

I am loath to leave Aunt Mina. She has taught me so much.

Will you continue to watch over her? I worry about her being alone. Yet another consequence of my behavior.

~~I shudder~~ Thank you again for your assistance today.

You are a good man. I hope you find what you are missing.

Respectfully,
Miss Elizabeth Garrett

Gideon read the letter twice. Was she truly remorseful, or was it another act? From the stricken expression she'd worn all evening, he leaned toward genuine remorse. The fact she intended to tell her father of her actions rather than letting another carry the tale showed she had matured from the girl who first arrived here.

Gideon turned down the lamp and knelt to petition the Almighty. The final plea was for Mr. Garrett to be given wisdom and for an extra dose of wisdom for himself.

What did she think he was missing?

Seventeen

ELIZABETH SMOOTHED AUNT MINA'S QUILT and tucked a lavender sachet under the pillow. She'd spent the last quarter hour dusting and straightening the room. Voices drifted through the open window.

One of the voices rose. Doctor Whiting wasn't pleased to find his cantankerous patient on the porch. Hoping to deflect some of his ire, Elizabeth hurried to the door. "Doctor Whiting, we didn't expect you this morning."

"Obviously not." The doctor glared at Mina.

The click of Aunt Mina's knitting needles was his only answer.

Elizabeth looked from one to the other. "Shall I go fetch Gideon to return my aunt to the house?"

Doctor Whiting shook his head. "No need, as long as she stays off her foot, she is welcome to sit where she pleases."

"Elizabeth, offer Doctor Whiting some of the cake you made this morning. Doctor, you may as well pull up a seat after traveling this far." Mina nodded to a chair and continued her knitting.

Elizabeth came back out of the house carrying a tray with diluted cider and two small plates of cake. She set them on the crate Gideon had rigged earlier as a table.

"Miss Garrett, join us. I told your aunt I expected her to stay off her foot for at least another three or four weeks. She shouldn't be gallivanting around the house."

Mina sputtered." I have not gallivanted anywhere in quite some time, Doctor."

Elizabeth shifted her weight from one foot to another. "I have been very careful to help her. Mr. Frost carried her out here before he left on his visits. He said he would be back within the hour."

The doctor harrumphed. "Are you any better following my orders than your aunt?

Elizabeth looked at her hands. Doctor Whiting followed her gaze. "Well, they at least do look better, and your speech is much clearer. I suspect all you need now is a little more time for the bruising to disappear." He stood and stepped toward Elizabeth. He tilted her head to the sunlight. "I am afraid, however, you shall have a small scar."

Elizabeth raised her hand to her cheek. Having a scar on her face was not the worst thing that could happen. The scars on her reputation were much deeper. More than one neighbor had ignored Elizabeth when coming to visit with Aunt Mina and check on her. The sin of wearing the crimson gown to church was apparently unforgivable.

Being ignored became preferable to the lecture she received from one matron, who put the blame for Mr. Butler's actions squarely on Elizabeth's shoulders. Somehow the event, like all events in the community, became common knowledge. Aunt Mina told Elizabeth to ignore the lecture. But the words still echoed through Elizabeth's nightmares. She shook them off to focus on what the doctor was saying.

"If it does not hurt your teeth or jaw, you may resume eating regular foods. I suggest you start with this cake. It is delicious."

"Thank you."

Mina looked up. "Go have a piece of cake now. I would like to consult with Doctor Whiting."

Doctor Whiting flagged Gideon down on High Street. "I'm not sure I liked finding Mrs. Richards on her front porch. But as long as you're willing to move her back and forth so she's not walking, I will allow it. Heaven knows her little wisp of a niece can't lift her."

"No, but Mina is shorter. I think they manage a bit of mobility without me." Gideon smiled at the doctor's frown.

"I need to ask your opinion on something. Mrs. Richards is of the opinion her niece may have been hurt more than she has let on. I understand from local gossip you were the one who interrupted Mr. Butler's advances. I must ask you again—are you sure she was not violated?"

Gideon closed his eyes, and the picture of Mr. Butler standing over the prone body of Elizabeth, his leg poised to kick her side, filled his mind. "I am sure. When I happened upon them, Mr. Butler was enraged. He seemed to be bent on beating her senseless. The top of her dress was torn, but her stays and shift were not. I would have expected more damage to her clothing, if—"

The doctor's brow furrowed. "Do you think Miss Garrett is acting peculiarly?"

"She has been quiet this week, but her facial injuries could account for that." *She also takes great pains not to look me in the face.* "I assume that also accounts for her not smiling as much."

"I told Mrs. Richards not to worry, but do keep an eye on the girl. Some women who have been violated fall into melancholy and have been known to take their own lives."

Gideon nodded.

The doctor flicked his reins and continued down the path.

Gideon suspected some of Elizabeth's worry originated from the letter she'd given him to post to her father last Monday morning. It lay safely tucked under the mattress in the barn's lean-to. The thickness of the missive made him question the amount of detail the letter contained—too much, by his guess. The way Elizabeth jumped to attention every time a carriage rolled past the house was a clear indication of its contents.

Knowing Mina's weekly Monday letter remained unwritten, he posted a short note of his own, focusing on Mina's fall and the excellent care Elizabeth provided. Mina sent a report yesterday. Before sending him to the post, she'd discussed her omission of Sunday morning with Gideon. Afraid Mr. Garrett would waste no time in retrieving Elizabeth and make matters worse, she saw no reason for her nephew to know too many details.

Gideon did not tell Mina of Elizabeth's hidden missive. It was the only thing he'd ever stolen in his life. In a week or two, when Mina felt better, and Elizabeth calmed, he would confess, and a new letter could be written.

⊷ ✳ ⊶

Gideon made the right choice when he encouraged Elizabeth to remain home with Mina. As predicted, the sermon focused on the virtue of women. Most of the congregants had managed to sneak a peek around the room, no doubt searching for the focal point of the minister's words.

Three rows back on the men's side, Mr. Butler listened to the pointed sermon, a smug smile on his lips. The idea of marching over to his pew and wiping the supercilious smirk off Butler's face with his fist crossed Gideon's mind more than once. There would be no sermon aimed at the man who'd donated enough money to complete the church building. Gideon added the inequity to his list of reasons to leave the ministry. Should a woman who dressed somewhat inappropriately for church be judged more harshly than the wealthy man who'd attacked her? If the situation were reversed and Elizabeth's attacker been one of the poor farmhands, would the sermon been the same? Or was it only the threat of losing the donation that excused Butler?

Gideon ground his teeth. Thus far he'd ignored the reverend's request to apologize for hitting Butler. He'd fought to defend a lady, not just engaged in a round of fisticuffs because he didn't like the arrogant man, a man with a history of ruining the reputations and lives of young women. However, since most of the girls were servants and had no recourse, they too took the blame. Was this really what the Bible taught? So far he had found no justification.

Perhaps Mina had the right idea. Worship God, but leave the different denominations out of it as the perfect church did not exist.

Gideon suppressed a sigh as the sermon wound down. He needed to make a decision about his future soon. Another letter from the seminary had arrived. He doubted he would be excommunicated for not apologizing to Butler, but he also doubted he would have the reverend's support. And a bad review would end his career as well. Gideon rather it be his choice.

Eighteen

GIDEON SET MINA DOWN IN the rocking chair, and Elizabeth propped her feet up. Mina winced more than necessary to keep up her pretense.

"I'll be back in a couple of hours."

"No, you won't. It is Wednesday, and you'll be going down Brockton way. Don't worry about me so much." Mina patted his cheek and turned her attention to her niece.

Gideon left the house through the kitchen.

Could the girl learn to use the loom without her standing behind? "Remember what I told you last week. It is like a dance."

Elizabeth sat on the stool.

"Pull your skirt up a bit." Mina bit her lip so as to not laugh at Elizabeth's shocked look. "Not that high. Now you can see the treadles easier."

Elizabeth took the shuttle in her left hand and studied the loom, then looked to Mina for instruction.

"Set it in the race. Now, which treadle do you start with?"

"The fourth." Elizabeth depressed the treadle and pulled the picking stick.

Zip. Clunk. The shuttle flew across the race.

Mina gave a little grin as Elizabeth jumped. "And now?"

"Batten." Elizabeth pulled the combed bar forward. "Then three." Elizabeth pressed the foot treadle and sent the shuttle flying through the warp threads. She looked up for confirmation as she pulled the batten forward again.

"I think you have it. Now think of it as a dance. Keep your right foot on the fourth and your left on the third treadle. And right, flick, pull, left, flick, pull. Dance, da, da, dance, da, da."

Elizabeth increased the speed with each zip of the shuttle.

Mina put her hand up, and Elizabeth stopped. "Very good. Now use a threaded shuttle."

Elizabeth pulled the empty shuttle out of the race and sputtered, "All the work I did was for naught?"

Mina smiled. "Better than having to fix a weaver's error. And you will always need to check your shuttle."

Elizabeth narrowed her eyes at the shuttle.

"An empty shuttle is like an empty soul. You can race around all day, but if you are empty inside at the start, you are empty still at the end."

Elizabeth raised a brow at her aunt's comment.

"Think on it. I get some of my best thinking done on the loom. It is too noisy to have a good conversation. Now back to it while I darn these stockings. Gideon will need them soon."

Gideon returned several hours later and entered the back door. He doubted they would hear him over the thunk, thump, zip of the loom if he knocked. He caught sight of Elizabeth at the loom first and paused to watch for a moment. A shadow hid the fading bruise. In the past two weeks, she'd matured more than she had in the first two months of her "retrenchment." If he had not known of her flirtatious past, he would assume she was as prim and proper as Joanna. More so, even. He grew weary of Joanna's little traps.

Gideon put the thought aside. He needed to deal with Joanna kindly and soon. He was not interested in finding a new wife yet. Perhaps his brother would have ideas regarding Joanna's pursuit when he met him in Boston tomorrow. If not for Mina's insistence, he would have canceled the trip. But she'd firmly announced that the Purdy boys would do the barn chores Thursday night and Friday morning while Elizabeth supervised. In exchange for his going, he extracted a promise from Mina to stay in her room—one he fully expected to be broken.

Elizabeth hummed a tune Gideon could not place as she continued to work. Thunk, thump, zip, thunk, thump, zip. How content she appeared. He took a step farther into the room.

Mina's chair sat empty.

Thunk, thump, zip, then silence.

Gideon looked up and met Elizabeth's wide-eyed gaze for a second before she disappeared behind the loom with a tiny yelp and a crash.

He hurried around the loom and found Elizabeth already setting the stool back in place. She smoothed her skirts and tucked a stray strand of hair behind her ear. The fall hadn't dislodged her hair. She'd taken to securing it better. How could he feel disappointed when he'd lectured her on the impropriety? "Sorry, I didn't mean to startle you."

Elizabeth didn't meet his eyes. She rarely had since that Sunday. "No, it was my fault."

"Where is Mina?"

"She wanted to lie down, so I helped her to her room. Don't worry. I was very careful, and she didn't step on her foot." Elizabeth's words poured out of her in a rush. She tried to scoot around him, practically plastering herself to the wall.

Gideon let her pass before turning and following her from the room.

Elizabeth cracked open her aunt's door and peeked inside, then stepped back, closed it, and continued to the kitchen. "Would you like something to eat?"

"Not now. I had food foisted upon me at three of my stops."

"Do you need anything else?"

"No, I came in to check on Mina. But I won't bother her if she is sleeping."

Elizabeth bobbed her head. "Then I shall return to the loom."

Gideon watched her retreating form and shook his head. Perhaps Jordan would be a better conversationalist, he mused as he headed to the barn.

＊

When she heard the kitchen door shut, Elizabeth breathed a sigh of relief, then settled back into her loom dance, letting the shuttle fly through the warp threads.

The daydreams her mind had wandered through prior to Gideon's interruption flooded back. Afraid he would see that he was the focus of those dreams, she'd dared not look at him. So gallant—more than gallant. The words she searched for failed to come to mind. Where her father would have continued to berate her every chance he got, Gideon had only allowed the subject of the red dress to become a part of the conversation once, on the morning after Mina's fall.

"Will you please post this for me?" She handed him two coins, unsure how much the thick missive would cost.

Gideon slipped the letter into his coat pocket but left the money.

"I'm sorry—"

Gideon held up his hand. "You don't need to apologize again. I was hard on you yesterday. Harder than I should have been. It is I who needs to ask your forgiveness."

"No, I—"

He stopped her again by lightly touching her shoulder. "We are agreed, we are both done apologizing and are both forgiven. There is no need to revisit that which is done. It will not change what happened."

Elizabeth was not sure if his words or his touch affected her more. The words comforted, but his touch made her heart beat a funny dance which started a longing for something beyond flirtation, that now and forever might be beyond her reach.

Thunk, thump, zip. Thunk, thump, zip.

No point in imagining Gideon in her future. Father had yet to reply to her letter. One advantage of the loom was that it drowned out the sound of passing carriages. The first week after she'd sent the letter, the sound of every carriage rumbling by the house caused her heart to race. Now she only held her breath if they slowed. Why hadn't Father reacted? She'd posted another letter yesterday but only mentioned Aunt Mina's improving health, glossing over the reverend's visit.

Last Wednesday, Reverend Porter had come to share in its entirety the sermon she'd missed. Elizabeth suspected he'd added a few more admonishments for her sake. Even a couple were directed at Aunt Mina. Only the firm expression on her aunt's face kept her from interrupting to defend Mina. Pompous man! Nothing like Reverend Woods. Aunt Mina had suggested the details of the conversation not be repeated in her letter home.

Thunk, thump, zip. Thunk, thump, zap. Tap.

The hollow sound caught Elizabeth's attention. The shuttle was empty, and the shadows in the room had lengthened.

Time to stop daydreaming and prepare supper.

Gideon mucked the last stall. He'd spent most of the time rehashing his conversation with Widow Snow over her pickled beets. Mina had been right to caution him against the widow's cooking. It was worse than Elizabeth's. That was unfair to Elizabeth, though, as her cooking skills improved each week. It was rare that she burned something these days. She'd even ventured to try some of the recipes in Mina's battered cookbook with success. He longed for seconds of her dried-apple pie.

Why did his mind keep wandering back to her? Of course Elizabeth had been the subject of the widow's diatribe. Gideon recalled the scene with a certain amount of satisfaction.

Widow Snow thumped her Bible onto the table next to the humongous bowl of beets. "Now you show me where in the Bible a man isn't held accountable for his own actions. You can't. It isn't there. Yet Reverend Porter carries on about how women must be virtuous. We all know he is talking about Miss Elizabeth. But there is not one word about men controlling their passions.

"No, Mr. Butler makes a big contribution to the church and he doesn't get a lecture at all. Yet everyone knows better than to let him near their daughters. He's ruined more than one girl. Poor Missy Meg. She never did say, but her son is the spitting image of Mr. Butler. And his mother went through more unsuitable housemaids than any other woman on the

South Shore. He's been taking what he wants from them since before he learned to shave."

The widow hadn't let him get in a word edgewise, but he agreed. Elizabeth's dress did not justify Mr. Butler's actions in the least. How could he remain silent on the matter? He'd shared his opinion with the reverend after Mina had recounted the lecture the minister had so piously delivered in her parlor only to be reminded he was on probation for a reason. The conversation had brought on further doubts about his future. He knew there were other denominations that would not have let Mr. Butler pay his way out of being publicly humiliated.

No wonder Mina did well not to join any church but spent time in her own Bible and attended for more social reasons. He knew many in his last church attended simply because it was the only church for five miles and they had no money to pay the fine for nonattendance.

Was the denomination important? Did it matter if he preached? But if he wasn't going to be a preacher, what would he do with his life? Could he be happy as a cobbler? The shoes he'd started for the Steward boy were passable, even without all his tools. But he needed shoe forms and a cobbler's bench.

Gideon wondered what tools Aaron would bring tomorrow.

Nineteen

ELIZABETH WRAPPED A LOAF OF bread and some cheese in a cloth. Despite her aunt's reassurances that the Purdy boys could handle the outside chores for two days, Elizabeth didn't want Gideon to leave. True, he hadn't stayed in the barn for over two weeks now, but it was reassuring knowing he wasn't too far if she needed him. Aunt Mina hopped around with help, but it was exhausting work helping her from the bedroom to the kitchen.

The back door opened, and Gideon stepped in, pulling off his hat. "It looks like it might storm. Perhaps I should cancel."

"Mr. Frost—"

"Elizabeth, we have discussed this. It's Gideon."

Couldn't he understand that she needed the distance? She was never going to flirt with anyone again. Of course, anytime now her father would show up and drag her home to marry the ne'er-do-well he'd threatened her with. Mother's last letter said as much. She took a deep breath. "I believe you should go. You needn't worry about Aunt Mina and me. I can do the barn chores if the Purdy boys don't come."

Gideon didn't answer but raised a brow.

"Well, I can do them well enough to ensure no animals will die before your return."

Gideon nodded. "Mina?"

"In the parlor." Elizabeth handed him the cloth-wrapped bundle. "It isn't much, but I am sure your sister will be planning a feast."

He accepted the food and walked into the parlor. Elizabeth didn't need to eavesdrop to know her aunt was telling him to stop dawdling and get going. Aunt Mina had already repeated herself three times this morning.

Minutes later Gideon passed back through the kitchen. "Take care and keep Mina down."

"I will. Enjoy your time."

And then he was gone.

⸻ ❈ ⸻

Gideon pulled his hat low to keep the rain from finding a way down his back. He made good time with the empty wagon and team he'd borrowed from Mina. Though, if he could have ridden Jordan, he would be at his sister's already. But the size of his tool chest and crate of shoe forms necessitated a wagon.

He should stop in at the seminary and give Reverend Ingram his answer, but until Mrs. Porter delivered the child and recovered, he would keep his promise to her. He would continue working to keep Reverend Porter from needing to travel to the outlying parishioners. The encouraging letters from Reverend Ingram did not have the effect the seminary director must have hoped for. Then it would be hard to counter the hollowness of yet another sermon on virtuous women when added to his previous questions.

Poor Elizabeth. She would need to return to church this Sunday to the third, and hopefully last, of the sermons Reverend Porter had planned. She'd missed only two weeks, but it would be hard to justify a third if Mina attended. Most of the congregants Gideon had visited with were divided on the subject. Some, like Widow Snow, felt Mr. Butler should have been reprimanded too and that Elizabeth bore no sin whatsoever. Gideon was torn. A year ago he would have also labeled Elizabeth as a temptress to be avoided. But he'd witnessed her hard work at the Stewards before the incident and her help with Mina after. Even if it were Elizabeth's fault, hadn't Jesus told the woman taken in adultery to go and sin no more? Why wasn't that being preached?

Wearing a fashionable dress did not equate with adultery. The only sin she'd committed was to be vain and prideful. And if all parishioners were to be judged on those counts, the little church would be empty.

The rain fell harder as he reached the outskirts of Boston. His sister's warm house was not far now.

─╫─ ✠ ─╫─

Ignoring his soaked raincoat, Gideon's sister held on to him as if she hadn't seen him in a decade, not just a year. "Constance, let me take off my coat before you drown."

"It has been too long." The fashionably dressed woman stepped back.

Gideon relinquished his coat to the house servant and resumed the hug. "Do you forgive me?"

"Always. After all, that is what big sisters do. Come into the parlor. Our brother should return soon. He went shopping for more leather." Constance rolled her eyes. She never did find joy in the smell or feel of the family trade.

Gideon wiped his feet an extra time before following his sister. She turned back to make sure he was following her.

"Constance, have you been feeling well? You look, er—"

"Fat?" She pressed her hands to her abdomen, pulled the fabric tight, and laughed.

"Not exactly. More like I shall soon be an uncle."

"Ah, I shall let you know in two months if you are correct. Now come and sit. We have not spoken since last fall. You have much to tell me."

"Not as much as you think. When I was dismissed from Greenwich, an old man told me to stop wallowing in my sorrow, which I am trying to do." He hoped she would take that as a warning not to meddle or matchmake as she had last fall. "I am on probation with the church, but I believe I will leave the clergy altogether. Hence the reason why I am here—to collect my tools."

"Won't you return home and work with our brother?"

"No. He has just enough work to support his family, and he doesn't need me splitting the profits."

Constance narrowed her eyes. Whatever she'd thought of saying, she let it pass. "How do you like your current position?"

"I am not enamored of Reverend Porter. If it had been their purpose to keep me in the church, they should have sent me elsewhere. However, I work half days at a Mrs. Richards's home. I do enjoy working there most of the time."

"Just most of the time?"

"She has this niece living with her who is, well, troublesome."

"Troublesome? What type of trouble does she give you, dear brother?" The corners of Constance's mouth turned up slightly.

"Not the type you are thinking of. She was sent to live with her aunt to be reformed. She'd never even laid a fire before arriving. I feared I might starve the week she came, waiting for her to learn to boil water."

Constance raised a brow. "How old is this niece?"

"Nineteen or so."

"I see."

The arrival of Aaron spared Gideon from knowing exactly what she saw. During supper his niece and nephew kept them entertained with tales of their schoolyard capers. James, Constance's husband, spoke of the changes in his shipping company, and Aaron discussed the latest techniques being used by shoemakers. Among them all, Gideon made sure Constance did not have time to speculate on his future.

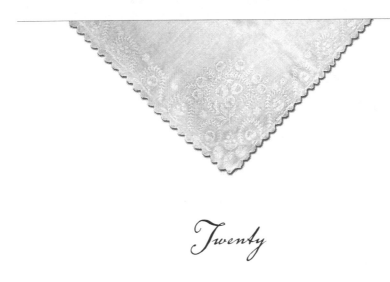

Twenty

SOMEWHERE A ROOSTER CROWED.

Easter Morning.

This year it fell on the second Sunday of April, a few days shy of the anniversaries of his son's birth and wife's death, and the pain hit with full force. The predawn darkness held the memories of unfulfilled dreams and threats of nightmares if he returned to sleep.

Gideon contemplated feigning illness. He had been unsettled since returning from his sister's a fortnight ago with the tools of his new trade. He found his faith in God's mercy growing even as his questions remained unanswered.

After years of Easter and Christmas being outlawed in Massachusetts and then the boycott during the war, many still did not celebrate the holy days of the Savior's birth and death. Only four months ago the United States Congress had met on Christmas Day. Determined to separate his congregation from their Puritan roots, Reverend Porter had encouraged celebrating Easter and Christmas as the Germans did. No reference was made to the lavish British commemorations in his admonitions. He'd only gone as far as having a vase of flowers put in the church and suggesting that families gather together and celebrate Easter. Gideon had endured listening to his sermon thrice already.

Gideon found himself wishing Easter remained outlawed, but the Bill of Rights ensured it would not be so again. *Maybe I should switch churches, too.*

Closing his eyes, he tried to recapture his fading dream. *Ruth tucked her head into his shoulder, then looked up at him with wide blue eyes.*

Blue?

Gideon shot upright. Ruth's eyes were brown, Elizabeth's blue.

He shook his head. Maybe he wouldn't need to feign illness. Elizabeth invading his dream was proof enough he was ill.

The scar on her cheek was the only reminder of her attack last month. The bruises were gone as was the calculated smile she'd often used. Mina's accident may have also been responsible for some of the changes. Elizabeth seemed even more and genuinely eager to help and learn.

Pretending was the word he was searching for. She wasn't pretending anymore.

Was *he*?

Today would be a day full of pretense for him. He would feign listening to the sermon and plaster on the requisite smile while his heart lay halfway across the commonwealth, mourning in the graveyard next to a little white church.

⇒ ✳ ⇐

A new bonnet—the first new piece of clothing Elizabeth had received since her mother smuggled the Christmas dress into her trunk four months ago. Elizabeth twisted to see it in the mirror.

Though the package came from Aunt Lydia, Mother had purchased it. The pale-blue ribbon matched her Christmas dress perfectly, and only one of the flowers was too ostentatious for her taste. Mother must be missing her to choose something in Elizabeth's style.

Elizabeth stayed up late the last three nights reworking the dress. The bodice sat too low—only a finger width higher than the red one—but the flounce provided the fabric to use in the transformation.

She tucked her embroidered muslin fichu securely into the collar. The gown's transformation was not drastic enough to forgo the use of a fichu but high enough to not cause embarrassment if the wind were to snatch the scarf away. Before securing the bonnet with a hat pin, she added one more pin to her hair. It would not fall today.

Elizabeth took one last look in the mirror. Her father would be surprised. There was nothing about her costume to embarrass him. Her cheeks reddened at the thought of the crimson gown. Had she ever thought it becoming?

Mother would be appalled at Elizabeth's disregard for fashion. She doubted either parent would believe the change wasn't some ruse. Aunt Mina might be a bit suspicious, but Elizabeth was determined. She could look beautiful without playing the strumpet. Not that there was anyone to be beautiful for, as her ragged reputation would keep all but the worst of rakes away. This left only Mr. Butler, whom she avoided by plastering herself to Mina's side.

Mindwell took another peek at her niece. She'd done an incredible job altering her dress. Mina had seen it shortly after Elizabeth's arrival when Elizabeth had attempted to remove the wrinkles from the gown. Where once the gown meant to allure and flatter, it was now subdued, some of the ruffles and trim having been removed. The neckline stood several inches higher, but try as she might, Mina could not see how the changes were made. Elizabeth had a talent for sewing. Perhaps she would get some cloth and ask Elizabeth to sew a dress for her, though she owned enough black dresses.

The sun burned off the early morning haze. As much as she wanted to walk, she took the carriage to church. Her ankle no longer pained her, but no one need know that yet. Using her cane more and having Gideon hitch up the carriage were not deceptions, per se. The doctor had told her to stay off her foot and encouraged her to use the carriage. Gideon insisted that she not attend church last week, citing the rain-soaked roads, but she suspected he'd done it as much to protect Elizabeth from gossip and more sermons on virtue. But that was the whole point of her delaying her recovery, wasn't it? Protecting Elizabeth.

If her nephew continued to insist Elizabeth only acted contrite, Mina could suggest Elizabeth earn a living with her sewing and stay with her. Ebenezer was as hard minded as a man could be. Splitting a hickory knot with an ax handle was easier than putting a single new idea into his mind. He refused to believe Elizabeth had retrenched in a single manner or design despite the weekly reports, claiming the changes had occurred much too fast to be real. Mina worried that once it was known her ankle was healed, her nephew would whisk Elizabeth away. His last correspondence hinted he might have found a way to solve Elizabeth's rebellions permanently. Mina trusted his solution would only work for his benefit and not her niece's.

The space in front of the church was half full of buggies and wagons when Elizabeth turned the carriage in. A good thing, as her niece's skill with the horse was not near that with the needle.

Gideon leaped down the church steps and hurried to the carriage. He guided the horse over to a shady spot and reached over to set the brake. Elizabeth dropped the reins and fisted her hands in her lap, but not before Mina caught the slight tremble.

Mina patted Elizabeth's arm. "You did fine. Going home will be easier."

Gideon came around and lifted Mina down, making sure she stood steady before offering a hand to Elizabeth.

Elizabeth darted a glance around before setting her gloved hand in his and stepping down. Mina hid a smile when both young people dropped their hands and stepped away from each other. She had a slower reaction pulling potatoes from the coals.

Gideon offered Mina his arm, Elizabeth following a step behind.

It struck Mina that she may need to do some interfering. Were both of them blind?

⥰ ✳ ⥆

Gideon didn't bother trying to focus on the sermon, letting his gaze wander over the congregation. At least two families he did not recognize attended today. One of the Patrick twins slipped off the bench next to his father and toddled toward his mother. An older brother placed his foot on the trailing apron string, stopping the little one with a jerk. The child sent up a chorus of howling when he fell on his hind end in the aisle. The mother handed the sleeping twin to another woman before slipping out of the bench and scooping up the crying boy. The withering look she cast her husband was not lost on the older son, but the father remained oblivious, his gaze fixed on the reverend. Only after the child had been escorted from the building did the father look around in puzzlement.

Segregation caused no end of troubles for the womenfolk. The mother reappeared a few moments later with the little boy in her arms, and Gideon's heart thudded to a stop. The child was about the age his own boy would have been. How would Ruth have handled his children as he preached? Would she have worn the same exasperated and tired look the mother did?

The mother set the little one down and aimed him back toward his older brother, holding on to the leading strings until the child had traversed the aisle and held his pudgy arms up to his sibling.

Gideon longed for his little one to reach his arms up to him to be held, but the child in his mind had curly blond hair and blue eyes—hair the color of the demure young woman sitting next to Mina. He allowed himself a moment to study Elizabeth, so changed from the girl who'd sat there a month ago playing with her fichu. Something about her face was different as well, and not just the absence of bruising. There was a peace, and she seemed engrossed in the sermon. Usually her eyes darted around the church. Today they remained focused on the man behind the lectern—mostly.

Her eyes skittered to his and quickly back to the reverend, and the faintest color bloomed in her cheeks. Gideon directed his own eyes to the center of the reverend's back, an altogether safer place to look.

Twenty-One

MINA SAT ON THE DIVAN, her foot dutifully propped up. Doctor Whiting eyed her suspiciously that morning while examining it. He was not as easily fooled as Gideon and Elizabeth.

Pity. Six weeks seemed to be the limit she could drag out the injury. This morning she'd found some forgotten wool and coached Elizabeth on carding it.

Elizabeth looked up from her carding paddles. "Too bad you can't see to read. We could finish Ann Eliza Bleecker's *History of Maria Kittle*." Mina did not miss the hopeful tone in Elizabeth's voice. Carding wool was tedious, but she would not switch her niece, even to learn of Maria's fate.

"It ends so sadly anyway. I could tell you the story of how I met your uncle. It's a much happier tale."

Elizabeth looked up, a smile on her face—all the encouragement Mina needed.

"I worked on the spinning floor of the old linen mill in Boston. We were celebrating the anniversary of the Society of Frugality. Some of the more forward-thinking men like Mr. Hancock saw the need for us to be less dependent on imports from England. That was back in August of '53, a terribly hot day for certain. About three hundred women toted our spinning wheels out to the Boston Common— all the girls from the factory as well as the married women who worked from their homes. We spent the entire day spinning as people watched. A minister preached and took up donations. One young man watched my friend, Martha. After awhile, he departed and returned around noon with his friend—Henry, of course. The first young man, Mr. Whittaker, peppered us with questions. 'How much flax do you spin a day?' 'How can you spin without looking at the wheel?' The two men asked if they could take us for supper after work. As the mill owner was providing a feast later that day, we declined. However, we determined the following Saturday afternoon we would meet them on the Common for a stroll and a picnic as it was our half day."

"Mr. Richards was the quieter of the two. He told me later he had been tongue-tied by my beauty." Mina giggled, a sound belying her years. "He never tired of using that excuse when he had little to say."

"As it turned out, he was visiting Boston on business for the day from Stoughton, where he still lived with his family. So returning on Saturday became a bit of a problem. But Mr. Whittaker put him up Saturday night, and we went to church together on Sunday before he returned home. After the first week, he managed to come to Boston almost every other weekend. On the weeks he couldn't come, he would write the most beautiful letters. Words may not have been able to come out of my Mr. Richards's mouth very fast, but they poured out of his pen."

Mina paused and looked out the window.

Elizabeth continued carding the wool. The soft scratch, scratch, scratch filled the silence.

"In time our mutual friends decided to wed. I'd been somewhat concerned for her as Mr. Whittaker was a widower and older than her by more than a decade. But they both seemed happy. She invited me to her little ceremony. Mr. Richards attended as well, as Mr. Whittaker had few other friends and no family here."

"Her parents hosted a small dinner in celebration of their nuptials. Henry asked if he might escort me home. He was more tongue-tied than usual and kept starting and stopping his sentences. Finally, as we rounded the last corner and saw my house, he pulled me to a stop and blurted, 'Mr. Whittaker has the right idea. I think we should wed.' Then he planted a kiss on my lips right there in front of God and everyone else. If I wanted to refuse, which I didn't, I wouldn't have dared after having almost my entire family witness the kiss. Your grandmother was scandalized." Mina laughed until she could barely breathe.

Elizabeth started on a new handful of wool. Mina calmed enough to restart her story.

"I was thrilled to wed only three weeks later, just to avoid your grandmother's constant scolding. I think she was jealous, as Mr. Richards had a talent for kissing." Mina felt the blush rising. She missed those kisses.

"We lived with his parents for a few months while he finished building this house. In time the Whittakers moved west. In fact, Mr. Whittaker sent Gideon to me with his recommendation."

"Is your friend still alive?"

"No, she passed some years ago, in childbirth. They were happy. Mr. Whittaker married at least twice more after that. Poor man. I think he is tired of outliving them all. We do keep up a correspondence."

Elizabeth let out a tiny gasp.

"Nothing romantic. He knows I won't leave the house Henry built for me, and he won't leave his grandchildren."

"Finished." Elizabeth laid aside the carding paddles with their sharp spikes.

"Good, now you can spin it. I think I shall go check on the bread and perhaps go take a nap." Mina's head was filled with memories she'd rather savor in the privacy of her room.

Elizabeth started the wheel with a flick of her wrist. It was ever so much faster than the drop spindle. It required more concentration to keep the fibers even, and the wool carried an odor the linen lacked, but the rhythm of her work brought a smile to her face.

She tried to picture her aunt spinning on the Boston Common. The wind must have made spinning difficult. But then again there may not have been much wind in late summer. August would have been hot out there under the sun. Had the Red-Coat soldiers stood by and watched? Had people scoffed at the laborers or applauded them? Elizabeth smiled at the memory of her aunt giggling like a girl. It hadn't been the practiced giggle Elizabeth had often employed. Aunt Mina's laugh was spontaneous.

Why would her great uncle or Mr. Whittaker fall for a woman who sat spinning? It wasn't very glamorous. Her thread broke, and she stopped the wheel to repair the spot before continuing. And how on earth had her aunt continued to spin with a handsome man watching her? If Gideon walked in now, she would break the thread for certain.

Not for the first time Elizabeth wished she could go back and change her life. She'd orchestrated every move and every interaction with every boy she'd met since she was ten. Only a few refused to do her bidding exactly as she wished. It no longer galled her that Samuel Wilson had ended their courting before it started. They would not have been happy. She would not pursue future suitors in the same manner. It was no fun to control every move a man made. Mother often cajoled Father, but neither seemed happy. The Stewards were happy in marriage, and Deborah hadn't harangued her husband. Aunt Mina talked of Henry with such fondness. All the advice her mother had ever given her came into question.

Elizabeth bit her lower lip and concentrated on feeding the fibers evenly into the hungry spindle. Assuming it was her aunt thumping about the kitchen, she did not look up when the footfalls stopped at the doorway.

Whir, click, click, whir, click, click. Elizabeth couldn't decide which was more mesmerizing—the sound of the spinning wheel or the whirling of the spokes.

A sound in the doorway drew her attention.

Gideon was leaning against the doorjamb.

Snap. Her hands jerked as the unattended thread broke.

⸺ ✳ ⸺

"Where is Mina?" Gideon's words came out raspy even to his own ears.

"I thought I heard her in the kitchen." Elizabeth fiddled with the broken thread, not raising her head to answer. Shame. Her wide blue eyes were so enchanting.

It must have been the way the wheel whirred when it spun that held him enthralled as he watched from the doorway. Was there another sight as calming as a woman spinning? Yes. His mind supplied memories of Ruth. But those moments were for a husband's joy. Spinning was different. He'd loved the sound of the wheel as a child, his mother spinning and humming.

"Do you need her?"

"Wha—No. I wanted her to know I think the goat will have her kids by morning. I am going over to let the reverend know I shall be staying in the barn tonight."

"Will you want supper with us?"

"Yes, please." Another kidney pie had been delivered to the Porters' and Gideon had no desire to return to dine with them.

Elizabeth slid the stool back and walked to the doorway. She waited until Gideon moved aside before going to the kitchen.

Gideon watched her retreat. He shook his head. Part of him was disappointed she kept a respectable distance. The other part applauded how she now acted circumspectly even in private.

⸺ ✳ ⸺

After a long night with the new mama goat and the second kid needing assistance in being born, Gideon's bed at Porters' was a welcome sight. He fell asleep without dreaming.

A crash downstairs woke Gideon. The reverend's heavy footfalls echoed on the stairs. Gideon was half out of bed by the time his door slammed open to reveal the reverend standing there in his nightshirt.

"Ride for the midwife!" The reverend ran back down the stairs without waiting for a response.

Not needing to be told a second time, Gideon pulled on his trousers and socks. It was about time the newest Porter arrived.

The midwife did not dress as quickly as Gideon had, and by the time they returned, Mrs. Porter held her new son in her arms. Gideon caught only a glimpse of the new baby before being ushered from the room along with Reverend Porter. Cries from the children upstairs alerted the reverend to his other duties, and Gideon was left alone to tend the kitchen fire.

A moment later, the midwife appeared with a squirming bundle. "Where is the reverend?"

Gideon pointed to the stairs.

"Well, then, you hold him for a moment."

Before Gideon could protest, the midwife thrust the tiny bundle into his hands. He adjusted his arms to keep from dropping the babe, who squawked in protest. Afraid to look down at the child, Gideon began walking toward the stairway when a pitiful mewing stopped him.

The red-faced child in his arms bore little resemblance to the child in his memory. The baby yawned and shook his little fist. Instinctively, Gideon held him closer. Wonder, not loss, filled him. For weeks he'd dreaded the moment he must see this newborn, and for naught. There was no pain, only awe.

Somewhere a cock crowed, and the midwife stood before him, hands outstretched. "I said I'll be taking the little fellow now. He needs to be with his parents."

Gideon handed over the sleeping child.

"Caught your eye, didn't he, Mr. Frost? About time you find yourself a wife and get one of your own. Miss Joanna would make you a fine one. Mark my word, she would." The midwife left the kitchen.

Gideon walked to the barn to milk the Porters' cow, knowing the reverend wouldn't be getting to his own chores today.

Twenty-Two

"IF YOU SEE THE BOTTOM of the paddle, it is too weak."

Elizabeth forced herself not to roll her eyes. Aunt Mina had repeated the same instructions at least a dozen times while the new linen cloth soaked in lye water for the past two days.

"If the mixture is too thick, like your stew, it will glob on the fabric and bleach unevenly." Aunt Mina continued.

It was as if she expected Elizabeth wouldn't "mind well." Elizabeth bit her lip to stifle the grin forming at her pun of her aunt's name.

"And whatever you do, do not splash the lye water on your skin. Nasty stuff. If you do, wash the lye off as fast as you can. Keep a bucket of water near. Are you wearing your oldest petticoat?" There was no need to ask about the decades-old dress Elizabeth wore. With any luck, she would ruin it today.

"Don't worry. I think I know what you want. I still believe it is impossible, but I'll do what you say. I am more worried about you doing too much. Making dinner and supper means being on your feet more than you have been." Elizabeth finished washing the breakfast dishes and dried her hands.

"Go on. And if you are making a mess of things, ask!" Aunt Mina waved her out of the kitchen.

Elizabeth hurried to the near side of the barn. Bleaching linen sounded no more complicated than any other recipe she learned in the past four months.

The lye water turned the color of weak tea. Using a long paddle, Elizabeth stirred the brownish muck. No use. It wasn't going to get any darker. The impossibility of bleaching the newly woven cloth using a cow-dung-and-lye cocktail! Brown, smelly, and downright disgusting, manure could not possibly bleach anything. Elizabeth would do one length of cloth bypassing this step to prove her point. Well, maybe she would do a quarter length. Because Aunt Mina wasn't often wrong.

Soaking the cloth in lye for two days made some sense. After all, lye did clean things. It was the main ingredient in soap. The possibility of bleaching anything in the dark water was ludicrous.

Elizabeth peered into the wooden barrel, the bottom of her paddle still visible. She grabbed the shovel and headed into the barn, wishing she'd brought out more than a shovelful earlier.

Fiddlesticks. The stalls were mucked clean, and the cow grazed in the pasture, so there was nothing left to collect. She stomped out the back of the barn where a pile of manure laced with bits of straw and hay composted in the sun. She circled the pile, looking for the latest additions. Some of the lumps seemed lumpier than others. Oh no! How could she differentiate cow droppings from horse or goat droppings? Or pig? Did Gideon muck the pigsty? What if she got the wrong kind of manure? Would it work? Not as if brown sludge were going to bleach anything anyway.

She'd paid no attention to the composition of the shovelful of dung she'd hauled from the cow's stall earlier, as she'd concentrated on not dropping the fresh manure on her person. Why hadn't she listened to Aunt Mina and gathered all of last night's droppings?

Gingerly, she separated a likely glob from the pile with the tip of the shovel, then brought the shovel closer to inspect her find.

Gravel crunched behind her. "Elizabe—" Gideon didn't have time to finish his sentence. Elizabeth whirled at the sound of his footfall, the momentum catapulting the patty off the end of the shovel and directly toward Gideon's chin.

Elizabeth gasped and stepped back, her left boot heel catching on a sun-dried flop. The projectile hit Gideon's jaw at the same moment her posterior connected with the sun-warmed hill.

Stunned, Elizabeth watched the brown glob linger for a moment before it dropped to Gideon's shirt and finally to the ground. Gideon's eyes followed the brown trail. After a moment, he brought his gaze up and locked it on hers. His left brow rose, followed by the corner of his mouth.

A laugh burst forth.

Elizabeth blinked in disbelief. He laughed now?

Gideon pulled a cloth from his back pocket and wiped his jaw. He extended his other hand to Elizabeth, his laughter filling the air.

Is he daft? That's manure on his face. How hard has he been hit?

Only as she stood did Elizabeth realize her own plight as her sodden dress clung to her backside. She twisted and tried to dislodge the mess by shaking her skirt.

Gideon's laughter grew, and he planted his palms on his knees to support himself.

He should be reprimanding her for another mindless act, not laughing like a madman. She sent him a scowl, but his eyes were all scrunched up, and he didn't seem to notice. Why, the man laughed so hard tears were falling!

"So-so-sor-r-ry." The words came out breathy as he continued to laugh. Elizabeth doubted he was sorry for anything. At least he wasn't yelling at her for—for—

A giggle worked its way up her throat and joined his laughing. Mirth filled the barnyard. Why on earth was she laughing? She'd flung dung at the preacher's assistant, and her backside was covered in it.

When they finally caught their breath, Elizabeth tried to look away from the still smiling man.

The bossy cow stuck her head over the fence, her large brown eyes blinking, her mooing low. Gideon looked at the cow, then at Elizabeth, and started laughing again.

—�֎—

Gideon sucked in a deep breath and stood up straight. He couldn't remember laughing that hard since his younger brother had found a skunk den.

Fortunately for them both, the fragrance of cow excrement would wash off easier than the stench had from his brother. Ma had banished his brother to the barn for days.

Elizabeth twisted to look at the back of her skirts, her nose wrinkling in dismay. She shook them harder.

Gideon gave his face another scrub with a clean corner of his handkerchief and bit his cheek to keep from laughing at Elizabeth's attempts to remove the muck from the back of her skirt.

He put his hand on her shoulder and spun her partway around. No amount of shaking would dislodge the mess clinging to her dress.

Gideon picked up the shovel. "Hold still."

Elizabeth took a step back, raising her hands. "What are you going to do?"

Gideon stared at the shovel in his hands and then at Elizabeth's pale face. "I was going to try to scrape some of the mess off your skirts."

"Oh." Elizabeth turned her back to him and pulled her skirt away from her body, stretching the fabric taut.

Gideon removed most of the onerous gunk with the tip of the shovel and said, "That's most of it. What were you doing in the dung pile?" He stepped back and leaned on the shovel.

"I didn't gather enough cow dung for the bleaching, and the stalls are clean. I was trying to figure out what clump would be the freshest manure. How do you tell cow from horse or goat dung?" Her nose wrinkled at the question.

"Well, at the moment, I know there is only cow dung in the wheelbarrow. So we could compare it, or you could take what I set aside for you and use it."

"You set some aside for me?" Elizabeth practically bounced over to the wheelbarrow to inspect its contents.

"Mina told me you might need it." Gideon schooled his features to keep another laugh from coming out. Elizabeth Garrett was bouncing with excitement that he saved cow dung for her. He grabbed the handles of the wheelbarrow and started around the barn. Elizabeth scrambled to keep up with him.

"How much do you need?" Gideon poised a shovelful above the barrel.

"I'm not sure. Maybe half that. Aunt Mina described what the liquid should look like when I am done, but she wasn't very clear on the amount of ingredients I need."

Gideon tipped the shovel, but Elizabeth stopped him with a hand on his arm. "Careful. You don't want it to splash. The lye water is very strong."

For the first time since meeting Elizabeth, he allowed himself to enjoy the warmth radiating up his arm as he eased the dung into the barrel without a splash.

⊷ ✳ ⊶

Mina set down the ladle. Was that laughter drifting through the open window? The only people who should be behind the house were Gideon and Elizabeth. She'd chased the Purdy boys away enough times they should know better.

Mina doubted Gideon capable of laughing. She cocked her head. Definitely laughter, and echoing from behind the barn.

The laughter faded. Mina longed to know what happened, but if she even set the tip of her cane out the door, her ruse would be up. Mina stepped to the window. No one stood in the barnyard.

The sound of voices followed the creak of the wheelbarrow. Gideon came into view first, with Elizabeth on his heels.

She knew Elizabeth would need more dung. Good thing she'd asked Gideon to set some aside. The couple worked together to mix the dung in the large barrel.

My heavens, what was wrong with Elizabeth's dress? Mina squinted. The brown patch might be mud, but it hadn't rained for several days.

The large, dark, wet patch looked almost as if she'd fallen in—surely not. Elizabeth would not stand in the vicinity of any man with her dress coated in manure.

Glory be, her niece was improving in the essentials. Instead of screeching about her predicament, Elizabeth was carrying on a conversation as if she were at a ball dressed in silk instead of ugly gray homespun stained with manure.

There, standing in the barnyard, was proof perfect. Ebenezer would never believe the change. Of course, his wife would be mortified. Mina smiled. Rebecca would be fanning herself and calling for the smelling salts.

Nevertheless, Elizabeth could not come in the house with that muck covering her dress.

While Gideon held the lengths of linen, Elizabeth used the paddle to introduce the fabric to the liquid-filled barrel. Mina smiled at the cooperation. The job was tough without some assistance. She'd hoped Gideon would step in and help.

The couple talked the entire time. More laughter filled the air. Gideon stayed by Elizabeth's side as they headed to the back door.

Mina hurried across the room to cut them off. Brown stains adorned the front of Gideon's shirt, matching the large one on Elizabeth's dress.

"Stop right there." Mina put her hand up and wrinkled her nose. "I am not having that odor foul up my kitchen."

"But, Aunt Mina, I need to change. I…fell." Elizabeth bit her lip and glanced at Gideon.

Gideon grinned. A full smile. Even having heard the laughter, Mina gasped at the sight.

He cleared his throat. "We had a little mishap in the compost pile. I'm headed out to go get a change of clothes, and Elizabeth is in desperate need of different attire."

A giggle escaped Elizabeth's lips. Gideon looked away, his smile growing even wider.

"Don't worry. I have already offered to wash his shirt and pants. They shouldn't wait until he can take them to the laundress."

The girl who'd arrived here only months ago with no laundry skills offering to do laundry? Her nephew would not believe her report.

"I need my brown dress and another peti—" Elizabeth closed her mouth, and her cheeks flamed. Gideon stared up at a nearby tree.

"I'll get them."

"But the doctor told you not to go upstairs!"

Mina closed her eyes. Her foot had healed, but to prove it at the moment might cause her plans to backfire.

Gideon cleared his throat. "I am not as…er…stained as Elizabeth. Perhaps if I retrieved the dress?"

Elizabeth's eyes widened.

Mina considered for a moment. It was not ideal, but Gideon had been married, so he was acquainted with women's clothing. She nodded.

Elizabeth shook her head and mouthed *No*.

Mina ignored her niece. "Best tell him what you need and where to find your things. You can change out in the barn's lean-to while Gideon heads up to his place to change."

Elizabeth kept her gaze on her toes as she described the location of the brown dress, another old petticoat, a shift, and stockings.

Gideon hurried past Mina and up the stairs.

Elizabeth studied the upper window while she waited.

Mina handed Elizabeth the bucket. "We best get some water boiling for the wash."

Gideon came down at the same time Elizabeth returned with a filled bucket. Mina took the clothing from him and noted he'd folded everything neatly inside the dress. "When you return, the water should be ready for the wash."

She handed the cloth bundle to Elizabeth. "Best wait until he gets Jordan out before you go in the barn."

Elizabeth nodded her understanding.

—⊷ ✳ ⊶—

Elizabeth shut the door behind her. The room was smaller than she expected. Since it was attached to the barn, she thought it might smell like a stall, but it didn't. Of course, the stench in her dress made smelling anything else impossible.

Mother would suffer apoplexy if she saw her now. Father's reaction was harder to guess. What had happened by the compost heap wasn't improper in the sense of her crimson gown, but it wasn't the type of thing a well-mannered woman did, either. She doubted Martha Washington had ever bleached linen. But Abigail Adams most likely had. She'd taken care of the entire farm during the war. Father couldn't fault her for bleaching linen if a president's wife had. Mrs. Adams preferred to live at their personal residence and not in Washington society. Father might not hold Abigail Adams as highly in regard as he did Mrs. Washington, but he praised her tenacity. Mrs. Adams's example would be enough to mollify Father.

While Father may approve of her to a point, flinging cow droppings in Mr. Frost's face was beyond the pale, even if he wasn't a real minister. She would need to be careful in her description in her weekly letter home. Not to mention Aunt Mina's report—although she suspected her aunt only detailed her actions in the best light to her father.

Elizabeth stepped out of the skirt. The damage was worse than she thought. Maybe the ugly thing was ruined. She hadn't even needed to spill any lye water on it. Not that she could have with Gideon standing next to her helping.

What must Gideon think of her?

His laugh.

The mess on her dress was worth hearing him laugh and witnessing his handsome smile. Gideon should smile more often. She thought of the bit of a dimple in his cheek that appeared when his smile widened.

She slipped off the rest of the soiled clothing, dumping them in a pile by the door.

She should have brought in a pitcher to wash. She could rinse in water from the trough only a few steps on the other side of the door, but if she were discovered by one of the neighbor boys or Gideon—

She pulled on the clean shift, sat on the bed to pull on her fresh stockings, and noticed a paper sticking out from under the straw tick.

Her hand hovered for a moment before she pulled it back. Gideon stayed in here from time to time. She shouldn't.

As she tied her petticoats on and wrapped a short gown over them, the corner of the paper waved, almost as if welcoming her scrutiny.

Peeking a little might not hurt. The paper might be important, and Gideon may need it.

She buttoned the first button. *No, I shouldn't.*

The second. *But what if it was lost . . .*

The third button. *No, I shouldn't.*

The forth. *It may be important . . .*

As luck would have it, her dress had eight buttons.

She lifted the mattress and pulled out the paper.

The writing was familiar. Very familiar.

It was hers.

Twenty-Three

GIDEON WHISTLED AS HE RODE Jordan down the street. A couple of boys stopped playing to stare at him, and he waved. One woman sweeping her porch looked up to see who passed by. She would have tales to tell her neighbor. Who would believe the taciturn under-preacher would whistle in public?

He came around the house to find Elizabeth already bent over the washtub, and dismounted. "I hope you don't mind. I put an extra shirt in here. I spilled some stew on it last night." He handed her the bundle of clothing.

Elizabeth took it without looking up.

Gideon stood dumbly. He'd only left a half hour ago, and they had been laughing. Now she wouldn't acknowledge him. Had she gotten embarrassed once she realized how filthy she was?

"Elizabeth?"

She scrubbed harder. If she wasn't careful, her skirt would rip long before it came clean.

"Has something happened?"

She lifted the sodden skirt from the water and inspected the location of the stain, then plunged the skirt back into the water with enough force to splash a good portion of the water out of the tub. Gideon jumped back to avoid his boots being soaked.

"Whoa there. Tell me what is wrong."

Elizabeth stopped scrubbing and stood up. She wiped her hands on her apron before settling fists on her hips.

"Do you really want to know? Or are you pretending to care? I thought you were a man of his word. You lied to me. Here you are some minister, and you lie like the rest of them."

"Wha—"

"You promised. Now what am I to do? Father will never believe me. At least now I know why he didn't come for me." She pulled a sealed packet from her pocket and held it up as a general would a rapier to signal the charge.

Gideon recognized it as the letter she'd asked him to post the morning after her attack. He'd forgotten about it when he'd left the lean-to and returned to Porters'. He reached for it, but she stepped out of his reach.

"You can't have it. I must post it now. But what am I to say? 'I gave it to the preacher to post, and he hid it?' Father will never believe it is the truth. Nor will he believe I confessed all in this letter with a tale like that. For weeks I have lived in dread that he would show up and find a new punishment for me, especially when I told him I see the error of my ways in my letter. I thought he must have believed me when he didn't come. But he never knew, did he?" Elizabeth cast an accusing glare at him.

Chastised, Gideon stared at his feet, trying to form an explanation. He'd meant to discuss the letter with her. He'd reasoned she'd been so upset when she wrote it she must have disclosed more than she intended to about the attack and Mina's fall. He opened his mouth to say so, but Elizabeth continued, her voice rising.

"He never knew of my shameful plan to prove to Joanna that she wasn't the only one who could catch you. Nor how embarrassed I was to realize I was no better than the strumpet he thought me to be, wishing I could sink into the floor of the church like a lost button between the floorboards. Nor how my own willfulness finally resulted in Mr. Butler's unwanted attentions. Then how my selfishness nearly killed my aunt. I begged for forgiveness for all of that. I realized my ruination lost me more than my good name because it lost me forever to you. How could I have told my father how much you helped me in one sentence, then blame you for not sending my letter? How?"

Gideon wasn't sure what to say. In the part of his heart that had died with Ruth, there was the smallest of movements, like a new plant forcing its way into the sunlight.

"I can't. I can't." Tears streamed down her face. "I'll be fortunate if he lets me marry a fishmonger now. He will never let me stay, and Aunt Mina needs me. For the first time in my life I am useful. Needed. And it's all going to end." A sob caught in Elizabeth's throat, her eyes filling with misery. She stared at him for a long moment before she turned and ran.

Gideon's first thought was to go after her, but chasing her down the street would not be easily explained. Instead he tied Jordan to the fence post. No point in unsaddling him. He'd give Elizabeth a few minutes to reach her rock and calm down before he found her and tried to explain.

From the parlor window, Mina watched the retreating form of her niece. Going to the thinking boulder, more than likely. She waited for Gideon to follow and grew more disappointed each minute the clock ticked by.

The back door opened, and Gideon called, "Mina?"

"In the parlor." Mina's hands worked a set of knitting needles. Gideon stood in the doorway and ran his hand through his hair. She looked at him, but her hands didn't slow. "Where did my girl go in such a hurry? You two didn't start a fire, did you?"

"No, but I upset her enough."

Mina's eyes narrowed, and her hands slowed.

Gideon squirmed like a schoolboy caught with a frog in his pocket. "She found the letter to her father she wrote after that terrible Sunday. She'd asked me to post it because of—" Gideon brought his hand to his face. "And with you injured, I told her I would, but thought I should wait a couple of days until one of my own letters could reach her father and maybe talk her into reconsidering what she wrote. I wanted her to reconsider what she had written to her father, so I didn't mail the letter. And I never got around to talking to her."

"You read it?"

"No. But she was so distraught I assumed her letter would be of the same tone."

The needles resumed their click, click, click in Mina's hands. "No wonder she was so worried about her father coming."

Click, click, click.

"So are you going?"

"Where?"

"After her! I assume she went to the rock below the ridge in the back field. At one time it was one of my favorite thinking spots."

Gideon raised a brow. "I can't imagine you sitting out there."

The clicking stopped. "I wasn't this old all my life. It is a lovely walk and a good spot to pray. Henry knew where to find me when we'd had a row. My Elizabeth is pretty smart to find my rock."

Gideon made no move to leave.

"Go on now."

"Before I go, I want to know if letting Elizabeth's, um, inner clothes soak in the tub will hurt them. I finished my things and her skirt, but—" Heat started to crawl up the back of his neck.

Mina bit back a smile. "They'll be just fine."

Gideon's boots echoed as he crossed through the kitchen. He paused at the door. "And Mina, don't you go finishing the laundry, or you may have more than the good doctor to answer to."

Mina chuckled. She had no intention of doing the laundry. Not when that particular boulder could be seen from the upstairs window.

⊰ ✳ ⊱

Cutting through the fields behind the barn was the fastest way to reach the boulder, but Mina rented out those fields, and his horse would damage the recently planted crops. So Gideon chose to go around by the road, as Elizabeth had. At least she'd left by the road. She could have gone elsewhere. He aimed Jordan up the road and kept a sedate pace. No point in setting tongues to wagging.

As he passed the building that served as both post office and stage stop, a sudden realization filled him with dread. He stepped inside. "Afternoon, Mr. Thomas."

"Ah, Mr. Frost, the post has come. I've not finished sorting it. Do you care to wait?"

Gideon shifted. "Did Miss Garrett happen to post anything today?"

"You know I am not supposed to answer any questions like that. But I suppose you are here to pay the penny she owes. I wouldn't have let her send it, but being Mrs. Richards is housebound, she probably didn't realize the thicker letter would cost more. Just made the post she did."

Gideon pulled a coin from his pocket and set it on the counter. No way he could retrieve the letter now. And if he wrote his own note, it would not likely catch up to Elizabeth's, but it was worth a try. He took another coin from his pocket. "May I have a piece of paper and the use of your pen?"

Mr. Thomas handed Gideon the inkwell and gestured to a waist-high shelf. "You can write over there."

Gideon dipped the nib in the ink.

28 April 1798

Magistrate Garrett,

You have no doubt received a missive from your daughter either this day or one past. The letter is dated two months ago. Please do not blame the delay on Elizabeth, as it was I who intercepted and detained the letter knowing she was overwrought when she wrote it. I know not what the letter contains, but I have a guess. Please know your daughter has much changed this spring in all her actions and deportment. Her presence here has been of much comfort and help to Mrs. Mindwell Richards. Please do not react to Elizabeth's letter in haste.

Your Servant—

Gideon paused. How should he sign it? The last short note to Mr. Garrett he signed "Reverend," as he wished not to explain how he knew about Mina's fall and Elizabeth's injuries. Although he had yet to officially declare his intention to leave the church, he felt guilt using the clerical title. But with what little he knew of the magistrate, he figured that using his title would help his cause the most. So for the last time in his life, Gideon signed,

Reverend G. Frost

⊷ ✳ ⊶

Elizabeth turned the sodden cloth over, but there was not a dry space to be found, so she used the corner of her apron instead. She should go back and apologize to Gideon and finish the laundry so Aunt Mina would not be tempted to do it, but her face was likely to be red and blotchy from crying, and she had no wish to be seen yet.

Her anger at Gideon had cooled. His interference had given her time with Aunt Mina, after all. If her father had come a few weeks ago, she would have had to leave Aunt Mina while she was still incapable of caring for herself. Her aunt got around much easier now, and it wouldn't weigh on her mind so when Father did come.

It was better she leave. She had all but blurted out her feelings for Gideon. She could never be a preacher's wife. Her reputation would ruin him. If she stayed longer, her fondness for him could only deepen. Discovering he could laugh—a pleasant surprise. She would miss him more than she would Aunt Mina. She could write her aunt, but not Gideon.

She turned her face to the sun and soaked in its warmth.

Another thing for Mother to be scandalized over—she was brown as an Indian, but a bit of tanned skin would match her work-worn hands. Once she'd thought less of the girls at home, like Lucy, who worked so hard. But now she knew there was something very satisfying about going to bed tired, watching Gideon ask for a second helping of supper, or seeing Aunt Mina's smile whenever she mastered a new skill.

Mother would never consent to allow her in the kitchen. Too bad—her bread was almost as good as Cook's. What would she do if she had to return home?

Had she been idle and vain because she'd had nothing else to do, or was it truly her nature to be so? Aunt Mina kept her too busy to while away her time. Not that she didn't have fun reading out loud or listening to her aunt's stories while spinning. But at home, she never did anything of note. Perhaps that was why she had behaved in so many regrettable ways.

If she did go home, there were many apologies to make. Some could be made by letters, she supposed. A few would need to be written. After all, hadn't what's-her-name moved to Ohio or someplace west with her husband? At least he'd married her despite the lie Elizabeth had circulated. Shame flooded her. She would compose a letter tonight. Perhaps her father would forward it. She would have to write one to him too. And what of Samuel and Lucy? Could she face them? She needed to say so much more to Lucy, whom she'd tormented all through school. It would be best done in person. Otherwise, they might not credit it.

Elizabeth counted the number of visits she would need to make after her father came to fetch her. She hoped he would give her time to complete them before packing her off someplace else. Tears filled her eyes as she chastised herself.

A footfall alerted her to Gideon's presence. Time to return. Aunt Mina needed her home. As she gathered her skirts to hop down, Gideon stepped close enough she couldn't make good her escape. He held out a fresh handkerchief.

"I am sorry." They said in unison, the ridge bouncing the words back to them.

Elizabeth shook her head. "You owe me nothing. I should not have berated you. I never asked you why. I assumed that—" She waved her hands in a helpless manner, the handkerchief fluttering about like a caged bird.

Gideon snagged the corner of the cloth, stilling the fabric. "Yes, I do. I presumed to interfere where I should not have. I did not mean to leave the letter this long. Only long enough you might have enough clarity to consider what you may have written."

"Did you read it, too, then?"

Gideon shook his head. "Given your distress and the thickness of the packet, I assumed you'd written of the events of that day in such a way as to make your role far worse than it was. I thought to protect you from your father's recriminations for a time as well."

Elizabeth stared at Gideon. She should have known he'd harbored no ill intent. She lowered her eyes. "I have made a mess of it again. You will be well rid of me, I think."

Gideon wrapped the end of the handkerchief around his finger, bringing his hand closer to Elizabeth's. "One is never well rid of a friend."

Elizabeth looked up, her eyes searching his. "Friend? After what I've done to you? If you knew what a vile creature I am, you would never claim such a thing. The crimson gown incident is nothing compared to what I have done. The people I have hurt and the chaos I have caused. I fear I have ruined more lives than my own. No, you cannot be my friend, Mr. Foster. It will only lower your esteem in the eyes of all those who know you."

He gave the cloth a final tug, bringing her hand into his, then held it for a moment before he answered. "I have no doubt that in your past you did things you are not proud to claim. But I have watched you these past months. You are so different from the angry, defiant girl who stood in Mina's kitchen attempting to wash clothes. You have done nothing to me save accuse me of hiding a letter, which I did. The greater shame in that Sunday does not lie with you, nor does it taint me, if that is what you speak of. Although those first few meals you prepared were want to kill me." His smile grew slowly, reaching his eyes.

Elizabeth pulled her hand away and covered her mouth in a vain attempt to hide the giggle. "I wasn't trying to make you ill."

Gideon leaned against the boulder, a chuckle on his lips. "But you did try to do that which you had never been asked to do, and you did so valiantly. I've cooked for myself for several months, and it did not improve as yours did."

Elizabeth tilted her head. "Why was that?"

"After my Ruth died and the baby with her, I became so sullen not a single congregant would invite me to dinner."

"You loved her very much, didn't you?"

Gideon studied the trees beyond the rock wall on the ridge. "At first I thought the pain would take me too. When it didn't, I was so lost. Working for Mina was what I needed. She taught me things about life no amount of study did."

"So, will you be leaving, then, to take your own church?"

"No. Now that I have my cobbler tools, I intend to set up shop or join one of the shops up in Randolph. But I will stay with Mina until she no longer needs me."

"I am glad of that. I would worry so if aunt were alone." *And perhaps I will know a little of your life, too, when I am gone. Surely Aunt Mina will write of you.*

"You are sure he will come for you?"

"He won't allow me to continue to sully his name here. If I remember half of what I wrote, I would expect him in no less than a week. Unless he has more pressing matters."

"Lizzy, I shall pray he does not come in haste."

"Lizzy? No one has called me Lizzy since I was six."

"Does it offend you? Elizabeth seems so pretentious sometimes."

Elizabeth furrowed her brow and shook her head. "No, I like Lizzy. My brother used to call me that until Mother lectured him. He still does if she is not around."

"Then come, Lizzy, we'd best get back before Mina attempts to finish the laundry."

Elizabeth scooted awkwardly to the edge of the rock, trying to keep her skirts in proper order. Gideon pushed himself away from where he leaned and reached out to her. "Allow me." He placed his hands on her waist and lifted her down, not immediately removing them when her feet touched the ground.

"Friends, Lizzy." He dropped a kiss on the top of her head and offered his arm for the walk across the field to where Jordan waited.

Mina dropped the lacy curtain back into place, wishing she could hear the conversation.

"Please bless them, Lord," she whispered as she headed for the stairs, adding a prayer for her descent as well.

Twenty-four

MAGISTRATE GARRETT TUGGED HIS VEST back into place and straightened his coat. His hat lay on the coach bench beside him. His little trip to Boston had extended for four days but had accomplished little. The coach wheel breaking north of Billerica had slowed his return by another half day. Another couple of miles and he would be home to face his wife's relentless tales of domesticity and idiotic questions. Chances were, as soon as his clerk learned of his return, he would come around to the house, ending his wife's chattering.

The absence of their children was felt keenly around the dining table. He hadn't realized how much intelligence Elizabeth had contributed to the conversation until she'd left.

Ebenezer asked the coachman to let him off at the front door and sent word to the town hall that he would be in the next morning. The message should be enough to send the clerk to his door in no less than three-quarters of an hour.

Rebecca appeared by his side before he closed the door. She raised a cheek for a kiss.

"I was worried when I did not receive word of your delay."

"You know politics—takes twice as long as you think it should."

A frown wrinkled his wife's brow. "But you could have sent word."

Ebenezer handed his coat and hat to the maid who'd appeared.

"Are you hungry, dear? I'll have Cook find you something."

"Yes, Mrs. Garrett."

His wife turned to the maid and requested a tray be brought to the parlor, where she herded her husband. Ebenezer glanced at the clock and hoped his clerk would hurry.

"We have a letter from our son. You will never guess."

"He is to marry this fall and stay in Philadelphia."

"How did you know?"

"He asked my advice last week when he was at his uncle's on business. I asked him to notify you as soon as the girl agreed."

"Oh." Rebecca took a sip of tea, clearly upset.

"What do you hear of Elizabeth?" He changed the subject.

"She wrote a letter to both of us. She has been bleaching linen and gave a detailed account. I do not see how using cow dung, which is brown, can make a fabric white. There was also a letter to you from Aunt Richards, and another looks to be in Elizabeth's hand, but as neither was addressed to me, I did not open them and left them on your desk."

Ebenezer took a bite of bread and nodded his thanks.

"I do long to see my girl. She has been away from us for more than four months now and sounds much improved. She does not complain about working like a slave for your aunt." Rebecca's voice took on the pleading lilt he detested.

"She is not working like a slave. She is only doing the work women without maids and cooks do."

"Which is working like a slave." Rebecca sipped her tea.

A knock at the door saved Ebenezer from turning the conversation into an argument. Only eleven minutes. He should reward his clerk. Ebenezer ushered the clerk into the study and shut the door as his wife slipped out.

"So there are things that couldn't wait for the morrow?" Ebenezer indicated a chair for the clerk and took his own behind the desk. The clerk placed a packet of papers on the desk.

"Just a few things needing a signature." He pointed to a space.

Ebenezer uncorked his inkwell and read the papers. "Oh, so Mary-Beth finally got herself a man."

"Yes, sir. They are to be wed in the morning and have been waiting for your signature certifying the intentions."

He signed the paper with a flourish.

"What is this? Abner Sidewall arrested again? And his sons?"

"The constable let the boys go home last night, but Abner is still in the lockup."

"The boys were stealing eggs?"

"They were hungry, sir. It seems Abner spent all the money on drink again. The good reverend came and got the boys. They will clean Mr. Wheeler's coop, and he won't press any charges this time. But everyone is quite upset about what is happening to the boys. If Abner has to stay in the lockup too long, people are saying we should send the boys off to relatives or some such."

The magistrate scanned the next paper. "Abner's done it this time. We will have to set up a trial. Tell me—did the other man live?"

Balanced on the edge of a straight-backed chair, the clerk looked more nervous than usual. "He seems much recovered, but Abner did break his arm."

"Let it be a lesson to you. Never drink in excess. Set the trial for Monday. That will give us the rest of the week to get a jury and for Abner to get someone to represent him. Shame. He wasn't like this when his wife, Millie, lived."

"Too bad you can't sentence him to be married, then. It would solve all our problems." The clerk gave a nervous laugh at his own suggestion.

Ebenezer sat back in his chair. It was a novel solution. Too bad he didn't have any females who'd committed a crime. He flipped through the other papers, adding his signature when needed.

"Is that all you have for me?"

"No, sir, your desk is full of things, but these were the most pressing."

"Very well, show yourself out. I will see you tomorrow."

The clerk hurried from the room, shutting the door behind him.

A stack of mail stood neatly on the corner of the desk. It would be better to read the missives than to return to his wife. He was soon lost in the pages of a news sheet sent from the capital.

—◦— ✳ —◦—

An hour later, Ebenezer opened a thin letter directed to Magistrate Garrett from some reverend in East Stoughton. He read it twice before searching the desk for the letters from Elizabeth and Mindwell. "React in haste? Who is this man to caution me in dealings with my daughter? Interfering reverend," he muttered as he moved papers aside.

On the opposite side of the desk, he found three letters—one from Mindwell and two from Elizabeth. The seal on the thicker missive remained unbroken.

He ripped open Mindwell's first, hoping his aunt would shed some light on why Reverend Frost might be writing. Mindwell's letter contained no dire news unless he considered learning to bleach linen newsworthy. She wrote again of Elizabeth's improvement. The same sort of thing she'd written about for the past several weeks.

Ebenezer broke the seal on the thick missive written in his daughter's hand and found six well-filled pages. Since most of her letters covered less than one, he turned up the lamp. Several of the pages bore spots, as if written in the rain. In a couple of places, the writing was illegible. The letter was indeed dated the first Sunday of March. Two months past. What had the preacher done to waylay it?

March 4

Dear Father,

I fear you shall be terribly disappointed in me when you read this. I thought I had been reformed, but maybe, as you have said, I am beyond all redemption. If I had listened to you and gotten rid of my crimson gown, none of this would have ever happened. Instead, I hid it in the secret compartment of great-grandfather's old trunk and had a jolly laugh. You gave me the trunk he used to smuggle his papers and clothing across the sea. That is not all I took with me to our aunt's without your knowledge, but the only thing that signifies at the moment. The other dress, which would have been my Christmas gift, I have never worn, and the forty dollars I hid in a little purse is mostly still there. Whether I have learned to be frugal, or there is no place to spend the money is probably the same. I have purchased some of the Baker's chocolate for our aunt as she loves it so and drinks it every morning, and a bowl to replace one I broke. I hope at least in this small thing you are not displeased.

There is a man here I find quite handsome but who ignores me because I do not have the qualities he desires. I was quite put out when this mouse of a girl started to catch his eye. So I determined I must get him for no other reason than I could. It was very foolish of me. After all, that is the part of me I have been trying to reform. I have no excuse because jealousy is not a good reason.

I determined my crimson gown would be the way to do it. It all seemed like a good idea—right up until this morning when I put on the dress. As I looked in the mirror, I was rather shocked to see how much of my breasts were exposed. Forgive me for speaking plainly, but I feel it is best I express myself clearly and leave no doubt as to every matter. I did, of course, wear a fichu, but the one I chose was of the lightest fabric and translucent. I should have chosen another, but I'd embroidered the flowers to match the dress.

The thought did occur to me to change entirely and leave off with my plans. It will not come as a surprise to you that this was a new idea entirely for me. I don't recall ever seriously questioning my actions before. However, the novelty of such a thought was not enough to change my course.

Aunt Mindwell did not say anything when I came down. She only gave me a somber look. Again, I nearly bounded up the stairs to change. But then through the front window I spied the girl I wished to best, walking with her parents to church. She had on a new hat. So I left for the church with our aunt. By the time we arrived in the churchyard, I felt very uncomfortable. More than one person stopped to stare, or rather, stare at me. But these were not the looks of admiration I usually receive. Most of the women looked as if they smelled something decomposing in the slop pail. Most of the men quickly looked away. The man I hoped to impress was clearly embarrassed for me. I was mortified.

I heard little of the sermon as I wished that I was small enough to fit through the chinks in the floor, or at least been wise enough to bring a shawl so I might cover myself better. There was another man who is quite wealthy, whose eye I did catch. Every time I looked up, I was aware of his perusal. But there was something almost sinister in his eye that made me even more conscious of how out of place my dress was. I became most desperate to cover myself more. A child in front of me cast off a blanket, and I would that I had used it to cover myself.

In the midst of this, I attempted to adjust my fichu to better cover me. To my horror, it came untucked completely. I hoped no one noticed as the sermon was still being given, but both the man I wanted to chase and the wealthy one saw. The first looked away, and I felt the shame of his thoughts. The second man looked at me just as our house cat looks at a mouse it has cornered.

As soon as we rose to sing the final hymn, I made my escape. There is a small copse of trees to the north of the church. I hid there, waiting for Aunt Mindwell. But as the people came out, I dared not go to her as I could hear them talking about me. I was evidently better hidden than I thought. I determined to remain until everyone left and then proceed home.

I was thus hidden, and listening for the last of the gossip to end, when my hiding place was discovered by the second man. Believing him to be a gentleman, I asked him to leave. He did not. Instead, he advanced on me. He proceeded to take liberties no man has formerly dared take. He forced a kiss on me that was as unwelcome as it was cruel. I slapped him for it. Instead of apologizing, he slapped me back and then proceeded to force me into another kiss viler than the first. His hands pulled at my gown.

I tried to hit him and scratch him, anything to make him stop. Somehow I managed to scratch his face hard enough that he pulled back for a moment before knocking me to the ground. I expected the worst then and knew I was being punished for all I've ever done. I dared not pray for help.

But help came in the form of the man I'd tried to impress. I was spared being violated. Once my attacker left, the other man offered me his coat. I was in desperate need of it as my bodice and sleeve were now torn so badly I could not hold them in place to cover myself. My fichu was gone, my hat trampled.

Then he walked me home or, rather, to our aunt's.

That is when the real punishment began. This man was so kind and solicitous. He didn't make me feel like a strumpet, although we both know I was. I saw him for the first time as not just a handsome face but as he is, which is something far better than I will ever be or deserve to ever have, even as an esteemed acquaintance.

Although I am not ruined in the full sense. I feel very much like I am. I cannot say how miserable I feel and ashamed of my actions. If this was the worst of it, I think I could endure. I cannot show my face in public for a few days as it is quite bruised and I have a cut which I am sure will scar. I almost hope it does so I will always remember what a terrible person I have become.

No, the worst of it is our aunt.

Knowing I was injured and hiding in my room, she came up to tend to my wounds. Something I could have done myself. She went back down the stairs before I did. And she fell.

If only I had been helping her as I should have. It is all my fault. Even now she lies in her room, pale and unmoving.

Our aunt cannot give you an account of my reckless and wanton actions of this day as she has not managed more than a few words. Doctor Whiting says she has hurt her ankle and her head. He is more worried about her head and fears at her age that the damage could be grave.

I have tried to give you the most accurate account of this day that I can. I have no doubt your disappointment in me is beyond all I can imagine. Please do not blame

Aunt Mindwell for anything that happened today. She bears no responsibility.

I am willing to take any penance you assign me and have little doubt you will soon retrieve me from East Stoughton to a situation you deem more fitting for a wanton daughter. I ask only that you allow me to stay at our aunt's bedside until she is able to be about the house again. She has a very responsible man who takes care of her few animals and needs, but while she is abed, there are some needs a man should simply not attend to. After that time, I will willingly submit to whatever orders you give me.

You are right. I am not even fit to be the fishmonger's wife.

Your daughter,
Elizabeth

PS. I have mastered the spinning wheel and am fit for that work ...

Ebenezer put down the letter. Why hadn't he been told of this by Aunt Mindwell?

A letter had arrived some weeks previous also from Reverend Frost, apprising him of Mindwell's fall and of the excellent care his daughter was giving her. There had been one line indicating that Elizabeth had been mildly injured in a separate incident but was recovering. Ebenezer had thought nothing of it at the time. Was the event he'd spoken of with the man who'd tried to take liberties with his daughter? His anger fluctuated between his daughter's attacker and her behavior. He wondered if the man had received any punishment for his actions beyond the beating her rescuer had given him. He doubted it. Too difficult to prosecute such a man, even if there were witnesses in a case like that. If the girl lost her virtue and been beaten, there was more of a case. A few cases, like the girls who had been raped by the deserters during the war, garnered general support from the neighbors, but most were blamed on the girl, and no action was taken. Of course, a particularly violent attack was easier to prosecute. If he could put the man in his jail—

"What had Elizabeth been thinking?" Ebenezer muttered as he paced the room. "I tried to tell her those dresses, especially that blasted red one, revealed too much of her figure and that men who did not have strong characters might think she offered herself not only to be seen but admired in more personal ways. Did my girl listen? No. But she is now."

None of this explained why his aunt had not mentioned the incident in her letters as she'd recovered. She must have concealed it from him knowing he would whisk Elizabeth away from her care. He'd never thought of his aunt as deceitful.

By all accounts, his aunt was up and about and had no more need of his daughter. He should go retrieve her, but he didn't want her at home with the lieutenant governor coming next week. He would wait until after that. Perhaps by then a solution would present itself.

Twenty-five

ELIZABETH SORTED THROUGH THE MAIL. There was a letter from Mr. Whittaker and one from someone she didn't recognize for her aunt. A letter for Gideon also waited in their box. Odd—his letters usually were sent to Reverend Porter's box. Nothing for her, but it was too soon. Yesterday would have been the earliest her letter could have reached Father. That meant he could come tomorrow, or even late tonight. She bit her lip and stepped out the door and into a human wall.

"Sorry." She looked up to see Gideon. Before he spoke, she held out his letter. When he took it, she skirted around him and rushed down the steps.

Gideon touched her elbow, and Elizabeth paused.

"Allow me to escort you back to Mina's."

Elizabeth nodded, afraid to speak lest her fears tumble out. She'd already bothered him too much.

"Just a moment while I untie Jordan."

Elizabeth stood on the walkway and waited. Jordan tossed his head, being led was not one of his favorite ways to travel. Gideon held out his arm for her, and she rested her hand on it.

"A letter from your father?"

"Not yet."

"You are worried." It wasn't a question, but she nodded and bit her lip.

"You are sure he will come?"

"I expect he must." Elizabeth swallowed the sigh that wanted to follow her answer.

Jordan bumped Gideon with his nose, but Gideon did not speed up. "What will you do?"

Elizabeth shrugged her shoulders. "What can I do but return and marry whomever he has chosen for me."

"Are you sure that's what he will do?" Gideon pulled a bit of carrot from his pocket for Jordan.

"He rarely makes threats he doesn't follow through on, and sending me away as someone's wife was the only other plan he's mentioned."

"But he can't legally force you to marry."

"Can he not? He is a magistrate. The intentions do not require my signature to be posted. He will use Mother to ensure I don't shame them by backing out. If she invites enough people, I won't dare hurt her."

"You would marry a man to not hurt her?"

Elizabeth shrugged. Didn't he see she had little choice? A fit of temper or refusal would only lead to something worse.

Gideon stopped. Jordan sidestepped in protest, and Elizabeth stepped back, nervously eyeing the large horse.

Gideon didn't speak again until she looked at him. "You should not marry for those reasons."

I know that, but I have little choice! The intensity of his eyes almost undid her. She would not cry. She released his arm and continued down the road.

Gideon caught up with her. "Elizabeth, you can't allow this to happen."

For more than two months she'd considered every alternative. Running away without a way to support herself would only put her in a situation as dire as her father would find for her. Refusing to leave Mina's would only hurt her aunt's reputation. Gideon Foster didn't know everything. Anger replaced fear. "How? How am I to do so without making things worse or hurting more people? I have had four months to find an alternative, and every plan I dream of falls apart when morning comes."

Silence followed them the rest of the way home. Elizabeth hadn't expected an answer.

Gideon's step quickened as they reached Mina's house. Thinking he was ready to be away from her, Elizabeth veered toward the front door, but Gideon stopped her with a hand. "I think I have an idea. Go find Mina. I'll be in as soon as I take care of Jordan."

Elizabeth watched him hurry to the barn. An idea? She shook her head. Impossible.

⇒ ✳ ⇐

Could it work? Legally it would help, but what about morally? It was a lie. But did not the prophet Abraham lie about his own wife to save them?

Gideon hurried to put up Jordan and jogged to the house. He found Elizabeth with her aunt in the parlor. Both women gave him a questioning look as he entered.

"Mina, Elizabeth is convinced her father will force her to marry, and perhaps move west. Do you think it is a possibility?"

Mina set aside her knitting needles and yarn. "It is most likely based on his correspondence."

Gideon looked from Mina to Elizabeth, who worried her lip. "I have an idea that will prevent that, for at least a year."

The women sat up straighter. Elizabeth tilted her head. "A year?"

"Yes, enough time to find a more permanent solution and prove to your father you are the person I know you to be."

Elizabeth looked to her aunt, too shocked to reply.

Mina recovered first. "Don't keep us in suspense. What is your plan?"

"We go to Stoughton and post our intentions."

"You want to marry me?" The hopeful note in her voice almost made him wish he did.

"No."

Elizabeth's face crumpled. Mina sat forward, a frown forming.

"I am not explaining this well. I mean to give you time. If you post intentions before your father can, the first will be valid, and you have a year from the date they are posted before they are no longer valid. Since ours is not the parish church, they need to only be displayed for fourteen days in public, at the post office. Then your father cannot force you to marry unless I release you and withdraw the intentions."

Mina sat back. "It could work, but everyone hereabouts would expect a wedding. Neither of you will fare well from a broken engagement."

Elizabeth sat quietly playing with the edge of her apron.

"If you like your father's choice, you need only ask to be released. If not, you have a reason to stay with Mina for the year." Gideon hoped it would convince her.

"What of you? What if you want to marry?" Elizabeth looked up.

"At the moment, I am not inclined to wed, and since I have yet to set up my cobbler shop, I have no means to marry again."

Mina picked back up her knitting. "Could you not rent the shop on High Street?"

"No, it is Butler's, and the other space belongs to one of the Curtises, but he has gone to Washington and is not expected back for a month."

"But you may want to marry someone else before the year is over. What will happen then?" The apron twisted into knots in Elizabeth's lap.

"I cannot court another woman once it is generally known I have declared intentions. It may be a favor to me, as some women will not be inclined to try to catch my eye." He left the name Joanna unsaid.

"I don't like that both of you would be living a lie. Preacher Boy, you may have given up your calling, but it is still a jump to lying for a year. Elizabeth, if it becomes known you lied about this, Ebenezer may come up with something much worse."

Elizabeth rose and paced the room. She stopped to look at Gideon and then again at her aunt. "I don't want to live a lie, but I like having a choice." Elizabeth stopped in the middle of the room and turned to Gideon. "Are you sure? This plan could go awry and leave you in such a mess."

It could, but it would be worth it. After all, if he'd dealt with the letter earlier, a sanitized version of events would have been sent and Elizabeth might not be facing a reprimand. "I am sure. It is my fault it was not sent sooner. We need not live much of a lie. Some couples decide not to marry and let the intentions lapse, merely going on with their lives. We would do the same, only faster."

Elizabeth drew in her lower lip and looked at her aunt.

"It is not as if you are marrying under false pretenses." Aunt Mina studied the clock. "If you leave now, you can appear before the clerk in Stoughton before they close." Mina pulled a purse from her pocket and counted out a few coins. "This will pay the fee. Take my buggy. Elizabeth go change your dress."

Elizabeth spared Gideon one more look before she hurried from the room.

Mina's voice stopped Gideon. "Preacher Boy, you must know I hoped you would declare intentions with my niece in a more honest fashion."

Gideon opened his mouth to protest, but Mina held up her hand.

"I know you still love Ruth and are not prepared to take a wife, but you now have a year to consider Elizabeth. I have watched you together. Friendship is not a bad foundation. Think on it."

Click, click, click. Mina had resumed her knitting.

Gideon hurried to the barn. He'd rather not think on it. His mind strayed too often to Mina's beautiful niece, but he could never support her in the way her father had. His house would know want. Marrying Elizabeth was not an option.

Elizabeth spent the drive to Stoughton looking at everything but Gideon, the one question she didn't dare ask continuously rolling through her head. What would happen if they decided the intentions were real? Would Gideon's shop be enough to support them in a year?

A ridiculous thought. Gideon's sharp "No" when she'd asked if he were proposing was more than enough to prove he could never think of her that way. The kiss he'd dropped on the top of her head only days ago, so like one of Nathaniel's, had been brotherly, not romantic—as much as she wished it were different. Her brother would like Gideon.

Her mother would never approve. There wasn't enough money in shoes. But money didn't matter, did it? The Stewards were happy together. Of course, more money might ease some things for them, but Aunt Mina loved her farmer husband, and his memory seemed to mean more to her than all the acreage in Curtis Corners.

She heard Gideon's voice and turned. "I was woolgathering. What did you say?"

"I asked what weighs so heavily on your mind."

"I was thinking of Aunt Mina." *Not a lie.* "Thank you for doing this. I will not have to leave her. I am loath to do that. Some days I think she pretends to be more feeble than she is, and other times I think she tries to be stronger."

"I have noticed the same. I am glad you will be able to stay with her."

"What of you? Will you leave her employ?"

"For now I will continue taking care of Mina's outside chores."

"What will your family think?"

"I will not tell them unless it becomes necessary, then I will tell them the truth of the situation. And you, what will you say?"

"As little as possible. Will you help me? Father is not likely to believe that anyone who has been in the ministry would have me. Especially after my wanton behavior."

"I promise you that you will not face your father alone in this." Gideon reined the horse to a stop and set the brake. He helped Elizabeth from the carriage, careful to not catch her dress in the wheel.

"Ready?"

Elizabeth straightened her skirt before taking Gideon's arm.

They found the clerk at his desk, a man of more than fifty with wire-rimmed glasses, his powdered wig sitting a bit askew. He looked up and shifted his gaze from Gideon to her.

"I assume you are here to post intentions, but neither of you are familiar to me."

"Miss Garrett and I reside over in East Stoughton and attend the church there."

The clerk pulled out a piece of paper. "Oh, very well. I shall have to write 'resides in Stoughton' as East Stoughton is not an incorporated body. Your name, sir?"

"Gideon Frost."

"Oh, yes, you are the assistant minister at the church over there. It isn't the parish church, but you will need to make sure your preacher announces the intentions just the same." The clerk turned to Elizabeth, not noticing the color drain from Gideon's face. "And you, miss, name and age?"

"E-Elizabeth Garrett. I obtained nineteen years last September."

"I am not familiar with the Garretts. Are you recently come to the area?"

"No, sir. I am living with my Aunt Mindwell Richards."

"And where does your father live?"

Elizabeth mumbled the town, and the clerk raised his brows. Had he heard of her father?

After a brief pause, the clerk wrote their names on a couple of printed forms and handed one to Gideon. "Give this to Reverend Porter for him to read. I will post this in the post office and have the Congregationalist minister read it here in the parish church. You may return on the..." the clerk consulted his calendar "...on the sixteenth to collect your certificate. Your intentions will have been publicly posted fourteen days by then, which is the minimum. Since you do not attend the parish church, we shall use that standard. I have put Miss Garrett's father's town instead of Stoughton as I believe this your permanent residence."

Nodding her acknowledgment, Elizabeth worried her father might be contacted but didn't dare ask the clerk.

Gideon handed the clerk a few coins, and they took their leave.

Once settled in the buggy, Elizabeth dared speak. "Do you think he will need to send a copy to my father's clerk?"

Gideon flicked the reins. "I don't believe so. I have never read any intentions from another parish."

Elizabeth relaxed and then recalled the way Gideon's face had paled. "You are sure about this? I noticed your reaction when he told you Reverend Porter would need to read the intentions."

"I assumed the public posting would be enough. I am worried that if Reverend Porter reads them, someone might object because of the incident with Mr. Butler."

"Could they do that?"

"There is no legal standing to protest the intentions because of that day. But the gossip may start, and I'd rather not see you hurt again." Gideon glanced her way, his eyes full of concern. Too bad the intentions were only pretended.

Twenty-Six

MAGISTRATE GARRETT TOOK ONE LOOK at the papers piled on his office desk and wished he were back home in his study reviewing plans for the lieutenant governor's visit. He knew most of the issues before him would be the same matters that came to his attention every month. His clerk had presented the few pressing items to him at his home yesterday.

He was glad he'd set Abner's trial for Monday. It would take him that long to clear his desk. Once, a decade or so ago, Abner had been a relatively quiet citizen. Never a beloved one, but he hadn't caused any trouble, either. He wanted Abner out of his court and out of town. There were rumors there were no living relatives to take in the boys. What would he do with them? Boys left to themselves often found mischief, and worse.

He put the matter out of his mind and concentrated on the top document in the left-hand pile.

Reverend Woods's sermon focused on marriage, a common subject for him each summer. No doubt the wedding of MaryBeth had prompted it a bit early this year. Ebenezer's wife whispered that, like many other couples, MaryBeth had begun her marriage planning to increase the family in less than nine months. The sermon dragged on, extolling the virtues of matrimony. Ebenezer didn't look at his wife.

At least she was still comely, if somewhat dull. Virtues of matrimony, indeed. It was nothing more than a means to an end.

The minister explained how men could benefit by the calming nurture a wife brought to him. Reverend Woods didn't live with Rebecca, nor would he be the one to marry Elizabeth. Pity the man!

Gideon elected to sit with the parishioners today rather than on the rostrum since Reverend Porter had relieved him of his duties when he turned in his official resignation the morning after posting intentions. The reverend insisted Gideon remain living with his family for propriety's sake. Gideon had agreed because it gave him the use of the entire lean-to as a temporary shop.

A baby cried. Mrs. Porter shifted the infant boy to her shoulder. Gideon chanced a glance at Elizabeth. One of the Steward girls sat on her lap, playing with a bit of string Elizabeth wove around her fingers.

The end of the sermon neared. Unfortunately, he still had to sit through the practice sessions, but the low rent was worth a few hours of listening.

"I have been asked to read the following intentions. Mr. Theodor Butler of Stoughton and Miss Charity Wixom of Brookline. Also Mr. Gideon Frost and Miss Elizabeth Garrett, both in residence here."

It was impossible to tell which couple's announcement stirred the most murmuring. Only about half the congregation managed to sing the final hymn.

After the prayer, a couple of men congratulated Gideon, but most avoided him. Across the aisle, he saw Elizabeth blush at something Mrs. Steward said. Mrs. Howell and Joanna pointedly ignored both Elizabeth and him, lifting their noses just high enough to make their point. He moved in Elizabeth's direction. No need to create more gossip.

Gideon's gut twisted as Mrs. Porter stopped to congratulate Elizabeth. What was he doing deceiving good people like Mrs. Porter?

Mr. Butler walked toward them, his hand on the back of a young woman dressed in silk. Gideon stiffened and moved closer to Elizabeth.

"Ah, Frost, what did they do, refuse to let you continue in the ministry after you announced you would marry her?"

Gideon balled his fists. Hitting a man in church would not help matters. "No, purely coincidental." *As you well know, I've been trying to rent your storefront for weeks.*

"My dear, let me introduce you to Mr. Frost and Miss Elizabeth Garrett. It appears they too shall be wed soon."

The woman smiled shyly at both of them, her hand resting at her waist. Was it the Parisian cut of her dress, or was she one of Butler's victims? The poor girl—apparently her family's wealth would force her into marriage with such a man.

Gideon assisted Mina into the buggy, keeping Elizabeth close lest Butler say something worse.

Mina looked at Mr. Butler's buggy and shook her head. "Poor girl, She has no idea and in the family way, too."

They rode to Mina's in silence.

—※—

The clerk ushered Abner Sidewall into the magistrate's office and gave the magistrate another quizzical look. The trial was not for an hour yet, and it was highly unusual for the magistrate to address someone before their trial.

At a nod of the magistrate's head, the clerk left the office, shutting the door.

"Have a seat, Abner."

Abner's eyes grew wide. Nevertheless, he sat down in the appointed chair.

"I have been giving your case much thought, and I think I have a proposal that will benefit us both."

Abner leaned slightly forward and listened.

An hour later, Mr. Sidewall pled guilty to all charges and was penalized by a fine. He agreed to return home to his sons that afternoon and toss all the liquor in the house down the privy. What's more, he would endeavor to sell his land and prepare to move to Ohio with his new bride in four weeks' time.

Twenty-Seven

SOUR MILK? AT LEAST IT was white, but it made as little sense to Elizabeth's mind as the cow dung. She counted the fact the milk was harvested the same day the dung collected as pure superstition. But she was not going to argue with her aunt on this point. The entire second batch of cloth received the dung-and-lye treatment.

She leaned over the milk-filled laundry tub and scrubbed away, then lifted the cloth out and set it to the side. Usually she would empty the large tub there in the yard, but Aunt Mindwell told her to use the liquid to water the lane to kill the weeds.

It smelled atrocious. She probably did too. She was up to her elbows in the sour-milk-and-dung residue. Some had sloshed onto her skirt. At least the skirt had a prior run-in with the dung, so it was of no great concern. She filled the watering can with the now-brown milk and started at the south end of the lane.

On her third trip, Gideon came around the barn. "I thought you were washing the linen today."

"I am. Aunt Mina told me to use the dirty sour milk to kill weeds when I was done."

His nose crinkled. "That is a pungent odor."

"Do you like it? I do believe I shall use it instead of a fancy perfume every day." She grinned up at him. "If you carry this, I bet you could wear some too." She tried to hand him the watering can.

Smiling, he stepped back. "Well, then, Miss Lizzy, I think I shall decline to help you." The expression on his face changed. "I have come from the post."

"Did Father…?"

Gideon shook his head. "No there is no letter from him for either of you."

Elizabeth bit her lip.

Gideon continued. "This is mine. I have been requested to go to the seminary and must answer to them in person."

"Oh." She tilted her head. "Why would they do that?"

"I don't know. I am going to speak with Mina and then leave this afternoon."

"Where will you go after?"

"Mina gave me leave to stay in the barn room for now, but I don't want to start gossip that might hurt your reputation with our intentions posted and all. I have been hoping to rent the empty shop on High Main Street. There are some rooms above it I can use as my home. Unfortunately, I must rent from Mr. Butler, and he has not been very easy to work with on the matter."

"I am sorry." Elizabeth shook the can to get out the last drops.

"It is not your fault. I think he just can't stand renting to someone who bested him at fisticuffs."

Elizabeth gave a wan smile. "Is there any other place?"

"There is one other building that would do. The truth is that it's better suited to a shoe shop. But I still have not heard from the Curtis family who owns it. His brother assures me he will let it to me."

"So you will not move north and go work with your brother?"

"No. I promised I would stay here for Mina as long as she needs me. And, to be honest, my brother married Ruth's sister. I don't know if I would like living near them."

"Her sister?"

"Yes. I told you it was a good family." He smiled. "Losing Ruth doesn't hurt the way it once did, but living under the same roof as her sister would dredge up painful memories I no longer wish to feel."

Elizabeth nodded. She knew what it felt like to be near someone who reminded you of all you could not have. "I wish you the best with your meeting."

"Can you do the chores tonight and in the morning? I should be back by tomorrow evening, or I can get the Purdy boys to come. "

"Yes, but if I need help, I will ask the Purdys."

"Until tomorrow, then." Gideon settled his hat on his head and left with a nod.

— ❋ —

It made no sense that Reverend Ingram insisted he come to Boston. A sense of foreboding had plagued Gideon since reading the letter three hours ago. Had Reverend Porter written of his impending nuptials? Should he tell the reverend the truth and risk the challenge to the intentions?

As Gideon headed north on Jordan, a familiar carriage passed him, but he could not place it. However, near the outskirts of Boston, he placed it as the carriage that had deposited Elizabeth at Mina's doorstep all those months ago.

— ❋ —

Mina instructed Elizabeth on how to stretch the linen over the mowed grass. "Keep it damp. Check on it several times a day and use the watering can. If it looks like rain …"

Elizabeth smiled. It was the third time her aunt had repeated the instructions.

Mina surveyed her niece's work. "I'm pleased. I never would have thought you could do this job when you first came. What are you going to do with the unbleached portion?"

Elizabeth straightened a corner of the cloth. "I thought to embroider table linens. I have a friend I owe a wedding gift."

"What of your own table?"

Elizabeth shrugged. "I don't know that I shall ever need them. I do not wish to return home after my year is over, and who would have me after all is done?"

Mina harrumphed.

A carriage pulled into the side yard, interrupting their conversation.

Elizabeth blanched and dropped the pail full of sour milk.

Father.

❈

"What is that horrendous smell?" Ebenezer put his handkerchief to his nose. What mess had his daughter made now?

"I am afraid it is me, Father. I rinsed the dung out of the linen with sour milk, and some of it spilled on me."

Milk, dung, and linen? What was his daughter doing with those? "Well, you'd better change before we leave. I will not smell that all the way back home."

"Leave?"

"Yes, leave. I wrote you last week all about your marriage."

"Marriage? Letter?" Elizabeth stepped back.

Ebenezer lowered the handkerchief. "Are you daft, girl? What did you think it said?"

Mina stepped between father and daughter. "Ebenezer, neither of us received a letter. What is this about a marriage?"

Ebenezer looked from one woman to the other, then ran his hand down his face. Had he sent it? The week had been a disaster, starting with the note from the lieutenant governor canceling his visit. Rebecca had been more than difficult since he'd disclosed his plans Monday night. He knew he'd written the letter. He was sure of it. And it should have arrived by now if he'd posted it. He patted his overcoat. Something in the right front pocket crinkled. He reached in and pulled out the addressed and sealed letter, then handed it to his daughter.

"How soon can you be packed?"

"I can't leave until tomorrow afternoon. Gid—Mr. Frost left for the day. He asked me to take care of his chores so Aunt Mina wouldn't try to milk the cow."

"You, milk a cow? And how dare you disrespect your Aunt Mindwell like that," he said, obviously having forgotten about Mina's insistence that Elizabeth use the more familiar moniker.

"Ebenezer ..." The warning in his aunt's voice gave him pause. "I have gone by Mina since long before you were born. Only your mother refused to call me by that name. Elizabeth did not disrespect me. And unless you have remembered how to take care of your own animal, I suggest you allow your daughter to do so. She has learned much these last few months. You may be surprised. Come into the house, and I'll get you something to drink."

Ebenezer followed his aunt through the back door. Over his shoulder he watched his daughter unhitch his horse and lead it to the barn.

"What is this nonsense about a marriage?"

Ebenezer settled into a chair and took the offered cup of cider. "The only nonsense I see is your education of my daughter."

Elizabeth tucked the letter in her pocket. Reading it now would not help. Aunt Mina had given her until tomorrow. Maybe if he saw her working, he would reconsider whatever plan he had.

Supper was a silent affair. Aunt Mina kept glaring at her father. The letter burned in her pocket as much as did the few bites of hot pie she choked down. She excused herself and went and readied the other upstairs bedroom for her father.

When she finished, she opened the door to her room, taking in the place that had become so comforting and familiar. A lump formed in her throat, and she shut the door before going downstairs.

She found Aunt Mina in the parlor rocking in her chair, her Bible in her lap. She looked around for her father.

Aunt Mina looked up. "He has gone on a walk."

Elizabeth's eyes filled with tears. She sat on the ottoman at her aunt's feet, laid her head in her aunt's lap, and began to cry.

Aunt Mina put her hand on her niece's, bent her head down, and let her own tears fall.

"Have you read the letter?"

Elizabeth shook her head.

Aunt Mina lifted Elizabeth's chin. "I think it is best to read it before your father returns."

The letter shook in Elizabeth's hands, and the words kept blurring. "Abner Sidewall? Before the end of the month?" Elizabeth clapped her hand over her mouth. Not Abner!

"Who is Mr. Sidewall?" The hand on Elizabeth's shoulder gave only the slightest comfort.

Elizabeth drew in a long breath before answering. "A widower with"—she drew in another breath—"with four unruly boys. Mr. Sidewall has been charged more than once for public drunkenness and for profaning the Lord's day." Elizabeth took another breath. "Mr. Sidewall has agreed to marry me before the month is out and remove his family to no closer than Ohio."

Elizabeth wiped her tears. "What can I do? Gideon is gone, and our intentions won't be certified for another week. If I tell Father, he will contest them."

"First we will pray. Gideon should return by noon tomorrow. We will try to put your Father off if we can. If not, I will send Gideon up there as soon as they are certified by the clerk. Did your father indicate he'd posted your intentions yet?"

"He doesn't mention it."

"That may give us time."

A noise on the lane alerted them to Ebenezer's return. "Go and pack your trunk. We don't want to appear to be dawdling."

⇥ ✳ ⇤

Gideon stared in disbelief at Reverend Ingram. "A trial? But I have already renounced my calling. How can I be defrocked?"

"And excommunicated." Reverend Ingram sat back in his chair, setting down the papers on his desk. "These charges are quite serious—fornication, profaning the Lord's day, and bearing false witness—all punishable under the laws of Massachusetts, but due to your position, we felt a church trial would be better suited to your crimes. If you are found guilty, the magistrate in Stoughton will be notified so you may pay the fines."

"I am innocent of all but fighting on the Lord's day, but that was to defend the honor of a young woman who was near to being ravaged."

Reverend Ingram frowned at the papers. "Who can attest to the truth of this?"

"Reverend Porter was told the whole of it within hours, as was Mrs. Richards. Who is it that accuses me?"

Papers rustled. "A Mr. Theodor Butler. I am sure you are acquainted with him. He has donated quite a sum to Reverend Porter's church fund."

"Did he mention it was he with whom I fought that Sunday?"

"Hmmm. Ah yes, here it is. 'Mr. Gideon Frost did in a malicious and unwarranted manner hit me in the face, causing my nose to bleed.'"

Gideon dropped his head to his hands. What was he to do?

"The trial will be at noon Friday. Until then you shall be given a private chamber so you may pray and contemplate. If you have any witnesses to request, a carrier will leave at dawn. That should give them time to appear, as East Stoughton is less than four-hour ride. They will have most of Thursday to prepare. I have already summoned Reverend Porter."

Gideon rose to leave.

"Gideon, I hope you can think of someone to testify on your behalf other than the women. Since Miss Garrett is also charged with fornication, her testimony bears little weight. Mr. Norton will show you to the room you will stay in. You are to take your meals there and not converse with my students."

Gideon nodded and stepped out the door to find Old Norton now acting as his jailer.

Twenty-Eight

ELIZABETH TOOK EXTRA TIME WITH the barn chores partly to delay the return north. She wanted Gideon to be proud of her, so she double-checked every job twice. Late last night she sat with pen and quill, trying to formulate a letter to him, but none of the words that came to mind were right. Either they were too stilted and entirely too proper, or they were not proper at all and revealed far too much of her heart.

She would miss the friendship they'd forged since the day he'd rescued her. She'd never imagined a man might be a friend, and she'd never had a true friend in her entire life, though there had been plenty of opportunities to have friends. She reminded herself she was not worthy of anything beyond friendship with Gideon. She hoped their friendship had not tarnished his reputation. The mess with the intentions would still need to be sorted out, but the sooner everyone knew he was not engaged, the better.

Every time she thought of her aunt, tears threatened. Aunt Mina had even congratulated her that morning on making the perfect cup of chocolate. Elizabeth thought it was the same as the batch she'd made the week previous, but Aunt Mina insisted otherwise. Elizabeth did not want to leave Aunt Mina alone. Gideon would take care of her, but it would not be the same. At least the two people she loved most in the world would be together, and, hopefully, Gideon's plan would give her time. But would being near him and knowing their intentions were false be any easier than going to Ohio as Mrs. Sidewall?

She leaned over the oat bin to make sure the lid was on tight when something crinkled in her pocket.

The letter. Perhaps she should read it again. So distraught was she last evening she had not gotten past the first few lines.

Elizabeth fished the letter from her pocket. The barn was not the right place to read it, so she hurried to the house.

Aunt Mina sat stirring something in the pot above the fire. She did not see her father. "I need to go read this," Elizabeth waved the letter in her hand, wishing she had one of Mina's hot mitts to hold it with. "Will you tell Father I have gone on a short walk?"

Mina straightened. "Cut through the pasture. He went on a walk himself and will likely stay on the road."

Elizabeth rounded the table and gave her aunt a kiss on the cheek before rushing out the door and to her rock.

She stepped carefully so as not to disturb the young plants. Her boulder welcomed her, already warm from the morning sun, but it was not enough to overcome the chill that coursed through her veins at her father's words.

Mr. Abner Sidewall is good enough for you, and his recent reversals in fortune should in no way prejudice you against him, nor should the fact he intends to take a farm in Ohio. The dowry I will bestow should be more than enough to pay his debts and leave you a bit to get started. It is well you have learned to cook and weave as there will be no servants for some time in his household, and with four of the most unruly boys in the county, you will be too busy to get into any more trouble.

He has sworn to take you despite knowing how your wanton behavior has caused your total ruination. I told him all, of course. He deserves to know of his wife's low reputation. It is a secret you can both keep as the area of Ohio where you are to live is unknown to both of us. There, neither of you shall sully my reputation further.

I have posted your intentions this day and have asked Reverend Woods to announce them in his next three meetings. Therefore, you shall marry on the twenty-third and depart that same day.

One week from the sixteenth. That gave Gideon time to protest the intentions.

A horse and rider thundered down the road. Through her tears, Elizabeth could not make out who it was, but she knew it must be Gideon. She leaped from her boulder, not worrying about showing her knees, and hurried to the house.

Two steps up, two steps back. The small room didn't have adequate room to pace. By now the brief note he'd addressed to Mrs. Mindwell Richards should be arriving. He prayed, not for the first time, that he had been mistaken about the identity of the carriage he'd passed yesterday afternoon.

Another promise broken. He'd told Elizabeth she would not have to face her father alone. Gideon ran his hands through his hair. Perhaps it would be better if Elizabeth's father took her home. Although she could attest to his innocence in some things, there was little chance the details of that fateful first Sunday of March would not cause her pain. He wondered if that day also haunted her nightmares.

Last night, he'd again dreamed that he had not interfered in time and found her bruised and broken body only after Butler had finished with her. In his dream, Elizabeth had died in his arms, as had Ruth. No dream of Ruth, not last night or the night before, had interrupted his sleep. Come to think of it, he hadn't dreamed of her or their son since the morning he'd held the Porters' wee one in their kitchen. Mr. Whittaker was right. There would be a time when he wouldn't long for Ruth. He would still miss her soft voice, but there was another woman with a quick wit filling a hole inside of him.

Gideon sat on the end of the bed. Elizabeth would become a question in tomorrow's court. What could he truthfully say without hurting her more?

⊶ ✳ ⊷

Leaning on her cane, Mindwell walked slowly to the front door. A slightly disheveled man she did not recognize stood on the porch.

"Mrs. Mindwell Richards?"

"Yes?"

The man thrust a paper at her. "This is for you."

Mina almost dropped the paper when the man turned and ran for his horse. She turned it over to see the address was in Gideon's writing. The back door slammed as she slid her finger under the wax seal of the seminary.

"Gideon?" Elizabeth's hopeful voice called from the kitchen. "Aunt Mina?" Her niece hurried through the house.

"I don't think he is coming, child. This was just delivered." Mina turned into the parlor to find a chair. Elizabeth followed.

Mina silently read the short note twice before looking at her niece. Fortunately he'd written in a large hand. Mina was thankful she'd not needed Elizabeth's help in reading it. "He isn't coming today. He is being detained. He has been brought up on charges, and the church leaders will hold a trial tomorrow."

"Surely not Gideon? What has he done?" Elizabeth reached for the letter, but Mina held it to her breast.

"I am afraid our Gideon has angered the wrong person."

"I can't leave you here alone."

"I am afraid you must. See there, your father has returned. I don't think we can put him off any longer."

The front door slammed. "Isn't your man back yet? The carriage isn't ready."

Elizabeth scrambled up from the ottoman. "I'll go and get it. Will you fetch my trunk?"

Ebenezer glowered but ascended the stairway.

Folding the letter, Mina slid it into her pocket before standing. She would need to pack a case too. She was going to Boston.

Twenty-Nine

Deep breaths. Deep breaths. Elizabeth refused to cry in front of her father. Her puffy eyes when she'd returned from her boulder to her aunt's were enough of an embarrassment. Her father hadn't spared her a moment. She'd barely had enough time to hug her aunt and whisper "I love you" in her ear.

It was just as well Brookline was not on the itinerary. She did not want to be fussed over by Aunt Lydia. There would be enough of that when they got home. No doubt her mother would fuss enough in the days before her wedding.

She had not felt this heavyhearted leaving her home last January. Perhaps it was her concern for Aunt Mina that made the pain in her heart expand until it filled her chest. Gideon might come for her before the week was out, but with a church trial, their intentions could be challenged and dismissed. Or he might not come, fearing her father would force an immediate marriage and he did not want her. She would pray Gideon would come, but she'd better not plan on it. If she were truthful, the lump in her throat that now threatened to strangle her was for Gideon's sake.

Fields and towns came and went, each town larger than the last until they reached Boston. Since her father had made no attempt to address her, she had not broken the silence. Elizabeth sat back in the carriage, not wanting to be gawked at. Still wearing her stained work dress and apron, she drew stares sitting next to her very well-dressed father. No one would ever believe her to be his daughter, especially if they saw her calloused, ungloved hands.

The new pale-blue muslin she'd intended to change into lay across her bed at Aunt Mina's. Perhaps her aunt would send it to her. She'd worked several nights to make the dress based on a fashion plate she'd seen at the milliner's. The straighter skirt needed fewer petticoats than the round gowns most women wore. The neckline lay a mere inch below the collarbone, and she'd embroidered the white bodice with pale-blue flowers. The higher waistline felt odd the first time she'd put it on, but it was surprisingly easy to move about in. When she found the money, one of the new style corsets would be purchased. She'd debated about making new petticoats and finally settled on modifying one of her sets to a narrower silhouette. The gown would not have been practical for the two-day carriage ride home, the fabric being muslin. In the next two weeks, she could sew another.

Even if Aunt Mina sent the new gown, Elizabeth didn't have the heart to wear it. Too much of the time she'd spent stitching the creation, she'd also entertained daydreams her heart knew could never be.

They passed through a street of dress shops she'd often frequented with her mother. While several of the windows featured the round gowns, only three displayed a dress like her creation. She sighed. Though she'd copied a recent Parisian fashion plate, it certainly was not the height of Boston fashion, yet. She was probably better off making more utilitarian wear anyway. Aunt Mina could sell the dress.

The gray-stone church and a long stone building next to it reminded her of Gideon's description of the seminary he attended. She searched the windows. A shadow moved behind a window. There was no way to know for certain, but Elizabeth raised her hand and bid the figure a silent farewell.

When dusk came, her father stopped at an inn that appeared to be no worse than a half dozen of the others they'd passed. The bed was far from comfortable, but at least she had a room to herself. The tears she'd hidden from her father poured out until she was empty.

Gideon watched people pass on the street below the window. It was too soon for anyone to answer his missives. A buggy with a woman in a gray dress as ugly as Elizabeth's soiled work one rolled past. The male driver seemed finely dressed. Could it be? He pressed closer to the window for a better view. The woman raised an ungloved hand and turned to look at the building.

Lizzy.

Why did his heart race so? There was no use going to the door and racing down the stairs. Old Norton had locked it after bringing his dinner more than two hours ago.

A wish. Nothing more. He had just wished her near. Though he knew her a changed woman, Elizabeth would never have ridden through East Stoughton, and definitely not through Boston, in a soiled dress. More than likely, she was stomping her foot someplace and cursing that he had not returned as scheduled. After all, it was nearing time for the evening chores, and the cow still gave Lizzy fits.

Gideon sat alone on the rostrum of the dining hall. The second largest room in the seminary, it had been converted into the courtroom. Next to him, a long table with five chairs awaited the ministers of his faith who would serve as judges. The students filed in to observe, knowing they might never see another proceeding like this. Only two other ministers of their denomination had ever been on trial to be defrocked and excommunicated. He recognized the four he'd met over the winter break. Fletcher nodded in acknowledgment. Dover and the others pointedly ignored him.

Reverend Ingram entered with four men in clerical collars, each man taking his seat at the table next to him. Gideon's shoulders fell a little more when Reverend Ingram took the farthest seat. He couldn't see the others well as his chair sat slightly forward, rudely forcing him to pivot if he wanted to see the faces of his judges.

Mr. Butler arrived alone. Reverend Porter entered with his wife on his arm, refusing to look his way, but Mrs. Porter smiled over the head of her infant son.

Hushed murmurs filled the room. *The Spanish Inquisition must have been much like this.* The thought nearly brought a smile to Gideon's face. The only thing he lacked were shackles around his ankles.

At the center of the table, the reverend picked up a gavel. Before he lowered it, the door opened again. Old Norton ushered in Doctor Whiting, along with Mina. Mr. Butler smirked. Mina leveled him with a stare that would've had any man with half a brain shaking in his boots. But Mr. Butler's smile turned condescending. Clearly he did not own half a brain. Old Norton rushed to get Mina a chair, donated rather unwillingly by one of the students, who was obliged to move to a bench.

The gavel dropped three times. The charges he'd heard privately in Reverend Ingram's office where now laid out before all. Murmuring from the students necessitated the gavel falling again.

"You have heard the charges. How do you plead?" The reverend in the center seemed to be the leader of the group.

Gideon stood and turned to address the five ministers. "With the exception of profaning the Lord's day, I am innocent of all charges. I did on the afternoon of the fourth of March, which was the Sabbath, set my fists upon a man in order to halt his attack of a young woman. Reverend Porter determined at the time that the dire situation called for such action, and I was therefore excused."

Murmuring again, followed by the strike of the gavel.

The balding minister nearest him addressed the front row. "Reverend Porter, to the charge of profaning the Lord's day, were you then, and are you now of the opinion that it should be dismissed?"

Reverend Porter stood. "I have considered the matter and—" The reverend stepped ever so slightly away from his wife. *Had she kicked him?*

Gideon schooled his features.

Porter continued. "—and I am of the opinion, due to the nature of the incident, that Mr. Frost had an obligation to intercede, though it is unfortunate he could not do so in a more peaceful manner."

A high, nasally voice from the oldest reverend at the table cut in. "Reverend Porter, on that date, did you see that the other participant in this brawl was charged by the local magistrate for his actions?"

"I did not."

"Not even for hitting a woman?"

"No. The character of the woman is of some question." This time Gideon was sure Mrs. Porter kicked her husband, as he wished he could.

Whispers rose, both at the table and from where the students sat. The reverend with the gavel hit it three more times. "I would like to remind those present that Reverend Porter is not on trial here. I move the charge of profaning the Lord's day be dropped from those brought against Mr. Frost, and no action is needed to report the instance to the civil authorities. Brethren, what say ye?"

"Aye."

"Aye."

"I would like to hear the particulars of the matter first," said the nasally voiced man.

"I concur." Reverend Ingram's agreement surprised Gideon. Could he not have allowed this to pass?

"Very well. Reverend Porter, did you witness this incident?"

"I did not."

Mr. Butler stood. "I witnessed it all."

"And you are?"

"Mr. Theodor Butler."

"Ah, the man bringing these charges. We have your statements, and unless we call on you, you are to remain silent."

"But I—"

Bam. The bang of the gavel silenced all in the room. "Mr. Butler, you are not a necessary part of this proceeding, as you have already given testimony. The exact line relating to this charge was, er—here it is. 'Mr. Gideon Frost did in a malicious and unwarranted manner hit me in the face causing my nose to bleed.' If indeed you struck a woman and Mr. Frost defended her, then his actions were neither malicious nor unwarranted."

"Bu—"

Bam. The gavel struck the table. "Sit down, sir, or be removed from the room."

Mr. Butler took his seat.

The reverend in charge looked around the room. "I gather the young woman in question is not here today."

Reverend Porter answered. "No, sir, she is not. Her father fetched her home, and she could not be reached."

Reverend Ingram leaned forward in his seat. "Did you see any evidence of an assault?"

"I visited the young woman three days after the incident to administer to her troubled spirit." Gideon balled his fists and bit his tongue. "At that time, there were several bruises on her face and a cut on the left cheek, which has since scarred."

"Did she make any accusations as to the identity of her attacker?" the balding one asked.

"She spoke not a word to me."

"Mr. Frost, other than yourself, is there any person here whom the young woman may have spoken to?" The tall, skinny reverend spoke for the first time.

"Her aunt, Mrs. Mindwell Richards, and Doctor Whiting."

"Mina?" the tall clergyman coughed out the name.

"Yes, Robert, 'tis I." Mina straightened to her full five-foot height and looked the taller man in the eye.

"What have you to do with this?" It was hard to tell if the color filling the tall reverend's face was a result of anger or of embarrassment for his apparent connection to Mina.

"The young lady in question is my grandniece and, yes, she named Mr. Butler as her attacker and said Mr. Frost is the man who saved her from further harm."

"Have you any proof of this, Mrs. Richards?"

"Only my niece's actions. She avoids Mr. Butler in all things."

"And, Doctor Whiting, what have you to say?" the nasally-voiced reverend asked.

The doctor helped Mina back into her seat before facing the board. "I was called to the Richards's house the evening of the first Sunday in March. I removed several large splinters from the young woman's back, which had been embedded there earlier that day. On her face were four large bruises—one above her left eye, another below, and bruises on either side of her jaw, as if some man had squeezed it tight." The doctor touched his own face to show the locations. "There was a cut along her left cheekbone that appeared to be from a large ring. Something like Mr. Butler wears on his right index finger."

"Did the young lady name Mr. Butler as her attacker?" asked Reverend Ingram.

"Not that evening, as she could barely speak due to the swelling on her face and jaw. However, on a subsequent visit, she was able to confirm the identity of her assailant as Mr. Butler."

"And what was the purpose of your visit?" The minister with the gavel took control of the questioning again.

"To check on the progress of her healing and to ascertain there had been no ravishment beyond that which Mr. Frost reported to me."

"And was there?"

"She denied there was, and since Mr. Frost was certain he'd stopped Mr. Butler before a rape occurred, I did not subject the young woman to further examination."

"I see. Why did you not go to the magistrate with charges?"

"The law only punishes where a rape by force has occurred. Mrs. Richards was of the mind that the charge of assault would generally be ignored, as has been the case in the past with Mr. Butler's indiscretions." The doctor cast a withering look at Mr. Butler as he concluded his testimony.

The five men at the table conferred in muted tones.

"Mr. Frost, we are dismissing the charge of profaning the Lord's day and also that of bearing false witness, as the charges seem to be in relation to the incidents of the same afternoon. The only person who might prove or disprove Mr. Butler's claim appears to be the young woman. Reverend Porter, at any time, has it been your belief that the damage to the young woman's face or person was caused by any other person besides Mr. Butler?"

Porter stood again. "No, sir."

"Mr. Butler, please stand. You claim Mr. Frost bore false witness as to your treatment of said young woman claiming she, quote, 'invited your intentions,' unquote. As all five of us are married or are widowers and two of us have fathered daughters, we know that invited intentions do not require the use of fists. Since several have testified that she was injured by your hand, we find no evidence of false witness."

Mr. Butler sat down but clenched his jaw so hard Gideon wondered if the man's teeth might not break.

"This brings us to the charge of fornication, which, Mr. Frost, if it occurred prior to your resignation, would be a serious charge in and of itself. Did you post intentions with a Miss Elizabeth Garrett on the second day of this month?"

"Yes."

"When did you ask for her hand?" asked Reverend Ingram.

"I did not."

The buzz in the hall rose. The gavel sounded several times. "A highly unusual circumstance. Most couples post their intentions after coming to an agreement about marriage. The accusation says you are marrying her only because she is 'with child' and there is no other reason. And, I quote, 'A gentleman of good standing would marry a trollop such as Miss Garrett has proven herself to be,' unquote. What say you of this?"

Gideon felt the weight of the gaze of every man in the room. Only Mrs. Porter and Mina gave encouraging smiles.

Crossing the room and throwing a punch at Mr. Butler's smug face was not an option, so Gideon balled his hands and turned to the tribunal. "First of all, I would like to defend Miss Garrett. In no way has the lady displayed wanton tendencies, nor is she of low moral character. Any of her missteps are no more than many a flirtatious miss has taken in trying to attract a husband. Having been on the receiving end of the flirtations of several women since my Ruth's passing, I am somewhat familiar with such things."

Several muted guffaws echoed from the back of the room.

"As far as any carnal relations, I have done naught but hold Miss Garrett's hand when assisting her, or allow her to take my arm when escorting her, as is proper."

The nasally one spoke up. "So you mean to tell me you have posted your intentions with a woman you have not proposed to, nor kissed?"

"Yes, sir."

"Perhaps it would save us time if you explained why your intentions have been posted," the tall minister asked.

"Miss Garrett's father finds some of her actions to be an embarrassment to his position. He—"

"What is his position?" The tall minister glanced at Mina as he asked the question.

"He is a magistrate."

The reverend waved the gavel in a motion for Gideon to continue.

"Her father has threatened on several occasions to marry her off to the next man he finds who will move to Ohio. Due in part to the circumstances of the first Sunday in March resulting in a somewhat distraught letter written by Miss Garrett to her father, both Mrs. Richards and Miss Garrett believed the fulfillment of such a threat was imminent. I offered the intentions as a way to give Miss Garrett a year's time with her aunt and to find a situation she would prefer."

Reverend Ingram frowned. "So you entered into your intentions under false pretenses?"

"Yes, but—"

"Make a note to have them withdr—" The balding minister picked up his pen.

"No, please. I intend to marry her if she will have me!" Gideon wasn't sure who was more surprised at his outburst. Mina looked too satisfied to be surprised, as did Mrs. Porter. The men in the room were another matter.

The gavel pounded twice.

"Are you saying you do intend to marry Miss Garrett?"

"Yes, I do."

"Just when did you decide this?" Reverend Ingram leaned forward, his brows raised.

When she flipped cow dung in my face? When she stood on her rock and shouted at her father? When she fell asleep on my shoulder after helping the Stewards? The day she tried to flirt by letting her hair drop? Just now?

"Mr. Frost?"

"Yesterday. I think I knew before, but definitely yesterday. I thought I saw her pass by my window wearing her hideous gray work dress, and I knew I wanted to marry her. She isn't Ruth, and that is as it should be. Though I don't know if she will have me."

The tallest minister spoke. "Judging by the expression on Mrs. Richards's face, I suspect her niece will have you."

Gideon chanced a look at Mina. Her grin was the brightest thing in the room.

The gavel struck once. "I move all charges be declared false and thrown out. Brethren?"

"Aye."

"Aye."

"Aye."

"Aye!"

The students cheered, and the gavel rang out once again.

"Mr. Frost, we accept your resignation as tendered, if that is still your wish, and we will allow you to stay a member of our sect if you so desire it. Reverend Porter, we advise you to instruct your parishioners on the proper way of bringing charges against a fellow member. In this case, we would like to point out that the accuser seems to be guilty of the false charges he's levied against Mr. Frost, including that of fornication. I believe this is the reason he is marrying one of my parishioner's granddaughters in two weeks' time. I advise you to hold council with Mr. Butler as soon as possible."

The gavel rapped three more times.

"Adjourned."

Mr. Butler escaped before anyone could stop him.

Gideon went to Mina's side and gathered her in a hug.

"Oh, my Preacher Boy, I knew you would come to your senses. I can hardly wait to call you nephew." She patted his cheek and turned to the doctor. "Do you think we can return home before the sun sets?"

The doctor offered his arm. "You forget I am used to driving in the dark. Mr. Frost, will you accompany us?"

"Let me gather my things, and I will catch up with you."

Mina stopped him. "Oh, Ebenezer did come for her. Oddly, she left in her gray work dress. I wonder—" She looked out the window for a moment before turning back to Gideon. "Since she is no longer living in my house, you are welcome to either of the upper bedrooms, if you would like to move out of the Porters' attic."

Gideon smiled. The thought of moving out of the Porters' brought immediate relief. He did not relish sitting across the table from the man who barely defended him, and then only at his wife's urging. "I'll be there."

Gideon turned to the Porters. "Thank you for coming."

Mrs. Porter smiled, and her husband almost didn't frown when he spoke. "Clive—I mean Reverend Ingram—has offered one of his students to help me this summer. We shall need your room."

Gideon nodded. "Mrs. Richards asked I move in with her since her niece is no longer there. When Elizabeth does return, I hope it is as my wife."

Mrs. Porter beamed as brightly as she had the day her son was born.

A hand clasped Gideon's shoulder, and he turned to find Reverend Ingram. "I am sorry about this. I told them it was nonsense, but—we will miss you. You are one of the finer orators this seminary has turned out. However, you look much happier than on New Year's Day. Go in peace, and someday I would like to meet this Miss Garrett."

"By then she will be Mrs. Frost."

"So she shall."

⟶ ✳ ⟵

Mother rushed out of the house as soon as her father reined the horse to a stop. If the idea was to bring her home quietly, her mother had not been apprised of it. Her mother's voice carried like the town criers. "Oh, my Elizabeth! Just look at you. That dress! Why, it is hideous!"

Elizabeth fell into her mother's arms, hoping to silence her more than anything. Afraid if she enjoyed the hug too long it would lead to more tears, she stepped back. She'd avoided conversation with her father for that very reason. Oddly, he'd become quite talkative this morning, extolling the whitewashed virtues of Abner Sidewall. To accomplish such a feat, her father had to reach very far back in time. Considering Abner was more than fifteen years her senior, discussing anything Abner had done before she'd learned to read seemed like ancient history. It was reassuring to know he'd distinguished himself near the end of the war when he was old enough to join up.

Her father had not attempted to do the same with Mr. Sidewall's sons, the oldest of whom was twelve—merely seven years her junior! There must be some law about the bride being closer in age to a man's children than himself. How would she ever tell a child taller than she anything he might listen to?

Father ushered them into the house and out of sight of any nosy neighbors. Mother insisted Elizabeth take a bath and rest. Her father simply glowered.

It would be a long two weeks.

Thirty

GIDEON STOOD AT THE DOOR to Elizabeth's room, his trunk on his shoulder, as the last rays of sun poured through the window. Could he sleep in her room? As it was, he'd spent too much time the past two days thinking of her, and she'd invaded his dreams for months. He would go to her as soon as the intentions were certified.

He looked at the door on the other side of the small hallway. The bed there was wider than the box bed at Porters' but shorter, and the room was littered with trunks and boxes he'd moved for Mina a few months ago. He could move tomorrow. After he got his Lizzy, there would be time to sort things out.

He stepped into the room and put his trunk down, but the action didn't make the chamber any more his. A dress lay across the bed. Lizzy must have meant to change before she'd left. If she had, he wouldn't have recognized her. Oh, that hideous gray dress. He closed his eyes and visualized her in it, smiling up at him. The intentions couldn't be certified fast enough.

He picked up the dress. The neckline was the higher sort Elizabeth had worn the past few months, but the rest of the dress seemed to have less fabric. It also wasn't multiple pieces like most women's clothing. Despite those differences, he thought it was…Never mind. He would not let his thoughts dwell further on the dress or its owner.

Was it really necessary for a woman to change her dress, petticoat, and stockings? He folded the last item quickly. They were too smooth, and the silk felt like something he need not think upon. The only place to set the gown was upon the small table.

The setting sun cast the room in an orange glow. Mindful of the lower ceiling, he walked to the window to witness the workings of God's hand. A dull light reflected off something in the field.

He watched the sun sink lower until the shadows swallowed Lizzy's rock.

⊶ ✳ ⊷

The clerk shrugged apologetically. "Magistrate Adams has an opening in an hour. I only know he received a complaint forbidding the banns of matrimony."

Gideon stepped back. There was only one person he could think of. He suppressed a growl. "I'll take the appointment."

"Be here at eleven o'clock, and don't keep Magistrate Adams waiting."

Without a word, Gideon left the building, noting that the time on the clock tower matched the time on his pocket watch. He walked down the street, looking at the wares for sale in the various shops when one display caught his eye. The bell over the door rang as he stepped in.

The proprietor tried to show Gideon several more items, but Gideon was only interested in the carved gold band that had caught his eye.

After a solid round of haggling, Gideon left the door several dollars poorer but with the ring in his breast pocket.

As the last bell tolled the hour, Gideon entered the magistrate's office. "Mr. Frost, I wondered if I might see you today. Do have a seat. Is Miss Garrett with you?"

"No, she is currently north with her family."

"Is she related to Ebenezer Garrett?"

"Yes, he is her father."

"Haven't seen him for years. I assume he is still hoping for a spot on the governor's staff or a bigger judgeship?"

"I wouldn't know, sir. We have never discussed the matter."

"Of course not. No doubt you are wondering why your banns of matrimony have been challenged."

"Yes, sir. I intended to get the certificate and leave for the Garrett's home this day."

"It has been alleged you published your intentions as a ruse to thwart the plans of the young lady's father."

"May I ask who my accuser is?"

"A Mr. Theo—"

"Butler."

"You are acquainted?"

"Unfortunately. The man has become a bit of a thorn in my side."

"Then this claim is false?"

"Mostly."

"Perhaps you should start at the beginning."

Gideon gave a condensed version of his church trial and the circumstances surrounding it.

"You say Reverend Porter was there?"

Gideon nodded. "Yes, as well as Doctor Whiting and Mrs. Richards."

"And you intend to engage yourself to Miss Garrett, and wed."

"As soon as possible." Gideon pulled the ring from his pocket. "I purchased this while waiting for my appointment."

The magistrate adjusted the glasses on the end of his nose. "An elegant ring." He moved his attention to an agenda. "Judge Smith and I can hold a hearing Wednesday next week to settle this matter."

"Do you have anything sooner?"

Magistrate Adams studied Gideon, then his calendar. "Friday morning the eighteenth at eight. Smith won't like it. If you ride straight through, you should be able to get there before nightfall, and hopefully before Ebenezer can get his daughter married off to someone else."

Gideon stood and shook the judge's hand.

"I'll have the clerk subpoena the reverend and Doctor Whiting. Knowing the doctor's unpredictable schedule, I will ask him to come in and give his testimony in front of one of us and a clerk, at his convenience."

Gideon left the courthouse less frustrated than he had been two hours ago. He prayed Friday would not be too late.

Mindwell watched the sunset. Another day and still things had not been set to rights. The wedding date set by her nephew drew ever closer. She was ready to head north and protest it herself. If things did not go well Friday morning, she would. Of course, Gideon would have to drive her. She was much too tired to do that herself.

She'd been busy the last few days setting her own plans in motion. She didn't have time to wait for Gideon to start earning a living making shoes.

If only her Henry were here. He'd set things to rights.

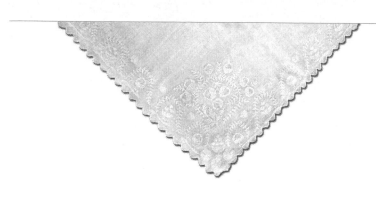

Thirty-One

ELIZABETH CLIPPED THE LAST THREAD on the cloth. She'd used most of the unbleached linen Aunt Mina had given her to make a tablecloth and twelve napkins. She hoped Gideon had helped Aunt Mina finish bleaching the linen she'd started. *Would Gideon see to such woman's work to save her aunt the trouble?*

He was Gideon. Of course he would.

She turned her focus back to the cloth. She'd promised herself she would not think of him. But, for the third time today, she'd broken her promise. If she had more to do, she wouldn't think of him as much. But Cook had shooed her out of the kitchen after Mother caught her kneading bread. The maid had gotten upset when she'd realized Elizabeth had dusted the parlor. Again. She hadn't dared try to work in the garden.

The tablecloth needed to be ironed. She hoped she would be allowed to do that. The only reason no one fussed at her for working on it was because Mother assumed it was for her future home.

She'd already managed to visit several of her old schoolmates and rendered apologies to them. Most of them had gaped at her, disbelieving, as they accepted the embroidered handkerchiefs she offered. Most of the offenses had been schoolgirl tricks—frogs in lunch pails, ink spilled on pinafores, and the like. A few had been slanderous—rumors of nonexistent warts or spreading gossip indicating a girl fancied by a certain boy was less than desirable.

The major offenses were harder. Emma Whittier had moved away after marrying. Considering the slanderous story she'd spread questioning Emma's virtue, she wasn't surprised. Elizabeth would have left town too. Her attempt to talk to Emma's parents had been met with a door slammed in her face. Short of standing up and announcing what she had done at the beginning of Church, she had no idea how to rectify the situation. She'd contemplated approaching Reverend Woods with such a plan but put it off, hoping another idea would come to mind.

She'd created a beautiful dress for Betsy Smythe and hoped she would wear it someday, even if she checked every seam twice. Elizabeth had double stitched most of the seams so there would be no possibility of this dress falling apart.

Cook was busy this time of the day, so it didn't take much to convince her ironing did not violate Mother's ban on housework. It took longer to iron the cloth napkins than she thought it would. The apple blossoms she'd embroidered required her to work slowly around the edges. Once finished, she wrapped the folded linens in a length of muslin and headed to the stable, hoping she could borrow the small buggy. If not, she would walk. It wasn't quite two miles.

⊷ ※ ⊶

Elizabeth reined the horse to a stop. She had not been out to the Marden—now the S. Wilson—farm since she was thirteen or so. Someone had built an addition on the old cabin. Movement in the garden caught her eye. Lucy's younger sister weeded among the cabbages.

Elizabeth stepped down from the carriage and reached for the muslin-wrapped bundle. The little girl came running from the garden to greet her.

"Is Lucy home?"

The girl did not respond. Instead she turned and ran around the side of the house. Elizabeth stood on the first step of the porch, uncertain whether to follow or knock on the door. She moved to the second step as Lucy came around the house.

Lucy stopped abruptly and placed her hand over her middle, the movement confirming the rumors. Samuel would soon be a father.

Elizabeth smiled what she hoped was a genuine smile. "Do you have a moment?"

Lucy glanced at the barn and gave a little shrug before coming around to the stairs. "Come in."

They crossed the doorway into the kitchen. "Pardon the sawdust. Samuel has been converting my old bedroom into a parlor. As soon as he is done, he will put a door in so people won't need to come through my kitchen."

Elizabeth waved her hand dismissively. "Don't worry about it. You may not believe it, but I have sat in much worse than a speck of sawdust in the past few months. Isn't the smell of those fresh-cut boards worth a bit of dust?" Elizabeth inhaled deeply and closed her eyes. "I do love that smell." She looked at Lucy. "Don't you?"

"Usually, yes, but the dust makes me sneeze and—" Achoo. She gestured to the rocking chairs by the window. "Have a seat. Would you like something to drink?"

"No, thank you. But do feel free to have something if you would like. I have come to offer a long-overdue apology, not to have you fuss over me." Elizabeth sat in the rocker near the door. Lucy sank into the other.

"I have wronged you so many times I know nothing I can say or do will ever make up for the frogs in your lunch pail, the stories I told…oh, and the ants. But by far the worst thing I ever did was trying to…um…" Her carefully planned words would not come to mind. "When I tried to take Samuel." Elizabeth felt her face heat as she thrust the bundle into Lucy's lap.

"I know this won't fix the mess I caused, but I want to give this to you to show you I am glad for your marriage. I made it myself. Well, not this fabric. I did weave linen and was in the process of bleaching it when my father came, but my aunt wove this." Elizabeth knew she was rambling, but she couldn't seem to help it. "I know everyone is saying I am only apologizing because my father is making me marry Mr. Sidewall, but I knew I needed to apologize to you weeks ago. When my aunt gave me the linen I wove, I thought giving it to you might show how sorry I was. At least to God. And you may appreciate the fact that I fell in the manure pile as I bleached the linen. Right in front of a man who is very kind and very handsome. Probably part of what I deserved after deliberately embarrassing girls in front of their beaus. Or for the ink I spilled." Elizabeth waved her hand uselessly, hoping all the words would just stop coming. "I am ever so sorry. It wouldn't be proper for me to say anything to Samuel, but if you would tell him—"

"Tell me what?"

Elizabeth spun in the chair. All the words tumbling out of her suddenly drying up like mud on a hot day, leaving her mouth feeling stiff and unable to work.

"Look, dear." Lucy held up the tablecloth. "Isn't it the most beautiful embroidery? Apple blossoms and lavender."

Samuel crossed the room to his wife's side and put his hand on her shoulder. To Elizabeth, the move seemed protective. Lucy reached up, patted his hand, and gave him a smile. "Dear, Elizabeth came here to provide us with this beautiful gift to commemorate our wedding. She also has apologized for many things and was asking me to extend an apology to you as well."

Samuel narrowed his eyes as he looked at Elizabeth. "Is this true?"

Elizabeth tried to swallow the lump in her throat, but the weight of every misdeed she'd ever perpetrated against Lucy and Samuel kept it there. She nodded.

Samuel's brows rose, and he continued to glare.

Elizabeth blinked back tears and tried to speak again. Her voice came out in a harsh squeak. "I am very sorry. I should have never—" Elizabeth's gaze dropped to her lap, where she twisted her dress in her hands. It took great effort to still her hands and smooth the dress. There would be no helping it—her tears would fall if she stayed any longer. She shot out of her seat and rushed to the door. Elizabeth paused with her hand on the knob. "Someday I hope you will forgive me. Even if I don't deserve it."

Slipping out of the door, Elizabeth ran to the buggy, her now-falling tears making it difficult to see. How inadequate her gift was. She'd thought all the hours she'd spent embroidering it would have given her absolution. So wrong. So very wrong.

"Miss Garrett—Elizabeth—stop!"

At the sound of Samuel's deep voice, Elizabeth halted with one foot high on the buggy's rung, the other on the ground.

"My wife has something more to say and asks that you stay for supper."

Elizabeth stepped back down and turned around. "I cannot stay as long as that—my father has already made arrangements."

Lucy stepped out of the door and came to stand by Samuel. "Can you come back in for a few minutes at least?"

Elizabeth took an uncertain step toward them. Lucy gave her husband a little push. "Samuel is going to go help Sarah finish the weeding."

Samuel gave Elizabeth a nod before stepping off the porch and heading for the garden.

Lucy beckoned for Elizabeth to quicken her steps, her smile more welcoming than Elizabeth expected.

Lucy shut the door behind them and gestured for Elizabeth to return to the rocker.

"Elizabeth, you need to know I forgave you long ago."

"Bu—"

Lucy held up her hand. "I know you didn't ask me to, but I learned I needed to forgive others so I could find contentment in my life. I needed to forgive Mr. Simms first. He wasn't a kind father. Then I needed to forgive the man who sired me."

Elizabeth tried to control her expression.

"Most of the town folk who lived here during the war know about it. Your rumor on my birth was more based in fact than you know. But my point is, I forgave a man who was dead, and a man my mother never knew so I could have peace. They didn't need to ask me. I forgave you in a similar way. I wanted to talk to you, but you disappeared after Christmas. So I wrote it in a letter. With all the gossip accompanying your disappearance, I wanted you to know that I held no grudge."

"Gossip?"

Lucy pinked. "Yes, gossip. What else did you think would happen when you disappeared?" Lucy didn't give Elizabeth the chance to answer. "Of course, your father refused to give me an address. He offered to mail it, but—" Lucy shrugged her shoulders. She took a folded and sealed paper from her writing desk and turned it over in her hands. "I wrote my forgiveness here. I never expected you to come begging my forgiveness when I wrote it, so much of what I wrote—" Lucy trailed off, waving her hand in a dismissive gesture. "But seeing you, I think you need more than my forgiveness. You need to forgive yourself. You have already been seeking God's forgiveness. I saw the difference in your demeanor last Sabbath. And I know you have visited every woman in town our age, looking for theirs." Lucy held out the letter.

Elizabeth took it and set it on her lap. She traced her name written on the front, giving herself a moment to call back the tears that threatened. "Thank you." The lump returned. Out of all the women she'd visited, Lucy—the one she'd most consistently abused and embarrassed over the years—was the only one to offer forgiveness.

Elizabeth went to stand and found herself wrapped in Lucy's arms. Lucy's tears mingled with hers. After a moment, they let each other go.

"I get so weepy." Lucy wiped her tears with a corner of her apron, then stilled. Her hand flew to her abdomen. She looked up, eyes wide. "He moved." A giggle escaped her, and her other hand covered her mouth.

Unsure what to say, Elizabeth merely smiled. What would it be like to carry a man's child when that man loved you like Samuel loved and protected Lucy? She would never know. She might well carry Abner's child one day, but she doubted they would ever have a relationship like Lucy and Samuel.

Tears filled her eyes again. She clutched the letter to her breast and whispered a good-bye. No one stopped her this time.

—⁘ ✠ ⁘—

By the light of her lamp, Elizabeth broke the seal on the letter Lucy handed her. After eating supper with her parents and Abner, she figured nothing could be worse today. The look of awe Lucy's eyes held when she'd felt the babe move would be forever etched in her mind.

An unbidden prayer went up. *Please help me to feel that way when I carry Abner's child.* She shivered. Abner looked at her much the way Mr. Butler had. He would do his best to make sure she carried his child. She'd dodged his kisses so far, pleading for some time to get to know him, hoping one day her skin wouldn't feel like little ants crawled all over it each time he touched her.

Lucy's letter did not repeat the gossip that reached her ears, only reassured her she knew it was not true, as did Samuel.

> *...Forgiveness is not something one gives because they are asked. It is something one gives because it is needed.*
>
> *I know you will probably never ask, but know all is forgiven. Including the little mouse in my desk. As for the mess with Samuel, how could you have believed we were really married when I myself did not? The situation was fraught with oddities.*
>
> *I hope someday you will find a man like Samuel. He finds all the good in me and makes me a better person. You may have tried to hide some of the good in you, but I am sure there is so much you have to share.*
>
> *Your friend,*
>
> *Lucy S. Wilson*
>
> *PS. Samuel forgives you too.*

Elizabeth set down the letter and cried.

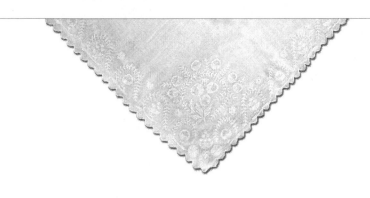

Thirty-Two

THE SIGNED INTENTION CERTIFICATE IN hand, along with a letter to
Elizabeth's father from Magistrate Adams, Gideon rode north. He
hadn't gone a mile before remembering Elizabeth's dress. Even if she
didn't accept his proposal, she would need it.

"Come on, Jordan, back to Mina's."

An empty kitchen and silence greeted him. Gideon checked the
other rooms.

Mina lay on the parlor floor, her eyes wide and staring.

She blinked.

Gideon knelt by her side. "Mina?"

The only answer he received was a moan.

Seeing no blood, he carried her to her bed, then smoothed her hair.
Apoplexy.

He prayed he was wrong. Lizzy would be devastated to not be here.
How quickly could he retrieve her? Would there be time? The doctor
would know better. He ran next door to send one of the Purdy boys
for Doctor Whiting, who indicated he would be doing rounds in the
area as they left the magistrate's chambers.

When he returned to the room, Mina gave him a wild look and
tried to move her mouth. The left side opened, but the right side
remained slack.

"Quiet now. The doctor is on his way."

"Zzzzztthh." She raised her left arm and grabbed his.

Gideon was surprised by the strength of her grasp. He patted her hand and tried more soothing words.

"Gaa zzzzth." She tried to push him this time.

"You want me to go get Elizabeth?"

Mina's eyes lit up.

"I'll go later."

"Nnnnnwww."

"You want me to go now?"

She squeezed his hand.

"I'll wait for the doctor, then I will leave."

Mrs. Purdy entered the room.

"Will you sit with Mina? I need to gather a few things. She wants me to go get Elizabeth." Mrs. Purdy didn't need to know he'd already set out to do that very thing earlier.

He hurried upstairs and grabbed Elizabeth's dress. In the barn, he mulled over hitching Jordan to Mina's buggy. Bringing Lizzy back riding double on Jordan wasn't an option. Even if it was an excuse to hold her close. He banished the thought.

Mina's buggy wouldn't stand hard riding. His brother lived less than fifteen miles south of Elizabeth's home. If he rode Jordan hard, then switched horses and borrowed a buggy at his brother's, he could be at Lizzy's by suppertime. Hopefully Jordan would rest enough for the return journey.

Gideon had just finished adding the dress to Jordan's saddle bag when Dr. Whiting pulled into the lane. Staying only long enough to have his suspicions confirmed, Gideon started north.

Thirty-Three

THE KNOCK CAME AN HOUR before they were to sit down for supper. Elizabeth bit back a groan. Abner was not supposed to come tonight. With four days left, she wanted to savor the last few days of just being herself.

The maid appeared. "Miss Elizabeth, there is a man here to see you."

Elizabeth descended halfway down the stairs before she realized the maid had not given a name. A voice came from her father's office.

She knew that voice.

Impossible.

Elizabeth slipped into the room and froze.

Both men turned and looked at her. She felt for the doorframe, afraid she might faint.

"Gideon."

"Lizzy." He stepped forward, grasped her elbow, and led her to a chair.

"Her name is Miss Garrett." The magistrate tried to step in between them. "Who gave you leave to call her otherwise?"

Gideon knelt before her and took her hands in his. Elizabeth wanted to smooth down his windblown hair, but she left her hands in his. For the first time in days, she felt like herself again.

"Mina is ill. She is asking for you. Will you come?"

"Aunt Mina? What—" A sob threatened to cut off her breath.

"Dr. Whiting thinks it is apoplexy. I found her this morning. She begged me to fetch you. Will you come?"

"Of course." *Gideon here? I must be dreaming, but Aunt Mina!*

"No, she can't."

Elizabeth looked at her father. "But Aunt Mina needs me."

"You are getting married in four days. It takes a day and a half to get there. You can't possibly get there and back." Redness crept up her father's face.

Gideon stood and addressed both father and daughter. "Then we should leave immediately. I have my brother's curricle. We can get to his house tonight. Then we can leave at dawn. By this time tomorrow, we'll be with Mrs. Richards."

"My trunk is packed. For my mar—I can be ready in a few minutes. Should we eat before we go? Supper is almost ready." Elizabeth stood, addressing only Gideon.

"Yes." Gideon reached for Elizabeth's hand.

"No!" Ebenezer's cane hit the floor with a resounding thump. "You can't go. What about Abner?"

"Aunt Mina needs me!"

Rebecca entered the room and looked from one face to the other.

"Father, please. I need to go."

"Sir, time is of the essence. If we are to get to my brother's tonight, we need to leave within the hour."

Rebecca gasped and fluttered her hands uselessly. "Elizabeth? You are not planning on leaving with this man? Unchaperoned?" Her mother's voice rose in panic.

"Aunt Mina. I must go." Elizabeth struggled with the words as the gravity of the situation settled around her heart. If only Gideon needed her too.

Her father turned to Gideon. "Mr. Frost, as a former clergyman, you should see how this would look to travel unaccompanied, and that little buggy of yours won't hold a chaperone."

Gideon looked from father to daughter to mother and back again. He turned to Elizabeth, once again taking her hands in his. "Lizzy." His gaze locked with hers.

Overwhelmed with the feeling that he was trying to communicate something very important, Elizabeth sucked in a breath. Could it be that Gideon was looking at her the way Samuel looked at Lucy? The way Aunt Mina looked when she spoke of her beloved Henry?

"Marry me?" The whispered question hung between them. "Please?"

"Yes."

Gideon leaned in to kiss her, but Ebenezer pulled Gideon back before their lips touched. "Just what do you think you are doing?"

"Sealing my proposal and her answer."

"But—but she is getting married." Rebecca fanned herself.

"Yes, to me." Gideon laid a protective arm around Elizabeth, pulling her into his side.

"I have an agreement with Abner Sidewall. She is marrying him in four days." Mr. Garrett thumped his cane again.

"I think, sir, you are correct. You have an agreement with Mr. Sidewall. One you made and your daughter is obeying. But has anyone ever asked her if she wanted to marry him?"

Elizabeth settled deeper into Gideon's side. He'd defended her.

Rebecca answered first. "No. This isn't her choice."

"Magistrate, by the laws of the Commonwealth, isn't your daughter allowed, by statute, to accept or reject her husband?"

"Technically." Ebenezer took a step back.

"She accepted my proposal." He turned to Elizabeth. "Am I correct in assuming you never accepted Mr. Sidewall's proposal?"

"He never proposed." In Gideon's arms Elizabeth found the strength to answer for herself.

Gideon turned back to the magistrate. "Please, sir. Marry us."

"Father, please?"

"But, Abner. Your dowry. He is leaving."

"Sir, I don't want the money. Let Mr. Sidewall keep it."

Elizabeth laid her hand on Gideon's arm and looked up into his face. "But you do need it to get a shop."

"It will work out. Let him have the money." The softness of his answer and the warmth in his eyes made her believe she could live without money for quite some time.

Elizabeth's breath caught. She looked at her father. "Please, you know Abner is more interested in the money."

Rebecca went to her husband's side. She didn't speak but looked at him for a long moment, then turned to Elizabeth. "Will you be happier with a poor man or a rich man?"

"I will be more content with a kind man. If he happens to be poor, then we will get by. After all, I can cook now." She turned to Gideon and smiled—a real one, not the ones she'd practiced so often in her mirror.

He smiled back. "And bleach linen."

Rebecca whispered in her husband's ear.

"Very well."

Elizabeth hugged Gideon and gave a tiny squeal.

"Stop! Let me finish! I'll have my clerk post your intentions, but you can't marry for more than two weeks, and you are not taking my daughter unchaperoned anyplace." A smug look covered her father's face. Elizabeth turned to Gideon.

Gideon reached into his pocket. "We already have our intentions certified, and I carry a letter from Magistrate Adams of Stoughton. I believe he is known to you."

Ebenezer snatched the documents. His face fell as he read them. Finally, he slumped in his desk chair and pointed to a shelf. "Mrs. Garrett, hand me that book."

Rebecca moved to a brown leather volume.

"No, the little one. Freeman's *Massachusetts Justice*." Ebenezer thumbed through the pages. "I can't find a legal ground to stop you from getting married. But Reverend Woods will need to perform the ceremony, as I refuse to."

Rebecca let out a gasp.

"His house is across the street. I suggest you go talk him into this, Mr. Frost. Good luck. He isn't one to perform marriages willy-nilly."

Unless you are Lucy and Samuel. Elizabeth kept the thought to herself. She wouldn't mind having something in common with the couple. And the way Gideon looked at her, she might have more in common than she thought possible.

Gideon leaned down to drop a kiss on Elizabeth's lips, but the sound of her mother's garbled squeak caused Elizabeth to step back.

"Later," he whispered. "Oh, you might need this." Gideon handed his bride the muslin-wrapped dress that lay on the bench.

Elizabeth looked out her window toward the reverend's house for the seventh time. Her mother and maid nudged her back to the dressing table. The blue dress turned out exactly as she envisioned.

"This dress is so modern. Are you sure it is what you want to wear?"

"Yes, Mother. I made it myself after a fashion plate only recently arrived from France. I saw a couple like it in the shop windows in Boston."

Male voices filtered up from below.

Rebecca turned to the maid. "Go see if they are ready."

Left alone with her mother, Elizabeth wanted one last hug. "I love you, Mother."

Rebecca dabbed at her eyes. "There was so much I was going to tell you in the next couple of days. To prepare you for—"

Elizabeth placed her fingers on her mother's lips. "I am prepared enough. Gideon has always been kind, and I want to be with him."

At the maid's knock, they opened the door and walked down the stairs, arm in arm.

Reverend Wood sat in the parlor talking to the magistrate. Gideon stood nearby. He noticed them first. His smile was quick. He cleared his throat, ending the conversation.

The reverend crossed the room. "Elizabeth, are you sure about this?"

"Yes. I love him."

"What of your commitment to Mr. Sidewall?"

"That is my father's agreement. No one ever asked me."

"Very well. I understand you must hurry back to your aunt's. Let's begin."

⇥ ✳ ⇤

Reverend Woods finished the ceremony and nodded to Gideon.

Just as Gideon's lips lowered and Elizabeth lifted to her toes to meet his kiss, the front door slammed against the wall. They both stepped back in dismay.

"What is this? You promised me the money!" Abner Sidewall advanced on the magistrate.

Reverend Woods rushed forward and stopped him with a restraining hand. "Shall we take this conversation to the magistrate's study?" The reverend followed Mr. Sidewall and Elizabeth's father into the office.

Gideon gave her a little shrug. "We should hurry so we can get to my brother's before it grows too dark."

Rebecca supervised the loading of the trunk and a basket of food from Cook's kitchen.

Elizabeth stood nervously with Gideon, waiting for the men to emerge from the office. She needed to say good-bye but didn't want to linger. Mina waited. On the other side of the door, the shouting dwindled.

Then the door opened and Abner emerged. The triumphant smile on his face scared Elizabeth. The man stopped before Gideon. "Good luck with the little strumpet. I got my money. Wouldn't have minded taming her, but you should get something out of the deal."

Gideon took a menacing step toward the man. "Don't you speak of my wife in such terms."

The good reverend reached Mr. Sidewall first and propelled him out the door, saving the groom from any misguided punches.

Ebenezer closed the door behind them. "You were right. He didn't care about my daughter." He offered his hand.

Gideon clasped it. "I will watch out for her."

"I know."

Elizabeth threw her arms around her father's neck, and for the first time in years he hugged her back. "You'd best be on your way."

⇥ ❋ ⇤

A mile south of town, the trees created a natural tunnel over the road. Gideon reined the horses to the side of the road.

"Is something wrong?"

"Very."

When Elizabeth twisted to try to look at the wheels, Gideon placed his hand on her shoulder and turned her back to face him.

"The buggy isn't the problem." He trailed a finger down the side of her face.

Elizabeth turned to look at the horses. With the pressure of a single finger, he brought her face back to look at him.

"The horses are fine."

"Then what is the problem?"

He cupped her face with his hand, and she leaned into his touch.

"The problem is, Mrs. Frost, I have tried to kiss you three times today. I only start"—he placed a very quick kiss on her lips—"to have it end." Another feather-light kiss. "Before I am"—the third kiss was soft as his whisper—"finished."

Gideon took his time giving his bride a chance to respond. When she did, he lingered, drawing out the middle of the kiss as long as possible. When he finished, he was pleased to find her fingers buried in his hair and her breath coming in little puffs.

He drew back. They needed to cover nineteen more miles tonight, and he had no intention of starting in the open conveyance that which was better shared in a more private setting.

He pulled Lizzy into his side and set the horses back on the road.

She sighed the smallest of sighs.

Gideon prayed the horses would fly like Pegasus and his brother would be able to make room for them someplace other than the barn loft.

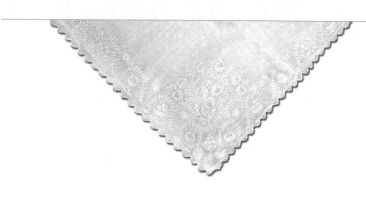

Thirty-four

THE COCK CROWED A SECOND time. Gideon helped Elizabeth down the loft ladder.

As they'd driven to Gideon's brother's last night, they'd determined they would leave as early as possible for Mina's. With his Lizzy tucked at his side, Gideon looked out the loft window, searching for some sign of dawn.

His Lizzy. He liked the sound of that. Yesterday, between their sudden marriage and news of Mina's condition, she not once suffered from vapors or any other nonsense, though she'd shed her share of tears for her dear aunt last night as he'd detailed what little he knew. He cleared the miles the best he could without stopping the buggy.

Lizzy's reaction last night to his sister-in-law's suggestion that the loft might not be a suitable sleeping place for a gentle woman warmed his heart.

Gideon's brother was willing to give up his own bed for Gideon and his unexpected new bride, but Elizabeth took one look at her sister-in-law's rounded form and refused the offer. Emma had then offered for Elizabeth to share her daughter's bed, but his Lizzy refused. "*Thank you for the kind offer of the bed in your children's room. I assure you I will be more than comfortable in the barn with my husband.*" In the end, Emma had insisted on sending them out with two extra quilts. His brother suggested, with a smirk, that the east end of the loft had the freshest hay.

As if reading his thoughts, Lizzy glanced at the loft, her cheeks pinking. She ducked her head. Gideon slid a finger down her cheek and lifted her chin. He whispered in her ear, and her blush deepened. When she turned her head and kissed him, Gideon deepened the kiss.

When he pulled back, he placed his hands on her shoulders. "Mrs. Frost, I think we should get going. Another kiss will delay us."

Elizabeth gathered the quilts and set them on the front porch. Gideon harnessed a none-too-happy Jordan to the light buggy, along with one of his brother's horses. His brother had little need of the curricle with his growing family and gave it to Gideon as a wedding gift. Gideon would return the horse later.

Lizzy stroked Jordan's muzzle. "I know you are not happy about this, but we must get to Aunt Mina's, and it would be hard on you to have us ride double all the way back."

Gideon doubted even a horse as smart as Jordan understood her words, but he did seem to calm. As he helped his wife up into the curricle, the morning chill lingered. Gideon slid closer to his wife, and they drove toward the turnpike as the first fingers of dawn emerged in the east.

Elizabeth never wished a ride through Boston to go faster. The window displays held no interest for her. It seemed every delivery wagon in the city was determined to slow them down. She only grudgingly agreed to stop north of the Charles River so the horses might rest. The yells and noises of the city made it impossible to carry on a conversation with Gideon, who watched for darting errand boys. She let out a sigh when the houses started to thin and Gideon's hold on the reins loosened. Only two more hours and they would be with Mina.

Over and over Elizabeth repeated her prayers for her aunt.

In time, the landmarks became familiar. Jordan seemed to realize they were near home, and his step became livelier.

As they crested the hill, East Stoughton spread out before them. Gideon squeezed her hand and brought it to his mouth for a kiss. "So, if I were to give you a kiss here, which do you think would reach Mina first, the gossip or us?"

"The gossips are not that bad, but I do prefer we tell her together. Perhaps you should wait on that kiss."

Gideon's face fell, but his eyes continued to twinkle. "I think she will be the only one in town not surprised by the news."

"Well, in that case . . ." Elizabeth turned in her seat and gave her husband a very thorough kiss. She later learned the kiss had been seen by one of the Curtis girls, who told their aunt. An hour later when the news reached High Street, Mrs. Purdy had her own tale to add.

―✕―

Gideon lifted Elizabeth from the curricle. "I'll be but a moment. I must get the horses unhitched." The Purdy boys noted his arrival and came running to collect the coins that were their due. He instructed them on the feeding of the horses, then ran to join his wife.

He found her standing outside of Mina's room talking to Mrs. Purdy in hushed tones. He came up behind them and took Elizabeth's hand. Mrs. Purdy's eyes widened, but neither of them offered an explanation before going to Mina's bedside.

"Aunt Mina?" Elizabeth knelt by the bed, taking her aunt's hand in hers. "I'm here." She lifted her aunt's hand to her cheek, where her tears bathed it. Gideon sat down in the chair behind Elizabeth and put his hand on her shoulder.

Mina's eyes fluttered.

"Aunt Mina?"

"Lizzzzbethh." The left corner of her mouth turned up in a grin, the right side remaining slack.

Elizabeth felt Gideon slide off the chair and move beside her, his arm coming around her waist.

"Mina, I am afraid we owe you an apology."

Mina didn't reply, but she pierced him with a glare.

"We got married last night and didn't invite you to our wedding."

There was no mistaking the joy on Mina's face. She tugged her hand out of Elizabeth's grasp and touched Elizabeth's face and then Gideon's hand.

"We hoped you would approve."

"A-about time." One corner of Aunt Mina's mouth lifted, and her eyes sparkled.

Elizabeth looked at Gideon and laughed. Gideon kissed her on the tip of her nose. "Yes, Mina, well past time."

"Now, what is this I hear about you refusing to eat Mrs. Purdy's food?"

"Ocolate."

"Ocolate?" Elizabeth puzzled for a moment. "Oh, chocolate. She didn't make it right, did she?"

Mina rolled her eyes.

"Shall I make you some now?"

Mina closed her eyes for a moment. "Yes."

Gideon helped Elizabeth to her feet.

Mina reached for Gideon and caught his trousers. "She pointed to the ceiling and made a sweeping motion. "Bed."

Gideon looked up. "You want me to move the bigger bed out of the storeroom and into Elizabeth's room."

"Your room."

"That was my plan too." Gideon dropped a kiss on the old woman's brow. "I guess I should call you Aunt Mina now."

Mina gave him a half smile.

━━ ❈ ━━

For the next two days, Gideon and Elizabeth took turns sitting with Aunt Mina. To Elizabeth, it seemed like the times Aunt Mina awoke were further and further apart. And she stayed awake for only a short time, barely long enough to have a sip of her chocolate and give a smile before slipping back into slumber.

In the darkest hours after midnight, Gideon convinced his wife to go rest upstairs while he took his turn in the bedside chair.

Just after dawn, Elizabeth awoke to her husband's kiss. Tears fell from his eyes. She didn't need to ask. She clung to him and wept as well.

⊶ ❋ ⊷

There wasn't a citizen who lived within ten miles who missed Mindwell Richards's funeral. Being a fine day in May with not a cloud in sight, there was little to keep anyone away.

Platters of food filled the house as friends told tales and remembered Mina fondly.

Gideon wondered if a few hadn't come to verify the rumors of his marriage as more than one question was asked regarding his nuptials. His wife stood in one of Mina's modified old black dresses at the other end of the parlor, speaking to Widow Snow. He must warn her not to eat the pickled beets the widow had set on the side table.

Mr. Butler approached, and Gideon stiffened, apparently the hefty fine was not enough to keep him away. "No wonder you tossed that punch. You wanted her for yourself. Tell me, was she good? Even a widowed former preacher should be able to tell."

Gideon fisted his hands. "I would thank you to not discuss my wife in such vulgar terms."

"The preacher and the strump—" Mr. Butler did not finish the sentence as a large man spun him around by the shoulder.

"I believe Mr. Frost asked you to not speak of his wife in such a manner." The man frog-walked Mr. Butler out the front door.

"Who is that?" Gideon asked the postmaster as he tried to stifle his anger for his wife's sake.

"That is Horald Becham. Lives west of here a bit. The gossips say Mr. Butler—er, um, Horald's sister died in childbirth. She was only fifteen." The postmaster's face reddened. "Mina took the girl in during—er, the time."

Gideon didn't need further translation.

The man returned. "Sorry about that. Didn't think he would have the nerve to come to Mrs. Richards's home. She didn't have much use for him."

"Thank you for your assistance. It would have distressed my wife if we'd come to blows. I don't believe we have met. I am Gideon Frost. Mina's niece is my wife, and I am the new cobbler."

"Horald Becham." The men shook hands. "Thought you were going to be a preacher."

"Not anymore. Hoping to set up shop soon, but—" Gideon waved his hand at the room. "Mr. Butler owns the only storefront in Curtis Corners to be let. The Curtis's do own a building I have been trying to look at, but the cousin who owns it has been out of town."

"Well, if you get a place, let me know. I make furniture and such."

"I will, Mr. Becham."

"Horald. Anything for Mrs. Richards's kinfolk." The man walked off in the direction of the food.

As the crowds were thinning, an older gentleman came forward to shake Gideon's hand. The man presented a card. "If you and Mrs. Richards's niece would stop by tomorrow, I would like to discuss the will with you."

"Will?"

"Yes, the will." The old man tipped his head and left.

Gideon turned over the card.

Burton Samuels, Esq. Stoughton, Massachusetts.

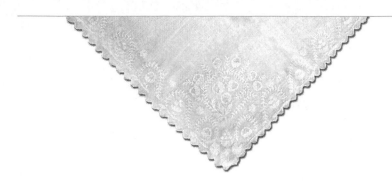

Thirty-Five

Elizabeth bit her lip and stared into her cup of chocolate. With all the food in the house, it was the only thing she wanted. She'd made it perfectly. She dared anyone to taste a difference between hers and Aunt Mina's. Yet she couldn't drink it.

Gideon laid his hand on her shoulder.

"Come take a walk with me?"

She stood, and he took her hand.

They walked through the fields to their boulder. Gideon lifted her up, then used the stepping stone to sit beside her.

"Shame the ridge hides the sunset."

Elizabeth nodded her agreement and nestled into his shoulder. "But it is a fair spot to watch the moon rise."

Gideon wrapped his arms around her and pulled her into his lap. "I did quite a bit of thinking out here after you left. Whenever I missed you, I would come out to this rock."

"Is that why you can climb up so quickly?"

He kissed the sassy grin. "Mina told me I was going to have to pave the path I was making."

Gideon wrapped his arms around her. "Any regrets, Mrs. Frost?"

Her answer waited while he kissed the tender spot behind her ear.

"Since we are still counting our marriage in terms of days, I am not sure I can have any yet." The teasing lilt to her voice and the accompanying kiss were more of an answer than her words.

The stars began to appear in the eastern sky. Elizabeth was not an astronomer, but she thought she recognized the few she watched through the barn's loft window. Warmth flooded her at the memories they made there, and she tried to think of other things. A kiss placed behind her ear did not help. Neither did the accompanying whisper.

"Next time we come out here, we should bring a blanket, and you should wear only four hairpins."

A shiver went up her spine, and she nodded in agreement.

Elizabeth wore the same hastily made-over black dress she'd worn the day before for the funeral, to go to the lawyers. Wearing something of Aunt Mina's kept her close. Gideon held her hand the entire way. He'd hitched the biddable mare to the curricle instead of Jordan, so the ride was slow and smooth.

The address was for a handsome house. Above the side door, a shingle declared that Lawyer Barton Samuels practiced here.

A clerk showed them to Mr. Samuels's office.

"Thank you for coming. Mrs. Richards called me out to the house about a month ago and initiated the sale of most of her land as well as changed her will, Miss Garrett."

"Mrs. *Frost*." Elizabeth sat taller at her declaration.

"Sorry, my apologies. All of the paperwork is in your maiden name. I have not had time to shift my thinking."

"Of course."

"Good. That will help move things along. You see, she signed the deed to the house and the remaining property over to you. Since you are married, you will, of course, add your husband's name to the deed. Having her sign the deed before her death makes most of the transfer easier."

"She left me the house?"

"And over fourteen acres. She sold off the other 106."

Gideon scratched his head. "Which fourteen? I can't think of a block that makes sense. I've only been caring for about four."

"I have a map I will give you when we get everything else taken care of." Mr. Samuels waved his hand at the papers on the desk.

"Now, Mr. Frost, she took part of the sale of her land in trade for a building on High Street, deeding the property to you. She was of the opinion it would make a good cobbler's shop and has left the remainder of the money in a number of bequests. I took the liberty of combining your shares. He slid an envelope to Gideon."

Gideon promptly gave it to Elizabeth. The lawyer raised his brows but didn't comment.

"All that is needed is for you to sign the deeds."

"I would like Elizabeth on the store deed as well."

Mr. Barton Samuels swallowed. "That is somewhat unusual. Are you sure, sir?"

"Yes, I am."

Mr. Samuels added a line to the deed.

When Gideon and Elizabeth signed the indicated spots, Mr. Samuels gave Gideon a set of keys. "These are to the store on High Street. I assume you have keys to the house. Also, I am to inform you both there are letters for you in her top drawer in a lockbox. Here is that key." He handed Elizabeth a tiny key on a ribbon.

"And the plot map?" Gideon shifted in his seat.

"Oh yes, here it is. Mrs. Richards insisted on keeping the acres behind the barn up to the ridge. Mr. Collins, the buyer, thought this odd as the ridge land is unfarmable, at any rate."

Elizabeth studied the map. "She placed her finger on a point. Gideon?" He looked where she directed. "Did you know Aunt Mina owned that?"

Gideon shook his head. He took her by the elbow and led her to the carriage.

Elizabeth gave her bun the slightest tap and pocketed the hairpin. She peeked out the corner of her eye to make sure Gideon had not noticed her move. They stopped walking at the boulder. Gideon dropped his bundle on the lee side of the big rock, then lifted her by the waist and set her on top. He didn't let go but stepped closer for a kiss.

Elizabeth gave the practiced shake of her head, causing him to pull back a few inches. When she shook her head again, her hair tumbled down her back as it should.

Gideon's eyes widened just as she hoped they would. "I see you only brought four hairpins, Mrs. Frost." His voice was low and husky as he claimed the previously denied kiss.

It was good there were only four hairpins. After being so thoroughly kissed with her husband's fingers wrapped in her hair, she doubted she would ever find them. She slowed the kiss so she could say what she had been thinking since the moment she'd seen the map on Barton Samuels's desk.

"Of all the things Aunt Mina gave me today, this rock means the most. My letter was wonderful, but this rock is where I discovered who I wanted to be, and it is where I found you. Do you think she knew that?"

"I think she did. She spied on us, you know."

Elizabeth let out a laugh. "How? When?"

"From your bedroom window. I saw the curtain move one day. It was the first day I wanted to kiss you."

Elizabeth thought about that a moment. "Why didn't you?"

"I am not sure. I know I had some excellent excuse, but now it seems rather silly." He leaned in for another kiss.

"Gideon?"

"Hmm?"

"If Aunt Mina could see us, do you think someone else can?"

"In the day, maybe, but by starlight? I don't believe so."

Elizabeth returned the kiss with more fervor as the stars twinkled above them.

The End

Historical Notes

Today, if one visits the town of Avon, Massachusetts, formerly known as East Stoughton, they can find Elizabeth's rock. Two decades ago I spent time sitting on that boulder pondering the origin of the rock wall below the ridge, life, and listening to a baby monitor. I wondered if, over the last few hundred years, anyone else ever sat on that rock. With that in mind, Avon became the natural setting for this story.

Although not incorporated until 1888, Avon traces its history to before the Revolutionary War. First settled by the Curtis family, it was known locally as Curtis Corners. The town failed to be incorporated despite multiple petitions to the Commonwealth and remained part of Stoughton. This placed some burden on the residents who had to travel several miles for services. A brick school house was built in the late 1790s, and today a modern replacement sits on the same street corner. The town Greenwich did exist in 1795, but was destroyed when Quabbin Reservoir was built in the 1930's.

Mindwell's stories are based in fact. There were at least two occasions between 1748 and 1754 when numerous women spun flax into linen thread on the Boston Common. Some historians have tried to link this to tax rebellion on the part of the colonists. However, this is unlikely as the demonstrations occurred more than a decade before the king of England levied a cloth tax. On the occasion of the second celebration, a pamphlet from an anonymous writer was circulated extolling the need for colonists to produce their own clothing goods, showing much foresight. And the name Mindwell was in the top twenty girls' names in 1720 New England.

About four years before the famous Boston Tea Party was held by the men, women from Boston and other parts of New England had their own "tea parties," where they signed compacts vowing not to drink or use tea. Thus, both drinking coffee and chocolate became a small patriotic act of rebellion. Baker's chocolate was supplying bars of unsweetened chocolate much like those we use today. It was used to make a chocolate drink that was considered a healthy breakfast. Some period recipes used milk and others water, but either way, the drink was not as sweet as the hot cocoa I like to curl up with while reading.

I tried to be as authentic as possible with the processes of spinning, weaving, and bleaching linen without taking over the story. Several period directions call for the use of lye and cow dung. Others call for urine as well as boiling. When I read the first instructions calling for dung, I knew Elizabeth needed it not only as bleach for the linen but as part of her reformation.

The parish church system existed in Massachusetts into the 1830s. Despite the adoption of the Bill of Rights, several states sponsored churches with tax money into the nineteenth century. Massachusetts was the last state to abolish the practice. Although most of these parish churches were Congregationalist, the evolutionary children of the Puritan Church, the First and Second Great Awakenings brought many new sects into being. While under the law, other sects could be parish churches. This could only occur when a congregation was large enough to warrant a church or the town voters voted for a church of a different sect. I combined beliefs of several of the various denominations into the imaginary sect where Gideon Frost became a minister. I did take the liberty of using an unfinished church building that existed near Curtis Corners at the time.

Under the parish church system, local magistrates could levy fines for those who did not attend church, who were of able body, for the space of three months. They also could fine those who acted rudely in a house of worship on the Lord's day. Both Mr. Butler and Gideon could have been fined for fighting on the Lord's day as well as Mr. Butler for striking Elizabeth. However, since there were no other witnesses to the fight, I chose not to have them charged with Lord's day violations as someone would have needed to file a complaint.

The Massachusetts Justice: being a collection of the laws of the Commonwealth of Massachusetts by Samuel Freeman, printed in 1795, has been an invaluable resource for this book, if not a bit trying to read as the *s*'s are printed as *f*s. It can be found online and lists a number of crimes that could not be enforced today.

Acknowledgments

THERE ARE NOT ENOUGH WAYS to thank those who helped me bring about this book. As always my cheerleaders Anita, Amber and Tammy, sorry if I talked your ears off.

Huge thanks to my beta readers; especially Nancy, Nanette, and Nicole who marked up every page of the manuscript and caught so many errors. I hope you recognize the book. The writer friends picked up on the way especially Sally, and Cindy, whose daily critiques and input have been invaluable. Thanks to all the writers in Cache Valley League of Utah writers, and iWriteNetwork, each of you has made me a better writer. Thank you for your part in my growth as a fledging writer.

Thanks also to Michele at Eschler Editing for the edits and finding oh so many little things to fix; any mistakes left in this book are not her fault. Nor are my excellent proof readers to be blamed. Thank you ladies!

My family, for sharing their home with the fictional characters who often got fed better than they did. And my husband who encouraged me every crazy step of the way, and who is my example for every love story I dream up. The real one is better.

And to my Father in Heaven for putting these wonderful people, and any I may have forgotten to mention, in my life. I am grateful for every experience and blessing I have been granted to form my life.

About the Author

LORIN GRACE WAS BORN IN Colorado and has been moving around the country ever since, living in eight states and several imaginary worlds. She graduated from Brigham Young University with a degree in Graphic Design.

Currently she lives in northern Utah with her husband, four children, and a dog who is insanely jealous of her laptop. When not writing Lorin enjoys creating graphics, visiting historical sites, museums, and reading.

Lorin is an active member of the League of Utah Writers and was awarded Honorable Mention in their 2016 creative writing contest short romance story category.

You can learn more about her, and sign up for her writers club at loringrace.com or at Facebook: LorinGraceWriter

Coming Summer 2017

Remembering Anna
A Novella

What is in the box Lucy found?

Join Lorin Grace's readers' group for your
free ebook (after release).

newsletter.loringrace.com

Enjoy it Now

Waking Lucy

Lucy dreamed of marrying Samuel,
until she woke up as his wife.

Don't miss the first book in the series.

Coming 2018

AMERICAN
HOMESPUN
THREE

Healing Sarah

LORIN GRACE

Healing Sarah

Summer 1816 never came.
The only thing colder is Sarah's heart.
Timothy can heal Sarah if given the chance.

49277370R00168

Made in the USA
San Bernardino, CA
18 May 2017